Holiday in the Hills

Lilac Mills lives on a Welsh mountain with her very patient husband and incredibly sweet dog, where she grows veggies (if the slugs don't get them), bakes (badly) and loves making things out of glitter and glue (a mess, usually). She's been an avid reader ever since she got her hands on a copy of *Noddy Goes to Toytown* when she was five, and she once tried to read everything in her local library starting with A and working her way through the alphabet. She loves long, hot summer days and cold winter ones snuggled in front of the fire, but whatever the weather she's usually writing or thinking about writing, with heartwarming romance and happy-ever-afters always on her mind.

Also by Lilac Mills

A Very Lucky Christmas
Sunshine at Cherry Tree Farm
Summer on the Turquoise Coast
Love in the City by the Sea

Tanglewood Village series

The Tanglewood Tea Shop
The Tanglewood Flower Shop
The Tanglewood Wedding Shop

Island Romance

Sunrise on the Coast
Holiday in the Hills
Sunset on the Square

LILAC MILLS

Holiday in the Hills

CANELO

First published in the the United Kingdom in 2020 by Canelo

This edition published in the United Kingdom in 2021 by

Canelo
31 Helen Road
Oxford OX2 0DF
United Kingdom

A CIP catalogue record for this book is available from the British Library.

Print ISBN 978 1 80032 226 4
Ebook ISBN 978 1 80032 140 3

Look for more great books at www.canelo.co

Printed and bound in Great Britain by Clays Ltd, Elcograf S.p.A.

Chapter 1

Ivy (it's-not-a-pen-name) Winter stepped out through
Tenerife Airport's sliding doors, caught sight of her pale
gaunt face in the glass, and hastily donned her oversized
sunglasses. Ugh, she really didn't need any reminders of
how drained and washed-out she felt, and certainly not
when all around there were happy faces and cheerful
voices.

'How far is it?' she asked the driver of the car that
had been hired for her journey from the airport to the
villa. It was on a hill somewhere, but from what she could
see of Tenerife so far, there were lots of hills, including
Mount Teide, the bloomin' great big one at the centre of
the island, so take your pick.

'One hour.' He held up a finger.

Great, she thought wearily. She'd already spent five
hours travelling, and that didn't include the obligatory
two-hour wait at Stansted. Then there had been the queue
at Passport Control this end, and the wait for her luggage
– there was quite a bit of it, and it had taken a while for
all three cases to appear. Now there was a further hour
to go before she could have a G&T and a lie-down in a
darkened room. Preferably both at the same time.

Ivy supposed she'd better let Nora know that she'd
arrived safely and was on her way to the villa. Part of the

'charm' of this writing retreat was the lack of phone signal or wifi to distract her (although Ivy did find this mildly alarming – what if she needed to make an urgent call?), so she'd better ring her agent while she had enough bars on her phone.

'Nora, it's me, Ivy.'

'Hello, hun. How are you?'

'Hot and cross.'

'I bet the weather is glorious.'

Through the car's tinted windows, Ivy could feel the heat of the sun, and its glare bored into her sunglass-clad eyes until her head pounded. With a deep sigh, she closed her eyes and rested her head against the back of the seat. A headache was nothing new, and she wasn't sure whether this one was a fresh ache, or was a continuation of the one she'd had since Daniel had dropped her – professionally and personally.

'I suppose,' she agreed, grudgingly.

'You are a cross-patch, aren't you? Wait until you see the villa. You'll love it.'

'Have you heard anything from Daniel?' The line was silent. Ivy listened for a few seconds, then opened her eyes. 'Hello, can you hear me?'

'I'm still here.'

'Good, I said—'

'Look, hun, I've got to go. Give me a call when you can, OK? Give yourself a few days to settle in and we'll speak later in the week – you can call me from the house phone.'

Ivy popped her mobile back in her bag and leant her head against the back of the seat again. A house phone was little consolation, but at least she could call someone in an emergency.

As for the matter of Daniel, it is said that an author is only as good as his or her latest book. Apparently, according to her royalties and the accolades she'd received, Ivy should be an absolute genius – if they were talking about published works, that is. The unpublished material – the manuscript she'd presented to her publisher two months ago, who had also been her lover at the time (not any more though, damn his rotten black heart) – was not so good. It was also nowhere near finished. All she had were the first six chapters, a rough outline, and Daniel's scrawled and scathing notes.

He'd disliked it, to put it mildly. The plot was full of holes, he'd told her, the style was saccharine, the main character insipid and unengaging, and the opening lines were bland and yawn-inducing. Don't hold back, will you, she'd thought at the time, hoping he was joking, knowing he was not. Even her incredibly supportive agent, Nora, had hummed and ahhed when she'd been presented with it.

Ivy had no one to blame but herself. She should never have bypassed Nora in the first place and shared her draft manuscript directly with her lover – and the man who also happened to be her publisher. Big mistake. On both counts. She should have waited until Nora had cast her beady and extremely critical eye over the outline. They could have polished it together until it shone (or not, but that was another matter).

Instead, Ivy had jumped the gun, riding high on her reputation as a highly successful and prolific writer, eager to share her work with Daniel. Her fans would buy anything she wrote – they always had.

But – and here was the rub, as Shakespeare had famously once written – her newest manuscript, the scrap that she'd managed to force out so far, was in fact dire. Her lead character, Libby, was flat and uninspiring – a fatal flaw for a protagonist who is meant to be a kick-arse vampire slayer – and the central romance was about as heated as a cup of tea left on the kitchen counter for an hour. Daniel was correct, although he needn't have been so harsh about it. The problem was, Ivy didn't have anything else in her. Nothing, nil, zero. The well of her imagination had run dry. It was as barren and withered as a blade of straw in the desert.

If her mind was blank, then her heart was, too. It had been scoured clean by Daniel's disbelief that she, of all people, could have written such mediocre rubbish (his words). He could have been gentler, more understanding, more supportive. He could have helped her work through it.

But he'd been too busy, she'd found out later, *supporting* another author. A younger, prettier, more dynamic author. One who was going places. One who was likely to win an international prize or two. Ivy was too mainstream for such an accolade; she wasn't literary enough. Authors of paranormal romance, sometimes with a touch of science fiction or steampunk, and always with a touch of naughtiness, didn't tend to be nominated for those sorts of things. Therefore, Daniel had set his sights on a better prospect, both professionally as she would boost his standing in the industry, and personally, cue the younger, prettier thing, and Ivy had been cast aside. That particular story was an old and very predictable one, and Ivy hated herself for being the victim in her own personal drama. She should have known better. She *did* know better. But it hadn't prevented her from being flattered by his attention and kidding herself that Daniel was different, that he loved her.

Right now, Ivy didn't have anything new for her agent to pitch to a publisher. Her current books were doing well, but not well enough for her to retire, and without fresh material to give to her readers, those followers might abandon her. Emails from her fans had been flooding in for months, demanding to know whether she was writing a brand-new series, and when the first book in said series would be out. But soon, the flood of interest would become a trickle, and then a drip, until it finally ceased altogether, along with most of the royalty payments as her sales dropped off. Then what would she do? The only thing she was any good at was writing – although even that was questionable right now. Without her writing, Ivy was nothing. Making up stories was who she was, it was what she did, it was her whole identity. And now she was in danger of losing it along with herself.

'We are here. Villa Colina,' the driver announced.

Ivy straightened up and took her glasses off in order to have a better look at the house where she'd be staying for the next six months. That was how long her agent had taken the lease out for. She guessed that if she hadn't produced anything meaningful at the end of that time, then she might as well take up a new career.

Ivy peered out of the window as the car crept between two iron gates, and pulled onto a longish drive before coming to halt outside a white-washed one-storey house with a red-tiled roof. Bougainvillea grew around the front door and pots of bright flowers were dotted around the outside. It certainly looked pleasing enough. She just hoped the inside matched the outside, and that there was a bottle of cold gin in the fridge.

'Look. *Vista*.' The driver opened her door and pointed out of the opposite window.

Ivy looked. She shuffled across to the other side of the car and blinked. Her mouth dropped open and her eyes grew wide.

The view was to die for.

The ground to the left of the drive dropped away dramatically to reveal a wide expanse of sea, with a small island near the shore, and a town or a large village nestled at the bottom of the mountainside she was on. God knows how many metres above sea level the villa was, but it had to be several hundred, if not a thousand. Maybe even more. The buildings below looked tiny. She could make out a harbour, several pools of the most magnificent turquoise, a church or two, and lots of higgledy-piggledy houses.

The miles and miles of sea hazed into the distance until the ocean and the sky became one, and Ivy was unable to see where one ended and the other began. The water was dotted with boats and white-crested waves raced across its surface, chased by a steadily blowing light breeze, which Ivy guessed was probably stronger further away from shore.

But it was the colours that stole her breath; she hadn't known there were so many shades of blue, from almost silver to a dark navy, which contrasted with the almost black rocks, the occasional green palm tree, and the white-washed, red-tiled houses.

Ivy climbed out of the car and stepped towards the sturdy wooden barrier at the cliff's edge for a closer look.

The scene was certainly magnificent and mesmerising, although whether it would get her creative juices flowing, was an altogether different matter. She'd probably be better off in a dungeon with only a desk and a lightbulb for company if she wanted to get any work done. It wasn't going to be easy writing about creatures of the night who liked to take a bite out of you and suck your blood, when you were facing scenery as spectacular as this, she thought. And in such brilliant sunshine and glorious temperatures, too.

Meanwhile the driver had retrieved her suitcases from the boot and was busily hauling them towards the front door, puffing and grunting.

Honestly, he needn't make such a fuss, Ivy thought – they weren't that heavy, and she couldn't have managed with less. After all, she was probably going to be here for half a year (unless by some miracle she completed the first draft of this damn manuscript sooner), so she needed plenty of clothes and other creature comforts that she didn't want to do without.

Ivy checked the printout that Nora had given her about the villa booking and scanned down the page until she came to the part where it mentioned the villa keys, and raised her eyebrows.

Apparently, the door to the villa was unlocked and the keys were on the table in the hall. *Really?* Had the owners never heard of burglars? She realised the villa was on the side of a rather large hill in the middle of nowhere, with the nearest village being a twenty-minute walk away, but honestly!

The driver dumped her cases by the generous-sized porch and muttered, 'Ninety-five euro.' He held out his hand and Ivy rooted in her bag until she found her purse, and handed some notes over, trying not to wince at the price. She thanked him and waited for him to get into his car and drive off, before turning to the villa with a sigh.

It might be wonderful, and she might be in a truly spectacular part of the world, but she was here to do a job, and she was dreading it. What if she was unable to write anything decent ever again? The thought sent icy fingers crawling down her back and, despite the heat, she shivered.

Pushing her misgivings aside, Ivy decided that today was not the best time to tackle her writing demons; she'd just endured a long journey, she was tired, dishevelled, and hungry. What she needed right now was to get her bearings, unpack, and have a gin and tonic before she addressed the issue of something to eat. Oh, and take some painkillers for this darned headache, though, to be fair, it was starting to ease on its own, probably due to the relief of having arrived at her destination.

Hesitantly, she grasped the ornate handle adorning the villa's door and turned it. It swung open silently and for a moment she stood listening for any sounds from within.

Silence.

That was good, wasn't it?

Hmm. Maybe it was too quiet. She wasn't used to it, and now that became another thing to add to the list of things she would worry about in the middle of the night, along with plot lines – or the lack of them.

But for now, curiosity got the better of her and she peered inside, seeing a corridor with rooms off to the left and to the right. At the end of it, brilliant sunlight flooded in through a set of French doors, drawing her towards them.

Stepping over the threshold, her gaze darted everywhere, taking in the buttermilk-coloured tiles on the floor, the shelves filled with books which lined the hall, the soft yellow walls and the muted turquoise doors, through which lay three large bedrooms and a family bathroom. With her suitcases lying forgotten on the porch, Ivy slowly made her way into the heart of the villa, her attention on the view through the glass doors.

She already knew from Nora that the villa had a pool, but she hadn't been expecting such a glittering, never-ending one with several sun loungers dotted invitingly on the terrace in front of it. The pool was cordoned off by a low garden wall which was covered by climbers, and a couple of gently waving palm trees threw much-needed shade in places. But what really took her breath away was the fact that one side of the pool area, the side looking out to the sea and that glorious view, was made up of clear glass panels. There was nothing obstructing the scenery and Ivy felt as though she was a part of it.

Surveying the rest of the pool area, she noticed a table and eight chairs situated under a wooden pergola with a sun canopy draped over it, along with a huge barbeque off to one side. Apart from the terrace, the area surrounding the pool was grassed, and Ivy could almost feel the cool tufts under her toes and the breeze ruffling through her hair.

Ivy had never been in an infinity pool before, and she was tempted to change into her swimming costume and dive right in, but she decided she'd better unpack first. Besides, a cold drink was much needed. Before that, though, there was the rest of the house to explore, and she slowly turned around to examine the room she was standing in.

Oh, this was nice, she thought. The living space was open plan, with a kitchen at one end and a sitting room at the other, with the transition between the two areas provided by a dining table and a desk with an office-type chair. There was a second set of French doors by the sofa, which also opened onto the terrace, and she could imagine how cool and airy the place would be with all of them open. The large desk was situated underneath a window which was positioned halfway between the two lots of French doors. Ivy could just imagine herself sitting there with her laptop, waiting for inspiration to strike while losing herself in the magnificent view.

The villa was light and airy, yet it had a cosy lived-in feel to it, which she put down to the little touches like the books in the hall, the paintings on the walls (some of them were exquisite and depicted scenes of what she assumed were the island's beauty spots), and the rug on the floor in front of the sofa – it felt like a home not a holiday rental, and she fell in love with it immediately.

Nora had told her that the villa's fridge and cupboards would be generously stocked by the rental company with essentials, enough to get her through the first few days, and when Nora had asked Ivy if there was anything in particular she wanted to add to the pre-arrival shopping list, the only thing Ivy could think of was marmalade and gin.

The marmalade was in one of the cupboards, she saw, after opening a few to check their contents, and the gin was in the fridge. Ivy took out the bottle and thoughtfully studied the rest of the items in there. Lots of salad stuff, vegetables, some mince, a couple of pieces of steak, chicken breasts, a selection of fruit, milk, fruit juice, eggs, cheese, Spanish-style ham… Plenty to make several meals from.

She opened the freezer door, expecting to see some ready meals, but instead came face to face with a drawer full of bags of ice and little else. Which meant that whoever had stocked her larder expected her to cook for herself, from scratch.

The idea didn't appeal all that much. She'd become far too used to dining out over the past couple of years – usually at some function or another that Daniel was obliged to go to – that she'd practically forgotten what a kitchen was for. Never mind, there was bound to be a restaurant or two within strolling distance – she'd explore later. For now, a cool G&T and a handful of strawberries would have to do.

Taking her drink and a bowl of fruit into the garden, Ivy sank down into a padded chair and heaved a sigh, a mixture of emotions whirling through her mind.

Putting the perfection of the villa and its location aside, she was here for one reason, and one reason only. This wasn't a holiday; this was work. And she was under no illusions that it would be *hard* work. Penning the outline for a whole new series in six months, with the expectation of at least one complete novel at the end of it, was daunting, especially since the novel in question was hardly her best work to date, and the meagre amount that she had written so far had to be seriously redone.

It was also terribly disturbing, because never before had she felt overwhelmed at the thought of writing. In the past, the stories had flown from her fingers, the words eager to be released into the world. Writing had never been just a job. She'd not seen it as a way to pay for a roof over her head and put food on the table (although it had, and then some). It had been essential, the tales within not letting her rest until she had released them from the prison of her mind, and she'd revelled in the excitement and sheer thrill of a new idea popping into her head, seemingly from nowhere.

Now, though, all she felt was unease and apprehension.

Because there *was* no new story in her head. Her mind was empty. Her heart was sore. And a future without her beloved storytelling terrified her.

Chapter 2

The setting of the sun took Ivy by surprise. It was only eight p.m., and it had already dropped behind the mountain on her left, although the sky was still relatively light. She bit her lip, wondering if it was wise to try to find a restaurant in an unfamiliar place when the villa was a decent walk from the nearest town and it would be dark shortly. There were other buildings in the distance, but from what she could see, they looked like private homes and even those were few and far between. Nora had informed her that the local village was a twenty-minute walk away, but Ivy wasn't sure of the direction and she didn't fancy negotiating such a steep hill at night.

Earlier, after she'd retrieved her luggage from the front door, Ivy had selected the largest bedroom and unpacked. She had set up her laptop on the desk under the window in the living room, along with a couple of notepads, a handful of pens, and her lucky charm – a battered and well-worn copy of the first book of hers that had been published. She kept this copy on her desk at home as a reminder of how far she'd come since those days of receiving rejection letter after rejection letter. Until, that is, Nora had seen her potential and had taken her under her wing.

Ivy had yet to emerge from under it.

As her tummy rumbled, Ivy made her way into the kitchen area, taking the information folder with her to read while she ate. She'd cook herself something, she decided. There were plenty of things to choose from, and she could always have something simple such as steak and salad.

Although it had been a long time since she had cooked a proper meal, as Ivy retrieved the meat from the fridge and popped it under the grill, and placed the makings of a salad on the countertop, she found it quite soothing. It was hard to pinpoint when she'd stopped cooking. It had been a gradual thing which had started slowly at first and had happened over the course of many months, until she was eating out most nights. With Daniel, obviously, not on her own, because that would be weird— But hang on, wasn't that what she'd intended to do this evening if she'd been able to locate a restaurant? The idea hadn't seemed so weird then. Maybe it was the odd mood she was in, because at the moment she didn't feel as though she was here to work; it felt more like she was on holiday, and she guessed she might struggle to get into the work zone tomorrow.

Maybe Nora should have found her a house in a remote part of Yorkshire instead, rather than a villa on an island renowned for sun, sea and sangria.

However, her agent knew her too well. Probably better than she knew herself, because if she'd stayed in the UK the bright lights and familiarity of London would have drawn her back. Not to mention Daniel... No, it was better this way. She was a couple of thousand miles from everything that was stopping her from writing, and if this retreat (no, it's not a holiday, she kept telling herself) didn't produce the goods, then nothing would.

Ivy cut off a slice of incredibly fresh bread. It smelled divine, and she found herself stuffing it in her mouth. Ooh, that was good, even without anything on it. She chewed and swallowed, then grabbed another piece. When was the last time she'd enjoyed such a simple thing as fresh bread? She'd been so busy watching her weight (her bum tended to spread if she didn't keep an eye on it), that she didn't usually eat many carbs.

Ah, well, she could always burn off the calories tomorrow in that wonderful infinity pool.

Tossing the salad in some olive oil and a little vinegar she found in one of the cupboards, she thought about the coming days and weeks. Holiday mode or not, she was here to work, and if she wanted to salvage her career then she had to be motivated. Tomorrow she'd start as she meant to go on, with a routine that was workable and one which she would be able to stick to. There was no point in setting herself ridiculous targets of writing ten thousand words a day (been there, done that, and she suspected she was now paying the price for that particularly expensive T-shirt). What she needed to do, was to strike a balance between writing and allowing herself to heal. Because no matter how tough she tried to be, in reality both her heart and her confidence were shattered.

But that wasn't all – and this was the thing that was so awful that she could hardly bear to think about – she had a horrible gut-wrenching feeling that she didn't actually enjoy writing any more. This fear cut deeper than Daniel's harsh (but accurate) critique, and his abandonment of her for a better prospect.

Ivy set the dining table and carried her meal over to it. Now that the grill was switched off and she was sitting relatively quietly, she was conscious once again of the silence both inside the villa and out. There wasn't even the sound of the sea to keep her company, and the breeze had dropped to little more than a whisper. The evening was warm, though, and she had both sets of doors open.

Perhaps she should have sat at the table outside and let the night air wash over her?

Shrugging and putting the idea aside for another time, Ivy tucked into her simple meal, washing it down with a glass of red wine from one of the bottles she'd discovered in the wine rack. One glass, that was all she'd allow herself, aware that she needed to be bright and alert in the morning.

Which reminded her – she should have a schedule.

She always used to write earlier on in the day, when the rest of the world was still slumbering and distractions were at a minimum. She used to do her best work then, from about six to nine a.m. Then she'd stop and have breakfast before tackling the rest of the things she needed to do, such as answering emails, editing a novel that was further along the publishing production line, approving a cover (or not), or doing some research (she didn't make *everything* up!). Gradually though, over the last few years, as she spent more evenings with Daniel, she'd gone to bed later, which meant she had got up later. She was also more often than not at Daniel's house, so before she started work she used to have to go home first, and it would be close to midday before she'd actually sat down to write anything…

Why had she let him affect her writing so much? He knew she was a morning person, but he tended to sulk if she said she wanted an early night. She should have put her foot down and not let her love for him dictate her schedule. It would have also helped if he had slept at her place more often, but he claimed it was too far out of the city and it took him too long to get into the office in the morning. He'd also claimed her mattress was uncomfortable and continued to complain about it even after she'd invested in a new one.

Right, she decided, now that she only had herself to please she would have an early night with the intention of rising early in the morning. She felt rather tired anyway, having spent the whole day travelling, so going to bed before ten o'clock shouldn't be a problem. Maybe returning to the routine that had been so conducive to writing for her in the past, might kick start her creativity.

Maybe…

Feeling better for having made some kind of a plan, she turned her attention to the villa's information pack. The sooner she discovered where she could get a decent mobile signal, the better. She felt lost without any contact with the outside world and rather twitchy when she thought of how many emails she'd have in her inbox just from being off the grid for one day. What about Twitter, Facebook, Instagram…? She shuddered to think how she'd keep up with social media if she couldn't access it easily.

Ah, that was better – she read that she would be able to get a signal in the nearby village, and then realised that she could incorporate this into her daily routine by taking a stroll to have lunch and use the local restaurant's wifi at the same time. A two birds with one stone kind of thing. Plus, she could pick up any supplies while she was there. She had enough fresh stuff to last a couple of days, but after that she'd need bread at the very least. And the exercise and change of scenery would do her good. Sometimes when she was stuck on a plot point, all it took was doing something physical to reboot her brain.

She read a little more and found that the villa was serviced each day by a maid (whose name was Alba) and when she saw that, Ivy had to remind herself once again that she was not at the start of a holiday, but instead she was about to begin a six-month writing marathon. Fancy having your bed made for you every morning! It felt positively decadent. And the pool and the grounds of the villa were checked daily by someone called Sebastián, the information pack told her, and any maintenance concerns should be directed to him.

OK, so she wasn't entirely isolated then, which made her feel a little better about her lack of immediate neighbours. Nora hadn't just dumped her here and forgotten about her. At least someone would notice if she fell and bumped her head or if she wasn't very well.

Feeling rather adrift, Ivy gathered up her dinner things and washed them, then had a shower and got ready for bed. It was only then that she realised there was no TV in the villa. The lack of which probably explained the library of books lining the hallway. With little else to do, there was no choice but to read. Or talk to the other people you were on holiday with – which wasn't an option for her, unless she wanted to hold a conversation with her characters. She'd actually been known to do that in the past, but right now the characters in the pathetic new manuscript that she'd submitted to Daniel were half-formed wretched things with very little appeal. And if she, as the author, wasn't remotely interested in Libby and her vampire lover, she could hardly expect her readers to be.

She took a look at the books instead, interested to see the wide variety of genres on display, in several different languages. They were neatly arranged, with Spanish books on one shelf, English on another, and so on. And there were board games too, she noticed, smiling as she saw Monopoly, a childhood favourite. She always used to be the hat counter – those tiny metal objects had proved fascinating to her eight-year-old self.

Her smile grew wider when she spotted the shelves of children's books. Enid Blyton! That was a blast from the past. It was this particular author who had ignited Ivy's love of reading, as her mum had encouraged her to read the stories she herself had loved as a child. They might be old-fashioned and hark back to another era, but there was something innately innocent about them.

Ivy wasn't going to read one now though, and instead she picked up a thriller – a genre she liked but didn't read a great deal of. Her reading was mostly dictated by the works of her peers as she tried to keep up with what was current and trending in paranormal romance. Not that she'd been keeping as up to date with her genre as she usually did; when she and Daniel had been together, most of her free time had been taken up by him, and her reading habits had fallen by the wayside.

Maybe that was the problem with Libby and her tame vampire? Had those pesky blood-suckers now fallen out of favour with the reading public? Had readers had their fill of sexy vamps? It was a thought, and one Ivy wasn't sure she was comfortable with. If she didn't write about vamps and the women they loved, what was she supposed to write about?

Pushing the worry to the back of her mind until tomorrow, she wandered around the villa, making sure the external doors were locked and the doors to the two empty bedrooms were firmly closed (her imagination was working overtime), before she retired to bed with her book.

Sleep, though, was a long time coming.

She wasn't used to it being so quiet. Or so dark.

And she wasn't used to being so alone with just her thoughts for company, either.

Chapter 3

Ivy woke to hear unfamiliar noises percolating through her bedroom window. Darn it, she'd slept later than she'd intended to.

She lay there for a moment, getting her bearings, before realising that the gurgling, sucky sounds were probably being made by the garden guy as he cleaned the pool. What was his name? Steve...? Sid...? Seb...? Sebastián! That was it.

Wanting to turn over and go back to sleep, but guessing that Alba, the maid, would be in shortly, Ivy forced herself to rise from the very comfy bed and staggered into the en suite for a swift shower.

Once she was dressed and had coiled her hair into a bun at the nape of her neck, she felt better equipped to deal with the day – and the strange man she could still hear pottering around outside. He wasn't making much noise, but it was so quiet at the villa that the slightest sound travelled. She hoped that neither he nor the maid would be coming around at this time every morning and disturbing her writing. Ideally, she would like to be up at six and at her computer by half-past, to get a solid four hours in before she had her first break of the day, and she didn't like the idea of being interrupted.

Something didn't feel quite right though, and when she checked her signal-less phone (old habits die hard), she realised she'd forgotten to set the alarm and it was gone eleven o'clock. Blimey, she must have been tired.

Vowing to set the alarm for tomorrow morning, she strolled into the kitchen, started the coffee percolator going and debated whether she should offer the service guy a cup. It seemed churlish not to; they'd probably be in contact quite a bit over the coming months, so she decided to go and make friends. Alba didn't appear to be here yet, but Ivy would ask her if she wanted one when she arrived.

The man had his back to her and was kneeling down near the far end of the pool. She thought he might be either pulling some weeds up or planting something, it was difficult to tell from this angle.

'Excuse me,' she called, taking a few steps onto the terrace and studying him as he half turned his head.

Realising he had company, he slowly got to his feet, and as he rose to his full height, Ivy saw he was at least six foot. Probably more. Definitely more. And wide-shouldered, with a broad back, slim waist and long legs. For some reason, she'd been expecting a young lad, a pool *boy*, not the man standing before her. She wasn't much good at guessing ages, but she estimated he was at least as old as she was, if not a year or two older, which would put him in his mid-forties.

Dusting his hands off against his jeans as he turned around, she got her first proper look at him, and it was as much as she could do not to let her jaw hit the floor.

He was handsome. Really attractive. Absurdly good-looking.

Thick dark hair curled around his ears, stubble which might have been designer (or maybe he couldn't be bothered to shave) shadowed his chin, and he had cheekbones that a model would kill for. Added to this, were dark eyes which were crinkled against the glare of the sun, a jaw Ivy wanted to run her fingers along, and a bronze tan from working outdoors. He was absolutely delectable.

As she got closer, she noticed a flash or two of silver at his temples and a tattoo snaking its way up his arm before it disappeared underneath the sleeve of his T-shirt.

'Hi, I'm er… I've just moved in. Not for good, obviously, but for the next few months.' Ivy gave a self-conscious laugh, thinking she couldn't recall the last time she'd stumbled over words as much.

'Ms Winter, I know. I am Sebastián.' His accent matched his good looks, and her heart skipped a beat. The way he said her name… Oh my goodness.

'Yes, I guessed as much. Here to clean the pool and…' She glanced at what he'd been doing a moment ago, '…gardening and stuff.'

'Yes. I'm sorry if I disturbed you, would you like me to come back another time?' His English was exceptionally good. Not only that, his voice was deep, sultry and rather gravelly.

'Oh, no, not at all, it's fine.' She waved a hand in the air. 'You didn't disturb me. I was just about to make myself a coffee, would you like one? I mean, if you're not too busy.' When he hesitated, she added, 'If it's allowed. I wouldn't want to get you into trouble, or anything. Only if you have the time, of course.'

'I can stop work for a few minutes, and thank you, a coffee would be good.'

'Great! How do you like it?'

'Strong, black, no sugar.'

Of course – she should have guessed. 'I'll, um, go and get you a cup.'

'Thank you. I'll finish this first.'

Ivy was glad to slip back indoors, and was grateful for the cooler air of the villa's living room on her skin. My, it had been warm out there and it wasn't even midday yet. Maybe she should think about slipping into a sun dress, instead of the loose blouse and capri pants she was wearing? It would be nice to feel the sun on her skin, and she couldn't wait to take a dip in that gorgeous pool. She'd wait until Sebastián had left, of course. He really didn't need to see her lily-white legs. Or any other lily-white part of her, for that matter.

'Sebastián,' she murmured aloud, rolling his name on her tongue. It didn't sound the same when she said it.

She watched from the window as he finished his task and strolled over to a small tap set near to the barbecue to run his hands under the water, and a thought hit her with such force she felt rather giddy.

He'd make a stunning vampire. Those sultry smouldering looks, the way he seemed to be at ease with himself, unlike all her stuttering and stammering…

No, not a vampire. An angel!

My God, *that was it*! That's what the story needed. Not a mamby-pamby vampire who falls in love with human women at the drop of a hat. It needed real conflict – the sort between pure good and pure evil, with Libby stuck in the middle. And the vampire wasn't going to be a vampire – he'd be a demon, and Sebastián would play the starring role as the good guy. But he couldn't be too good; not with that face and body.

A fallen angel then – one who had to redeem himself, but along the way he'd fall in love with Libby, because…? Hmm. Clearly she still had a great deal more thinking to do and lots of things to work out, but it was a start! And for the first time in months (maybe years) she felt genuinely excited about her writing.

'Sebastián,' she said again, almost dreamily. He'd be—

'*Sí*, Sebastián. *Y yo soy Alba*,' a female voice said from behind her and Ivy nearly leapt out of her skin.

Heart thumping, she turned to face the speaker and saw a tiny woman with a face wreathed in wrinkles, holding a mop and bucket.

'Crikey, you almost scared me to death,' Ivy said, her hand on her chest. 'I didn't know you had arrived.'

'*Sí, sí.*' Alba nodded enthusiastically, smiling widely. Then she held up her mop. '*Puedo?*'

'Er… yes. *Puedo*. Great!'

'She means, do you mind if she carries on with her cleaning,' Sebastián said, and Ivy yelped and whirled around to discover the service guy standing by one of the sets of French doors.

'*Puedo* means "may I",' he explained.

Alba then started speaking to him in rapid Spanish, her eyes darting to Ivy then back to Sebastián, and once or twice she shook her mop.

'She wants to know if she should come back later. And she also says she is pleased to meet you.'

Ivy marvelled again at the rich depth of his voice, noticing it had a melodious quality to it. She had an unsettling feeling that she could listen to him talk for hours, just to hear the sound of it.

Her angel – let's call him Nathaniel for now, she thought – should sound just like him; throaty, a little sexy (but not too much) and most definitely not all silvery and tinkly. He had to sound human, but more so—

'*Señora?*' Both Sebastián and Alba were looking at her expectantly, although Ivy thought she could see an undercurrent of concern on Sebastián's face.

'Oh, sorry, I was miles away for a minute. Uh, yes, of course she should carry on.' Ivy smiled widely at the maid, trying to convey a sense of friendliness. 'I wouldn't want to stop her from doing her job.'

Sebastián stared at her for a second longer than necessary, then spoke to Alba, who shot her a quick smile, nodded, and shuffled off into the hall with her mop and bucket.

'Please, call me Ivy,' she said to Sebastián. 'Alba, too, if you could tell her for me? There's no need for this *señora* business, especially since I'm going to be around for a good few months.'

'OK.'

But he didn't sound certain, and Ivy guessed she'd probably still get called Ms Winter or *señora*; it was probably written into his contract or something, that the staff shouldn't be overfamiliar with the guests.

'I was making coffee, wasn't I?' she said, shaking her head at herself, and poured some out of the pot into two cups. 'Would Alba like one?'

'She can have mine,' Sebastián offered. 'I have to see to my next property.'

'Oh, of course.' She hadn't even considered that he might have somewhere else to be. 'I'll leave it here for her, shall I? Please can you tell her it's here?'

'Of course.' He stepped through the doors and suddenly the previously airy open-plan kitchen area felt cramped and full.

He was quite a large man, and it was impossible not to notice him. Good looks aside, he was charismatic and sex appeal rolled off him in waves. A bit like George Clooney, only younger, and more brooding, and definitely more attractive. My God, if only she could capture that raw power in her writing – but she wasn't sure she could do him justice.

She was itching to try however, and as she watched him walk through the living room and into the hall, she studied his every move. The way his shoulders rolled slightly, the way his hands hung loosely by his sides, his long legs, the set of his head – she tried to memorise every last inch of him. Thankfully, he seemed unaware of her scrutiny. As he disappeared from view for a second, she took a deep breath, excitement coursing through her. In a few moments he was back.

'Thank you for the offer of the coffee. It is very kind of you. Maybe tomorrow,' he said, and as he walked past her, she caught the faintest scent of him: masculine and slightly earthy, with an undertone of the sea, and possibly deodorant or shampoo. It was quite a heady, intoxicating smell and she was relieved when he moved out of sniffing range, although she was tempted to ask him what after-shave he used. Maybe she could buy some for Daniel—

Damn! She really must try to stop thinking about him. They were over. He was in her past and that's where he should stay. Allowing him to hijack her thoughts was taking a step back in her emotional recovery, not forwards.

'Yes, OK, great. Tomorrow it is,' she replied, absently.

Then he was gone, and Ivy was left feeling a bit of a twit at the way he'd made her go all tongue-tied and awkward. All she hoped was that he didn't think she fancied him or anything, and that was the reason for her being so gauche. Actually, she suspected she'd sounded more like someone's elderly aunt rather than a teenager with a crush, and she wasn't sure which was worse.

Quickly, she hurried to her desk and opened her laptop. She needed to get her thoughts and impressions of Sebastián – woops, Nathaniel – written down before she forgot them.

But, as she was tapping away, Ivy had a rather disconcerting feeling that she wasn't going to forget the slightest detail about him any time soon. She was convinced she could still detect the lingering smell of him, despite the breeze from the open doors and the waft of whatever Alba was using to clean the floors.

As she worked, Ivy's excitement began to build; she simply knew her readers were going to adore this new character of hers. She, herself, was half in lust with him already...

Chapter 4

Ivy sat up straight in her chair and arched her back, grimacing as her spine realigned itself after she had been sitting in one position for so long. After a couple of clicks which made her wince, she rotated her neck and reached out her arms, laced her fingers together, and stretched. It hurt, but in a good way, and she clambered stiffly to her feet.

Not so long ago, she'd have sprung out of her chair like a rabbit popping out of its burrow, but these days she was a bit more careful on the springing front, as her body didn't bounce back as easily as it once did. She thought she might also need glasses soon. Ever since she'd hit the big four-O, things had started to go downhill. If she wasn't careful, she'd soon be keeping her teeth in a glass by the side of the bed.

Boy, was she hungry and she desperately needed a drink, too. When she checked the time, she saw why – it was mid-afternoon, and she hadn't had breakfast, or lunch either. All she'd consumed since she'd got up was a single cup of coffee.

Ivy took a few steps towards the kitchen side of the room and felt her limbs starting to loosen. She realised she was exhausted, not physically, but mentally, although she did feel emotionally exuberant.

For the first time in many, many months she felt connected to her writing. Today, she'd poured her heart and soul into it, and she believed it showed. She wouldn't really be able to tell until she read back what she had written (and maybe not even then, because she wasn't sure she trusted her own judgement any more), but what had started off as making notes and observations about Nathaniel, had turned into the first two chapters of the revised manuscript. And, even better, she knew where she was headed with the rest of the book; she even had an inkling how the other novels in the proposed series might pan out.

She might be tired, she might be hungry, thirsty and mentally drained, but she was filled with a lightness and a sense of achievement that had been missing from her life for far too long.

She felt *fulfilled*. And it was wonderfully liberating.

She also felt vaguely restless and rather envious of a revamped Libby, who was no longer insipid, but was rather wicked in an innocent way and who was on the cusp of being downright evil.

That was what the story was about – Nathaniel's fight to save Libby from the demon who wanted to claim her. And Ivy anticipated having great fun with role reversals galore right the way through the story. Nathaniel, was inherently good, but came across as sexy and dangerous, with more than a little of the bad boy about him. On the other hand, Dante, the demon, was evil personified, but played the nice guy to perfection.

Ivy really wanted to return to her writing desk and pick up where she'd left off, but she knew from past experience that she needed a break, and not only to refuel. Her brain needed time to recharge as well, because every time she tried to think about Nathaniel's character, all she could see in her mind was the colour of Sebastián's eyes.

After wolfing down a sandwich while standing in the kitchen and leaning against the counter (she'd had enough of sitting down for a while), she threw the last drops of orange juice down her throat and decided to go for a walk to the village. She needed to stretch her legs and she also needed to reconnect with the rest of the world. Logically, she knew that Nora would call her on the landline if there was anything wrong or if something urgently needed her attention, but now that the idea was in her head, she simply had to check the notifications on her phone.

She decided to have a look at the restaurants while she was there too, and if she wasn't too tired she'd take a stroll back to the village later this evening for a spot of dinner. As she swapped her sandals for trainers, she idly considered what the local taxi situation was like. She hadn't noticed a number for one in the information pack, but she hadn't really had a decent look. She'd check in the village later, she thought. Maybe there was a taxi rank there? If so, she'd get their number because she seriously didn't want to have to walk back every night in the dark.

According to the map she had seen in the info pack, Ivy headed to the right out of the villa's gates and down the hill for a couple of paces. To her dismay, there was no pavement, so she was forced to walk on the road and every time a car went past she grimaced, hoping it wouldn't come too close. Not only that, but what looked like a short dab on the map was actually a decent walk, as the estimated twenty minutes turned into three-quarters of an hour.

Then there was the fact that she almost walked straight through the village and out the other side before she understood that the hamlet which she thought must be on the way to the village, actually *was* the village. There was hardly anything to it, just a single main street with a couple of shops, a café with a higgledy-piggledy pile of tables and chairs out the front where several elderly gentlemen sat, and a bus stop.

In desperation, she halted and turned in a full circle.

Several small streets radiated off the main one, but they looked like little more than residential roads. However, she picked the nearest and trotted down it, and it wasn't long before it swept around and ended in a little square.

This was more like it, although the few businesses in it – and there weren't many – appeared to be shut too. The only thing open were the church doors and, as if on cue, the bells began to toll, making her jump.

It was then that she realised today was Sunday – the shops hadn't gone out of business, but were in fact closed, and on closer inspection of what appeared to be a small supermarket, the sign on the door said it was closed between one and four p.m.

Ivy had always thought the Spanish siesta was a myth. Clearly not in this place. It was alive and kicking and currently having its mid-afternoon nap.

It seemed she had a few choices: go back to the villa, pay the church a visit, or join the handful of old men drinking coffee and smoking outside the café situated on the main road. She chose the latter in the hope that it had free wifi.

To her relief it did, and she also had a couple of bars of signal on her phone. So, the first thing she did after she'd ordered coffee and a pastry, was to call Nora.

'Hi, hon, how are you? Settled in yet?' Nora asked.

It was odd to hear her agent's voice; anyone would think Ivy had been away for weeks, not just a couple of days. But England already seemed so long ago and so far away.

'It's lovely,' Ivy gushed. 'You should see the villa – the views are stunning. I'm not too keen on the lack of phone signal though.'

'You've got a landline – what are you complaining about! By the way, there's no need to check in every day. You're there to work, remember?'

'Speaking of work…' Ivy lowered her voice as much as she could. 'I've met the most gorgeous man, and I'm using him as a basis for one of the main characters in my new series.'

'You are? That's brilliant. Hang on a sec, what do you mean you've "met a gorgeous man"?'

'He's the guy who sees to the pool and the garden. Don't worry, I'm not going to jump into a relationship with him. I've only just come out of one, remember? Speaking of which, have you had any contact with Daniel recently?' she asked, fully expecting Nora to make an excuse to end the call like she'd done yesterday.

'Ivy, you know I have, darling. I've got other authors with him.' She said it gently enough, but Ivy heard the warning and vowed to heed it. She shouldn't have asked in the first place. It wasn't fair to expect Nora to gossip about a publisher, even if that publisher had been sleeping with her most lucrative author for the past year and a half.

'Tell me more about this series,' Nora said, changing the subject.

'Not yet, but suffice it to say, there's a demon, an angel and a feisty heroine involved.'

'That's great! Isolation is working for you, then. See, Aunty Nora is always right.'

Ivy snorted – Aunty Nora indeed. 'I'm older than you,' she pointed out.

'Not by much, and it's still possible. Now, this agony aunt has work to do, and yes, I know it's Sunday, but an agent's work is never done.'

Just as Ivy ended the call, her coffee and pastry arrived and she smiled her thanks at the waitress. 'Could I have the wifi password, please?'

The woman rattled off a string of words and Ivy stared blankly at her. 'I'm sorry, could you repeat that, please?'

'*Escríbelo,*' one of the elderly gentlemen said to the woman and mimed writing on his hand.

The waitress nodded, darting into the café and returning a second later with a piece of paper with the password written on it. Ivy took it gratefully.

'Thank you so much, and thank you, too,' she added, speaking to the old gent.

'*De nada,* you are welcome,' he replied in heavily accented English. 'If you need help, ask. I speak a little English, *un poco.*' He raised his hand and showed her a finger and thumb close together. 'Pilar has not so good English. My name is Jorge. Are you on *vacaciones*?'

'On holiday? Not really; I'm staying at Villa Colina,' she said. 'My name's Ivy.' She assumed Pilar must be the waitress.

'*Hola*, Ivy. *Salud.*' He held up a tiny glass of golden liquid.

Ivy did the same with her cup and took a sip of coffee. She connected to the café's wifi and, thinking it was lucky that Jorge spoke a little English, was about to ask him where the nearest restaurant was, when her attention was claimed by her phone telling her she had email.

Surprisingly, the world had carried on perfectly well without her for the past two days and nothing much seemed to have happened. She responded to a few comments on Twitter, uploaded a photo of her new writing space to Instagram with the hashtag #working-hard and made sure to tag the holiday company, Dream Villas, in it, before answering a couple of emails. She then checked her sales ranking on Amazon and was pleased to see it was holding steady.

Thinking ahead, she decided she needed to prepare a few posts in advance, ready for her next trip into the village, and she'd also take some photos too. Readers loved to have little glimpses of her life, and although she didn't want to boast about her writing retreat, she did want to share titbits with them to remind them she still existed. Some hints about a new series on the horizon wouldn't go amiss either.

It was very pleasant sitting at a pavement café, she thought, tipping her head back and lifting her face to the sun, which was quite hot without the breeze to take some of the warmth out of it. She sat there for a while longer watching the world go by slowly as the village gradually came to life. Not all of the businesses on the main street opened after siesta time and she guessed today being a Sunday had something to do with it, but about half of the shops raised their shutters or opened their doors, and she was pleased to see a butcher, a grocer, a delicatessen, a couple of small general stores and a bank. The bank remained closed, but it was nice to know it was there in case she needed to withdraw some funds.

She suspected she'd have to replenish her own food stocks once she started to run out, so it was a relief to discover that she could probably obtain most of what she wanted right here. However, she couldn't see any restaurants or other places to eat apart from the café she was currently sitting in, and there didn't appear to be a taxi rank either, so she paid her bill, leaving a generous tip, and explored the rest of the village, certain she'd stumble across at least one or the other.

But there was no restaurant, not that she could see, although there was a bar which served food and another small café down one of the other side streets. There was no taxi rank either, to her dismay. And when she tried to decipher the times of the buses, she was disappointed to see they were scarce on a Sunday, and not much better during the rest of the week, although early morning and evenings seemed to fare better on the public transport front.

It was as though the village had gone back in time fifty years and Ivy didn't know whether to celebrate it, or cry. One thing she did know was that being here had already done wonders for her creativity and she couldn't wait to get back to the villa for round two with the laptop. Surely, cooking her own dinner two evenings in a row was a small price to pay for the resurrection of her creativity?

Chapter 5

Her fourth full day in Tenerife was going to be much like the previous three and Ivy had a feeling that her time spent on the island would give *Groundhog Day* a run for its money. Without a car she was limited in what she could do. Of course she could always hire one, but she didn't drive a great deal – let's face it, you didn't need to if you lived in London – and she didn't feel confident at the thought of having to drive on the opposite side of the road. She reasoned that she could take the bus if necessary, but there was the worry that she'd get stranded and wouldn't be able to get home. Taxis were a viable option, but only for shortish distances otherwise the cost would soon become silly and she was conscious that she still had a tax bill to pay.

Therefore, she was stuck.

It was a nice stuck, not a nasty stuck, but stuck all the same.

This morning she had already been working for three hours when she heard noises outside, and guessed it was Sebastián. Anticipating the imminent arrival of Alba too, Ivy decided it was time for a break – coffee, fresh bread, butter and jam was on the breakfast menu today, so she quickly primed the coffee machine and set out the food.

She intended to eat on the terrace, under the shade of the pergola and maybe read a book for a while. She was getting quite into the thriller she'd started the other night and the break from writing would do her good. Besides, she'd almost finished the paperback and there was a huge climax building up that she had to see resolved soon. After that, she planned to put in another couple of hours work – this time on plotting and structure – before calling it a day and having a late lunch. She hoped to follow this with a spot of sunbathing and a few dips in the pool, before a shower and a walk to the village to have coffee and to check her emails. She'd better take a look at the new releases too and download any that looked promising – it always helped to keep up with what her fellow authors were publishing. Just because she was sequestered away to write her own stuff, it didn't mean that she shouldn't keep abreast of what was hot and happening in the world of paranormal romance, and now was the ideal time to do this, without the distractions of the internet, Daniel, living in London…

As usual, Ivy couldn't help taking a sneaky peek at Sebastián as he cleaned the pool and swept up any fallen leaves. He was as handsome and as striking as the first time she'd met him. Every encounter gave her new material for Nathaniel's character, although that wasn't the sole reason she looked forward to his visits, and to Alba's, of course. For someone who enjoyed her own company and who was a confirmed introvert, Ivy was also lonely at times. It was all very well holding numerous and quite detailed conversations in her head with her characters, but she had a feeling she was doing it far too often than was healthy. And her extremely limited Spanish (aka, non-existent) meant that she didn't find it easy to converse with the gaggle of old men who seemed to be a permanent fixture outside the café, unless Jorge was there – which he wasn't always, and the others tended to come and go, too. They always smiled at her though, and raised their coffee cups in greeting.

While the coffee was brewing, Ivy ran to the bathroom to check her hair. She'd taken to wearing very little make-up, just a swipe of mascara, and she was pleased to notice that her skin was starting to take on a healthy outdoor glow.

That was the problem with a job which kept you tied to your desk all day – there was a tendency not to go outside much. But with the glorious weather on Tenerife and the lure of the infinity pool, plus her daily walk to the village and back (thankfully, she'd found a short cut which was along a dirt track and not the road, and only took the promised twenty-minutes), Ivy was starting to look and feel exceptionally healthy. It also helped that she had to make her dinner from scratch, using fresh ingredients, and as she wasn't the most sophisticated cook in the world, they tended to be simple yet nutritious meals, involving a considerable amount of salad, with fresh fruit to follow. She also allowed herself a glass of wine with her meal, often taking the half-finished glass outside afterwards, where she sat and watched the twinkling lights of the town below.

Garachico, that's what it was called according to the map, and she made a promise to visit it before long. God knows how much a taxi would cost, but she wasn't exactly spending a great deal in this ivory tower on the side of the hill, so she should be able to stretch to it as long as she didn't make a habit of it.

As she left the bathroom, a movement from inside her bedroom caught her attention, and she called out, 'Good morning, Alba. Coffee?'

She almost leapt out of her skin when a deep, throaty voice replied, 'Thank you. I would like that.'

What the hell was Sebastián doing in her bedroom?

For a second, she was quite put out until she realised he was probably checking every room in the property for problems such as sticking windows or blown light bulbs. He seemed to be an all-round handyman, as well as gardener and pool cleaner.

The thought of him in her bedroom did make her heart race though, no matter how innocent the reason. Curious to see how he looked in the room (the image would do wonders for her writing, she told herself), she pushed the door open – to find him manhandling her sheets!

'What are you doing?' she demanded. It was all well and good her having the odd daydream about Sebastián in his role as the sexy main male character in her new novel, but it was quite another to think of his hands all over the bed she slept in. It made her tingle and she wasn't sure that getting all tingly over him was a good idea.

'Alba is not here today, so I am cleaning the villa.' He whipped a pillowcase off and dropped it on the floor with the rest of the bed linen destined for the wash.

Ah, that explained it. Ivy wasn't particularly happy at having him change her sheets, though, but there wasn't anything to be done about it now. 'Is it her day off?'

Sebastián glanced at her and shook his head. 'No, she has gone to Santa Cruz to visit her sister who is not well.

I think she might not be back for a few weeks, maybe longer.'

'Let me do that,' Ivy said, stepping forward to gather up the dirty sheets.

'No, it is for me to do,' Sebastián said firmly. 'Maid service is every day, so today I am Alba.'

'But there's a washing machine in the kitchen,' she objected. 'I'm perfectly capable of shoving a few things in it and turning it on.'

'*Sí*, I know this. But,' he was smiling at her, 'maid service is part of the package.'

'At least let me make the bed.'

'No.' He shook his head, still smiling. 'My job.'

'I *am* allowed to make you coffee, right?' she asked, a little facetiously.

'You are. Black, no sugar, please,' he reminded her.

As if she could forget – she'd been making him and Alba coffee for the past few days. She hesitated before she went to the kitchen, hoping she hadn't left any underwear lying around in the bedroom. Not that she had, but now that the thought had popped into her head, she couldn't shift it. It was a bit like wondering if you'd really locked the front door – once you considered the possibility that you hadn't, then you had no choice but to go back and check.

Which was precisely what she wanted to do now, but couldn't because Sebastián was in there and she didn't want him to know that she was hunting for stray pairs of knickers or the odd bra.

Cursing silently, she made the coffee.

It took him a while to join her, and as she pottered around in the kitchen her ears followed his progress from

41

her bedroom to the bathroom, where she heard water running and guessed he was cleaning it. All she could do was to hope she hadn't left anything embarrassing lying around in there, either. No doubt he'd seen worse things in the past than Ivy's smalls and the odd packet of tampons, but for some reason she didn't want Sebastián to see anything like that of hers.

At least she was tidy and kept the villa clean in between Alba's visits. Apart from the desk which had papers strewn across it and post-it notes stuck around the window frame above it, there wasn't a thing out of place.

Eventually, he came back into the main part of the house, wiping his hands on a towel. 'All finished,' he said. 'Or is there anything else you need?'

'If you can do my shopping and cooking, that would be great,' she replied, deadpan.

'What is it you need? I can buy it from the shop if you tell me what you want.'

'Will you cook it for me too?'

'If you wish.'

Oh... she'd been joking obviously, but he was taking her seriously. This was awkward. Him doing her shopping might be handy, although so far she'd been able to get everything she needed from the selection of little shops in the village, but as for the cooking part...

Then she saw the twinkle in his eye and she understood that he was the one who was teasing her.

She rolled her eyes. 'Touché.'

Sebastián dipped his head in acknowledgement and grinned at her. Oh my God, just look at those dimples in his cheeks. They were too much! If she'd thought he was sexy before, then he was downright gorgeous when he grinned like that.

She'd have to make Nathaniel grin. Not often, because he was supposed to be dark and brooding, but just now and again, enough to get Libby all hot and bothered. Just like Ivy herself was becoming…

'Seriously,' she said, trying to round up her wayward emotions before they ran away with her. 'There isn't a restaurant in the village, is there? If there is, I haven't found it.'

'No, but I can recommend El Huerto Secreto. It is in El Tanque. You will have passed through the town on your way from the airport. It is about five kilometres that way.' He pointed further up the hill.

'Thanks, I might try that tonight. I'm getting rather fed up with my own cooking.'

'You don't like to cook?'

Ivy wrinkled her nose. 'I do… it's just that I'm not very good at it. Lack of practice probably. I tend – *tended* – to eat out a lot in England. It was easier and I couldn't be bothered to prepare a meal just for one.'

Daniel had never come to her house for dinner. Breakfast on the odd occasion, but not dinner. He was usually too busy schmoozing clients or attending fairs or conferences to eat at either his place or hers. And if she hadn't gone with him (which was rare, because he liked to have her by his side) then she hadn't usually bothered to make herself anything more complex than a plate of cheese and crackers. Or she hadn't eaten at all. Was he taking Rebekkah Rain (*definitely* a pen name) out this evening, and if he was, would he end up in her bed or his? Ivy hoped it was Rebekkah's, because she didn't want to think

43

about another woman in the space she had not all that long ago occupied.

Crossly, she shook her head to rid her mind of her fickle ex. Daniel had no business being in her thoughts, not after the way he'd treated her. It was her own fault – she should have realised what he was like. After all, his reputation for being ruthless was well known, as were the number of girlfriends he'd had in the past. At her age, she would have thought she wouldn't have been stupid enough to think that she'd be the one to tame him, to persuade him to settle down. He was in his late forties and he had remained unmarried for years (there was an ex-wife somewhere in his dim and distant past), so why on earth did she think she'd be the one to get him to the altar again?

She came back to herself to find Sebastián studying her, a flicker of disquiet in his eyes.

'Are you OK?' he asked.

'Of course. I'm fine.' She poured the coffee and handed him a cup, but his attention wasn't on the rich, dark liquid. It was on her.

'I shall cook for you tonight,' Sebastián announced abruptly.

'Excuse me?'

'I,' he patted his broad chest, 'shall prepare a meal for you.'

'Oh no, I couldn't let you do that!' She was quite taken aback by the offer. It was very sweet of him, but he was the guy who cleaned the pool (and he was also now the guy who made her bed – but she didn't want to dwell on that). He was probably quite good with his hands too (nope, she didn't want to dwell on that, either), and she had the feeling he could fix most things, but she certainly wasn't going to let him cook dinner for her.

'I am a good cook,' he said. 'Very good.'

'I'm not doubting that for a second, but I'm not going to let you cook for me.'

'Why not?' He seemed genuinely perplexed.

'It's not your job.'

'I have cooked for guests before.'

'You have?' She wasn't sure if he was winding her up or not.

'Yes. Many times. The villa comes with the option of meals included.'

'It does?' She still wasn't comfortable with the idea. However, she couldn't decide if it was because Sebastián would be the one doing the cooking. Maybe if he'd had provided a meal on the first evening she was there, it would seem perfectly normal. Or maybe if she was staying here with a group of other people, Sebastián cooking their meal wouldn't seem quite so intimate.

She honestly didn't think she could lounge around the living room while he slaved over a hot stove. And then what would happen once the meal was ready? Would she be expected to eat it while he hovered in the background, clutching a bottle of wine in case her glass needed topping up?

Nope. This was so not going to happen.

'It's fine, really.' She'd prefer to eat at that restaurant he'd recommended.

'If you are sure? It's no problem for me to make you dinner.'

Oh yes, it is, she thought.

He finished his drink and placed the cup in the dishwasher. 'Thank you for the coffee,' he said. Then, on his way out with an armful of sheets off her bed, he added, 'I have left my mobile number on the table in the hall. This is my personal number, not for work. If you change your mind, call me.'

She nodded, having no intention of calling him at all. For anything. Not even if the oven exploded. The way he was making her insides tumble over, she didn't trust herself to be in the same village as him, let alone be in the same room, watching him prepare dinner for her.

'Get over yourself,' she muttered, as she sat down at the dining table and buttered a thick wedge of bread. He wasn't interested in her – he was just being polite. And he was probably married with a handful of kids and a dutiful wife, and was working all hours of the day and night to provide for them.

Feeling a need to ground herself and stop thinking such silly thoughts, she used the landline to give her agent a call.

'Sweetie, how's it going?' Nora gushed. 'Hang on a sec...' Ivy heard some muffled talking as she covered the phone, and she waited patiently for Nora to finish whatever conversation she was having.

'It's going really well,' Ivy said once she'd reclaimed Nora's attention, filling her in on what she had achieved so far.

'I'm glad. You seem to have got your mojo back.'

'I most definitely have! I can't wait to show you what I've got for you, but that's several weeks away yet.'

'You know the score – as soon as you've got a synopsis, send it across with some sample chapters and I can start approaching a few publishers.' She hesitated, and Ivy sensed there was something going on.

'What is it?'

'Nothing much. Honestly, don't worry.'

'About what? What is it that I don't need to worry about?'

'It's nothing.'

'You can't leave me in suspense, that's not fair.'

Nora let out a sigh. 'It's Daniel. He's been putting it about that you're old hat, and that you've run out of ideas.'

Ivy was stunned. 'The nasty, spiteful, horrid— Ooh! Words fail me.'

'I think that's exactly what he's been hinting at,' Nora replied dryly, and despite herself Ivy laughed.

'He's going to be in for a shock when he sees my new book on the shelves,' she declared.

'I've never heard you so confident. Is it really that good?'

'I'd like to think so.' It was Ivy's turn to hesitate. Was this fledgling novel any good, or was she kidding herself? She wouldn't really know until she gave it to Nora, but her heart was telling her it was the best she'd written to date.

'I can't wait to read it, and to think you haven't been there a full week yet. There must be something in the air.'

Oh, there was something all right, but it wasn't the air...

Chapter 6

It turned out that El Huerto Secreto was very popular indeed. So popular that booking was advised, and Ivy was regretfully informed that they didn't have a table free for tonight. Nor tomorrow, or the following few days. They were closed on Mondays, but would next Tuesday do?

It would have to, she grumbled to herself as she confirmed the booking and went back outside. The taxi that had picked her up from the villa had disappeared, but rather than ring for another one straight away, she decided to have a wander around the small town in the hopes of finding sustenance elsewhere.

But no matter how far she trotted up and down its steep streets, she only found one other place to eat – a pizzeria. It was busy and too full of parents with children for her liking; she didn't fancy sitting at a table on her own while everyone else played happy families around her and gave her sympathetic looks, so she chose the only other option and called for a cab to take her back to the villa.

'It's not possible,' a man's voice told her over the phone. 'Two hours. There is a… *celebración*. Big, big *celebración*. All taxis busy. Two hours. Maybe one and one half.'

Great. She might as well walk back to the villa, and while she was at it, she could plan what she was going to cook tonight because it didn't look like she was going to eat out.

'Ms Winter? Ivy?'

She whirled around at the sound of her name, to find Sebastián standing at the door of the pizzeria, clutching the hand of a small girl and staring quizzically at her.

'Oh, hi, I was um, just, um...'

'El Huerto Secreto?' he guessed, taking a step towards her.

'Er, yes. Hello,' she said to the child, who was hanging back, half hiding behind her father's legs and with a thumb corked firmly in her mouth.

She was the prettiest little girl Ivy had ever seen, with dark hair caught up in a curling ponytail on the top of her head and huge brown eyes which regarded her solemnly. She might have known any child of Sebastián's would be as gorgeous as he was. She also might have known that Sebastián was taken.

'This is Emilia. She is three years old and very shy. Except when it comes to making fun of her Uncle Sebastián,' he said.

'Uncle—? Ah, she's not yours, then?'

'No, but she has my heart anyway.' He bent down and scooped her up, balancing her on his hip, and the child took her thumb out of her mouth to wind her arms around his neck. Sebastián kissed the little girl's cheek and Ivy almost melted. What an adorable pair they made – the large handsome man and the cute little girl. And there was also something very appealing about a man who loved small children. Daniel had never liked kids. He didn't have any of his own and he tended not to frequent the kinds of places children went to. Which hadn't bothered her, because for her the option of having children had long gone. Forty-three was too old for her to start a family, and when she had been of an age to consider having kids, the timing had never been right. Besides, she hadn't met a man she wanted to have children with, and she was traditional enough to want to do things the old-fashioned way. So, no children, and it was the one real regret in her life.

'Do you have any children of your own, Sebastián?'

'No, but I am uncle to this little one, and she's enough for anyone, no? And I have two nephews, also.' He nuzzled his nose into Emilia's hair, making her giggle. 'Do you have children?' he asked, then added hurriedly, 'Apologies, I should not ask guests personal questions.'

'That's OK, I don't mind. No, no kids.'

Their gazes met and held with a flash of something that Ivy – whose profession was based on finding just the right word – couldn't put a name to. Whatever it was, it was gone almost as soon as it had arrived, and she looked away quickly, hoping he didn't see her attraction to him written all over her face.

For goodness' sake, she said to herself; she was here to work, not to fall in lust. And she'd only just come out of a relationship which she was still smarting from – why on earth would she want to enter into another?

'Are you coming inside?' he asked, jerking his head at the door.

'No, I'm going to head back to the villa. I've booked a table at El Huerto Secreto for Tuesday,' she added brightly.

'It means secret garden,' Sebastián told her. 'I know the owner, Miguel. Would you like me to phone him and see if he can fit you in tonight?'

'That's so kind of you, but please don't bother. I'll wait until Tuesday. Honestly, it's fine.'

'I am sure if Miguel knew who you are—'

Ivy blushed and fluttered a hand in front of her face. 'No, really, he's probably never heard of me, and why would he? I'm not that famous, and it would be so embarrassing.'

Sebastián's expression was puzzled, and even Emilia was studying her curiously. 'I will tell him you are a guest at Villa Colina, and he will find you a table as a favour to me. He has done this before. There is no reason to be embarrassed.'

Ivy winced inwardly; oh yes, there was! She'd stupidly assumed that Sebastián had heard of her and was going to use her small and limited fame to get her a table. Her cheeks grew hotter and she knew she must be glowing as red as the sunset. What an idiot she'd made of herself.

'Seriously, it's fine,' she said. 'There's plenty of food in the villa and I'm happy to make myself something.'

Sebastián raised an eyebrow, and Ivy bit her lip.

'Come eat at the pizzeria, with us,' he suggested and she was even more mortified.

He was feeling sorry for her and he'd seen straight through her white lie. Both of them knew she wasn't going to cook anything tonight. What she would 'make' was a sandwich, not a meal.

'Thank you, it's a nice offer, but I don't want to intrude—'

'Come eat with *me*,' he said, softly.

Emilia was starting to squirm, and the little girl whispered something in her uncle's ear. 'Emilia wants to go back inside and she said she wants the nice lady to come with us,' he translated.

Ivy gave him a disbelieving look. 'She didn't say that.'

'She did! We are about to order, so please join us. There is wine…' He smiled invitingly.

'I don't think I should.'

'Please?'

She took a deep breath and let it out slowly. If she continued to refuse, she was going to appear churlish and stand-offish, and she had many more months of seeing him at the villa. But if she accepted, she might be opening a can of worms. She may well fancy Sebastián, but she didn't know him as a person and she wasn't sure she *should* get to know him. He was employed by the owners of the villa and it might throw up a whole load of problems if she was to socialise with him, however innocently. Though she was fairly sure Sebastián's offer was perfectly innocent. In fact, she got the feeling that he felt sorry for her. She didn't know what Nora had told Dream Villas when she'd booked the property, and she guessed that the company assumed she was on an extended holiday. On her own. Alone. When she looked at her retreat from the world in that context, she understood that she might come across as rather sad and pitiful.

'OK, but let me pay,' she said.

Sebastián narrowed his eyes and slowly shook his head. 'You are my guest. Anyway, we order the food to share – there is no one meal you can pay for. Pizza, tapas, fries, garlic bread… it is put in the middle of the table for everyone to take.'

That wasn't what she meant. Her offer had been to pay for everyone, not just for her own food. But as she nervously followed him and Emilia inside, she was glad he'd taken it the wrong way as she didn't want to appear to be throwing her money around magnanimously, especially when Sebastián's job was probably low paid. The last thing she wanted to do was to offend him.

The pizzeria was just as busy as earlier on. Sebastián, still carrying Emilia, wound his way through the crowded restaurant to a long table towards the rear, near doors that opened onto an outside seating area with swings and slides.

The table had eleven chairs around it, four of them empty and as Sebastián set Emilia down he said something to a waiter, who went to fetch another chair. Emilia dashed off outside to join a pair of small boys who were chasing each other around the slide, and soon their squeals and laughter drifted in through the open door.

Six pairs of eyes gazed at her curiously as Sebastián introduced her in Spanish. Then he switched to English and went around the table.

'This is my sister, Cristina, and her husband, Sergio; Yolanda, my other sister, and her husband—'

After the third person was introduced, Ivy knew she didn't stand a cat in hell's chance of remembering any of their names, apart from Sebastián's and Emilia's, but everyone was friendly and they nodded and smiled, and said hello. A chair was brought for her and placed in between Sebastián and his grandmother. His parents were at either end of the table and one of his sisters and her husband were seated on the same side as Ivy, with the other sister and her husband seated on the opposite side, along with three empty seats which she guessed must belong to the children.

The conversation soon started up again, and Ivy sat quietly trying to take it all in, thankful for Sebastián's comforting presence.

The old lady said something to her, and Ivy smiled and shook her head to show she didn't understand.

'My grandmother wants to know if you are married, do you have children?' He leaned across her slightly and spoke to his grandmother, and Ivy breathed deeply as the enticing scent of him drifted over her. He smelt divine. When he straightened up it was to tell her that Marta, his grandmother, was being nosey and that Ivy didn't have to answer if she didn't want to.

'That's OK. Please can you tell her that I'm not married and I don't have any children.'

'I already told her about having no children, but I didn't know about the other,' he said.

Marta spoke again.

Sebastián translated. 'She wants to know have you ever been married, and if not, why not? Or are you one of those modern women who has a lover?' He rolled his eyes, and spoke to the old lady again, then turned back to Ivy. 'Sorry, I told her it is not polite to say "lover". The correct thing to say is "partner".'

Marta snorted. 'Lover,' she said in very heavily accented English, drawing out the word and rolling the r at the end.

'She is...' Sebastián pulled a face and shrugged apologetically, and was then subjected to a barrage of Spanish and a wagged finger. 'She says it is not for me to apologise for her, and that she is not sorry.'

Ivy grinned. She was beginning to like this old lady.

The brother-in-law sitting opposite Ivy caught her eye and asked her, in fairly good English, how long she was on holiday for.

'I'm not on holiday,' she replied, 'although it does feel like it most of the time. I'm here to work.'

'Ah, I see. And where is that? What company?' he asked, and she wished she could remember his name.

'I work for myself. I'm a writer.'

'For a magazine?' This was from his wife. She was chic and attractive, with wings of dark hair framing her face, and she was made-up perfectly. Ivy felt a little dowdy in comparison. She could certainly see the family resemblance to Sebastián in the shape of the woman's full lips and the height of her cheekbones.

'I write novels. Books,' she added, in case Sebastián's sister didn't understand.

'Sí, a writer,' she nodded.

Sebastián leant towards Ivy. 'Is this where I ask if I have read any of your books?' He was teasing her, she thought.

'It depends on whether you read paranormal romances,' she said archly, then immediately wished she hadn't. What if, at some point in the future when the manuscript she was working on was published, he actually read it out of curiosity about the author who'd once stayed in the villa he serviced? She'd be horrified if he recognised himself in Nathaniel.

'I like romance,' his sister said, fluttering her eyelashes. 'Romantic films with handsome men, such as *A Lavender Summer.*' She pulled a face at her brother, and Sebastián shot her a narrow-eyed look.

Her husband shook his head. 'I was handsome before I had a wife and children,' he said and sighed dramatically, rubbing at his receding hairline ruefully and earning himself a nudge in the ribs from his wife.

Sebastián's father asked Ivy, 'You like Villa Colina?'

'Very much. It's superbly appointed and the views are amazing.'

'Good. I told him he should buy—'

'*Papá*,' Sebastián broke in, staring intently at his father. '*Ella no sabe.*'

Francisco raised his eyebrows. '*Nada?*'

Sebastián shook his head. His father glanced at Ivy, then back to Sebastián and shrugged. He said something else in Spanish, and Sebastián smiled and patted him on the arm.

What on earth was that all about? Maybe his father didn't like him doing the job he was doing? Or maybe he was telling Sebastián that one day he might own a place like that. Ivy certainly wished she had the funds to buy a villa like that herself, although she suspected it was well out of her price range. Maybe if she sold her house in London…?

'Sorry, I don't mean to be rude, but you know what parents are like,' Sebastián said to her.

She certainly did. Both of hers were dead now; her father only having passed away a year or so ago, but her mum had been gone a long time. It must be nice to have such a large family, she thought. She didn't have anyone at all, apart from some distant cousins on her mother's side who still sent Christmas cards, but whom she hadn't seen for years.

The sense of affection and love around the table was palpable and it gave her a warm glow even if she wasn't part of it. Everyone made her feel incredibly welcome though, and even Sebastián's mother, who didn't speak English, kept shooting beaming smiles at her and nodding. And Marta, Sebastián's grandmother, kept passing her plates of food and, via sign language, urging her to eat more of the delicious dishes.

Sebastián had been right – there was an abundance of food and everyone dived in happily, swapping one dish for another as they passed the plates around, bickering amicably. The noise was incredible as everyone seemed to be speaking at once, and not one of them appeared to listen to what anyone else had to say. It was lovely to see that the three children were allowed to join in and be as raucous as they liked, without being told to be quiet, and Ivy noticed that all the other families in the pizzeria behaved the same way. Dinner time in this part of the world was very much a noisy, family affair.

When she eventually sat back, full to the point of bursting, she realised she was having a really good time. The food was wonderful, the wine flowed, and the conversation was lively, even if most of it was incomprehensible to her. Sebastián did his best to keep up with the translation, but most of the conversation was too quick-fire and rapid, and sometimes he had to search for the right word, and by the time he'd found it, the conversation had moved on.

After he'd tried to explain a convoluted and detailed story regarding Álvaro, who was one of his brothers-in-law, a goat, and the owner of a bar, she found herself laughing so hard at the end of it that she had tears in her eyes – and not because she'd followed the story, but because of Sebastián's attempts to explain it to her. He couldn't translate the words fast enough and had ended up pretending to be a goat and then miming the bar owner's rage.

'You crack me up,' she giggled. 'It's almost as if the goat is here right now, and as for the poor owner...' She dissolved into giggles again, along with the children who clearly thought the world of their uncle and his ridiculous antics.

'You should be on the stage,' she declared, wiping her eyes. 'You'd go down a storm in a pantomime.' Not that she'd been to a panto since she was a child, but she guessed they probably hadn't changed all that much.

An abrupt lull in the conversation made her look around the table, and she caught a couple of glances being exchanged, but she couldn't decipher their meaning. Then Marta said something, Sebastián's mum replied, and everything was back to normal so quickly that Ivy wondered whether she'd imagined it.

Sebastián, clearly exhausted from pretending to be a goat, was sipping his water and staring into space, his expression blank.

Feeling a little awkward, she said, 'I really must learn a few phrases in Spanish.'

He blinked and swivelled slightly in his chair so he was facing her. 'You are here for many months, so it is a good idea and a good opportunity to learn the language. I could teach you, if you like.'

She didn't mean for him to teach her – she was thinking about maybe downloading an app for that – although now he'd mentioned it, she liked the idea. But, she had to ask herself, was it because she liked him (more than liked him, if she was being honest), or because he spoke good English and was at the villa every day? In fact, she didn't think he'd had a day off since she'd arrived, and he was still cleaning the inside of the house too, because Alba had yet to return.

Was it fair of her to burden him with yet another chore?

'Thanks for the offer, but you've got enough on your plate as it is,' she said.

He looked at the empty plate on the table on front of him and frowned, and Ivy stifled a laugh. 'I mean, you have enough work, without me giving you more to do.'

His expression when he lifted his gaze to her face, was warm. 'It will not be work for me to teach you. It will be pleasure.'

Aw, he was so polite and accommodating. It wouldn't be that much of a pleasure to teach her, because she wasn't a very patient pupil, and she didn't want to subject him to her inevitable annoyance when her learning wasn't progressing at a swift enough pace. Ivy knew what she was like as a pupil; chess had been a prime example – Daniel had tried to teach her once and she'd given up long before she'd got the hang of it, because the whole experience had made both of them cross.

Still, it wouldn't do any harm if they exchanged simple things such as, 'good morning' and 'how are you' in Spanish, and then she could practice secretly on her own and surprise him one day.

'That would be great,' she said, 'but only if you're sure, and only if it doesn't interfere with your job. Speaking of jobs, I should phone for a taxi. It's getting late, and I want to be up early tomorrow. I have a book to write and early mornings are my most productive.' She got to her feet. 'Can you tell everyone that it was delightful to meet them, and thank them from me for making me feel so welcome? And thank you, too,' she added. 'I've really enjoyed myself.'

'So have I.' He did as she asked, explaining that she was leaving, but before the words had even left his mouth, she was swamped by everyone wanting to hug her and kiss her cheeks in farewell.

It was a good twenty minutes before she was able to leave. 'I should have phoned for a taxi earlier,' she lamented, as she gathered up her bag.

'I shall take you home,' Sebastián said, waving to his family and dodging yet more hugs and kisses with an ease born of long practice. 'Quick, if we don't leave now, we might have to stay until midnight.' He ushered her to the door, ignoring her half-hearted protests that he needn't trouble himself, and that she could just as easily get a taxi. 'I insist,' he said. 'It is no trouble.'

Once outside, she hesitated, wondering which of the many cars was his, having only ever seen him drive the Dream Villa van, then she froze when he walked towards a fearsome-looking motorbike and halted beside it.

'That's yours?' she asked, her voice a higher pitch than usual, and she swallowed convulsively. She'd never ridden on a motorbike before and she wasn't sure she wanted to do so now.

Sebastián was rooting around in a box on the back and he produced a helmet with a flourish. 'It is big, but it will be OK for now, and I promise to drive carefully.'

She sent him a doubtful look. 'I don't know...'

'You've not been on a bike before, no?'

'No.'

'It will be good, you'll see. I will take care of you.' He held the helmet out.

She took it and stood uncertainly, until he reached out and removed her handbag from her shoulder and popped it in the box. Then he moved closer, took the helmet back and slowly, gently, placed it on her head, his fingers tucking her hair up underneath it.

She shivered, his touch making her heart thud. His face was mere inches away from hers as he concentrated on making sure the strap was adjusted under her chin. The scent of him filled her nose, a delicious light, clean smell with a hint of sandalwood and musk, and she closed her eyes, trying not to inhale too deeply in case he realised the effect he was having on her.

Suddenly, their eyes locked.

For a second, she gazed into his and she noticed lighter flecks hidden in the dark-chocolate depths. He caught his bottom lip with his teeth and her attention was drawn to his mouth, and all she wanted to do was to kiss him, to taste him—

'Here, you will need this.' The mood was abruptly broken as he turned away and unhooked a black leather jacket from where it was hanging on the handlebars.

It smelt of him, she noticed, as she caught hold of it. 'Don't you need it?'

'Not as much as you. I am used to the bike; you are not.'

She shrugged her way into it, feeling the heaviness of the material on her shoulders and the silkiness of the lining against her bare arms. She almost felt as though she was wearing his skin – it was incredibly intimate.

'I'll get on first, and you sit behind me,' he said, swinging a leg over the bike.

She was reminded of a gunslinger in the American Mid-West when he mounted a horse, and Sebastián's casual grace and unconscious confidence stirred something deep within her. Trembling slightly, she cocked her leg over the seat and settled herself behind him, trying not to get too close.

'You will need to put your arms around my waist and hold on tight,' he instructed, wedging his own helmet on his head.

Having no choice, Ivy scooted closer until her chest was pressed up against his back, and she felt the warmth of him seeping through her dress where she hadn't zipped the jacket up. Taking a steadying breath and wondering what the hell had got into her, she slid her arms around his waist and held on.

God, he felt good. She already knew he was fit, but what she hadn't realised was how lean and muscular he was. His stomach muscles felt solid under her fingers and there didn't seem to be an ounce of fat on him. She tried to not let her imagination run riot as she imagined what he'd look like without his T-shirt, but it wasn't easy when she was cosied up against his back and if it wasn't for the damned helmet, she'd be able to run her tongue up the back of his neck—

Stop it! She seriously had to get a grip on her runaway libido and her wayward imagination. This was the guy who serviced the villa, for goodness' sake. She was nothing more than a guest to him, and he'd probably be horrified if he knew the kinds of thoughts she was having about him.

But she couldn't seem to help herself and it was quite disconcerting. She blamed it on this new series and the delectable Nathaniel – perhaps basing her sexy main character on someone real hadn't been such a good idea, especially when she was currently cuddled up against his back and wishing there wasn't a dirty great big helmet between her lips and his neck.

It was all very well to think that the sooner she finished this book the better, so that she could stop having such thoughts about him, but her current manuscript was only the first of a whole series featuring a Sebastián look-alike; plus she was set to remain at the villa for close to six months; *plus* she was doing the best writing she'd ever done, and that was the most important thing. Her writing was everything to her, and she was currently on a wave of creativity which she hadn't experienced since those early heady years of seeing her work published for the first time. All this meant that she wouldn't be able to escape Sebastián anytime soon, even if she did manage to put physical distance between them, because he was still very much in her head.

Ivy wasn't prepared for the abrupt jerk backwards as the bike began to move, and she let out a little squeak, grabbing Sebastián tightly as they picked up speed. She felt a rumble in his chest and realised he was chuckling, so she squeezed him harder and shouted, 'That was mean!'

This time she heard his laugh as well as felt it, and she narrowed her eyes. Her head told her she was perfectly safe and they were travelling quite slowly, and it also told her that Sebastián wouldn't let anything happen to her; but her heart was thumping, her hands felt clammy, and her stomach was doing a backward flip.

By the time the bike slowed and turned gently into the villa's drive, she was a complete wreck. She had to force her reluctant arms to unwind themselves from his waist, her legs felt like jelly as she clambered stiffly and inelegantly off the machine, and her head was spinning. Yet she also felt excited and exhilarated, and she hadn't wanted the brief journey to come to an end.

'That was fun,' she said after she'd managed to find her voice.

Sebastián switched off the engine, eased the kickstand down then got off the bike. Ivy waited patiently for him to unbuckle her helmet and ease it over her head before she removed the jacket, rather unwillingly, and handed it back. As he put it on, she had to admit that it probably looked much better on him than it had done on her. Black jeans, black helmet, black leather jacket, dark eyes which looked almost black too, and her mouth was suddenly dry.

'I'll wait for you to go inside,' he said, and all she could do was nod. When she reached the door to the villa, she halted and turned back to him.

'Thank you for bringing me home and thank you for inviting me to share dinner with you. You have an adorable family and I really enjoyed myself.'

His face was in shadow but his eyes glittered, and she caught a flash of teeth as he smiled. 'Me, too. Very much.'

Then he snapped the visor into position, and she stood in the doorway to her luxury villa feeling totally confused as she watched him drive away.

After a few moments, she retreated inside, made her way to her desk and began to write.

Chapter 7

Seeing Sebastián the next morning felt awkward – for her, not for him. He didn't appear to be in the least bit fazed. Unlike Ivy, who was fazed to hell. It didn't help that she had only managed four hours' sleep, because after he'd dropped her off, she'd sat at her desk until three a.m., her fingers flying over the keyboard as the words poured from her brain and onto the page.

He behaved exactly the same as he had done every other morning so far, getting on with the job of cleaning the pool and the garden, before making his way indoors to sweep and mop the floors. Since Alba's disappearance and that first morning when she'd caught him changing the sheets on her bed, she made her own. She also cleaned the bathroom too, although he often did it again anyway as part of his rounds. He hadn't commented on her bedmaking skills and neither had he tried to remake it again, but she fully expected him to bring her fresh sheets again today, and the thought of slipping into sheets he'd handled made her feel rather weird.

He mightn't have been bothered about last night, but for Ivy it was a different matter. Feeling self-conscious, she busied herself in the kitchen while he did what he needed to do outside, then she took her coffee onto the terrace while he cleaned the villa. She really hoped he would stop doing that; she was perfectly capable of cleaning the place herself. She didn't need anyone else to do it for her, especially not Sebastián. This villa was her home for the next five and a half months and she wanted to treat it as though she was actually living here, rather than taking a vacation in it.

Gathering her scattered wits, she sauntered casually into the kitchen (feeling anything but casual) and waited for Sebastián to emerge from her bedroom where she could hear him running some water in the en suite.

'I made you a coffee,' she said when he appeared, and she pushed the cup towards him.

He took it with a nod and a smile. She waited for him to have a sip, then she said, 'I don't want you to clean the villa any more.'

The hurt and confusion on his face was evident, so she hastily added, 'I'd really like to do it myself. It would make me feel more like I am actually living here, rather than on my holibobs.'

His blank expression told her that he hadn't understood that last bit.

'"Holibobs" is slang for holidays. I appreciate what you're doing, and I understand it's part of the rental package, but I can't just write all day, or sit around by the pool. Looking after the villa and doing my own washing will give me something to do when I'm waiting for inspiration to strike.' It was only a half-lie – she honestly did find that the change of pace from sitting at a desk to doing household chores helped her think. It was as though the physical, mundane stuff rebooted her brain, and in the past she'd often spring-cleaned her way out of a sticky plot situation. The lie bit was that she didn't currently have a problem with the plot. On the contrary, her plotting was going extremely well, and as for the writing itself, she was already over a third of the way through the story and she was itching to get back to it after she'd had her breakfast.

'OK, but only if I can do something else for you instead,' he replied slowly.

Ivy was taken aback. 'It depends,' she said, her tone cautious.

'Let me cook for you tonight.'

'Oh, um, no, that's awfully kind of you, but—'

He grinned disarmingly at her as he interrupted her in mid-flow, 'You do not like to cook. I do.'

'Yes, but—'

'I have to do something to earn my wages, and if you won't let me clean the villa...' He paused, letting his words sink in.

Oh hell, she hadn't been expecting that. Wishing she hadn't said anything about cleaning the villa and realising that she couldn't take the words back without sounding an idiot, she blurted, 'You can cook but only if you eat with me.' Where had that come from? She had not intended to say anything of the sort. Mentally face-palming herself, she tried to give him a genuine smile and not the grimace that was itching to show itself.

'You have a deal,' he said.

She watched him go to the fridge and peer inside it. He rooted around in it for a second or two, then he did the same thing with the freezer.

'What are you planning?' she asked. 'And is there anything you need me to do?'

'I am not telling you, and no, there is nothing for you to do except eat it when it is cooked.'

'I'll be popping to the village later, is there anything I can pick up while I'm there?'

'No, thank you. You have everything here.'

She did? OK, then. But after he'd left, she couldn't help having a look inside to guess what might have taken his fancy, but she was none the wiser.

The rest of the day followed the same leisurely pattern of all the other days so far, and Ivy discovered that she liked the routine she had set for herself. The absence of social media or any other online distractions was liberating and it forced her to concentrate when she might otherwise have been surfing and messing about. To be fair, she didn't normally do a great deal of that when she was writing (she wouldn't be so prolific if she spent all her time on the internet), but the temptation had always been there in the background to check her emails, or sign up for another book promotion.

After a simple lunch of eggs, olives, cheese and bread, she took herself off to the cafe for her usual two cups of coffee and access to the free wifi.

'My word, you're looking well!' Nora exclaimed when Ivy FaceTimed her while she sat at her usual table.

'I'm feeling well,' she admitted.

'How's the writing going?' Nora asked.

'Great, more than great, wonderful.'

'When will you have something for me to look at?'

'I've just sent you an email with a synopsis attached, and the first five chapters,' she said. 'I've written more, but I want to tweak them a bit first before you take a look at them.' Five whole chapters (and a bit more) already! She was most definitely on a roll. She could usually manage to write about two thousand words a day on average, but since she'd been living at the villa, she'd more than doubled that.

'Got it,' Nora said after a pause. 'I'll have a look at it this evening and let you know if I think you're on the right track.'

Nora had been a godsend throughout Ivy's career and she was as good an editor as anyone employed by any of the big publishing houses. Editing her clients' work wasn't strictly part of her remit as an agent, but Nora always ran her critical eye over any manuscript that came her way, and she was an expert in knowing what editors were looking for and whether the story sitting on her desk was one which she could successfully submit to a publisher. All of which was the reason why Ivy would be on tenterhooks until she received Nora's feedback. Ivy might believe this was the best writing she'd ever done, but Nora might not agree.

What would she do if Nora hated it? Or if there were so many issues that it would take a major reworking to address them?

Absently, Ivy scrolled through Twitter while she pondered the problem.

There would be only one option available to her — she'd have to throw in the towel, close her laptop, and put her special writing pen back in the box. Because if her writerly instincts were so wrong on this one, then there would be little point in writing anything more. She'd have to find something else to do with the rest of her life.

It was only when one of the elderly gentlemen patted her on the arm, a concerned look on his face, that she realised she had been sitting outside the cafe, her coffee untouched on the table in front of her, with tears trickling down her face – because without her writing, her life wouldn't be worth living.

Chapter 8

'Why are you crying?' Jorge wanted to know. He was awkwardly bending over and peering anxiously at her.

With his limited English and her non-existent Spanish (she really should avail herself of Sebastián's offer to teach her, she thought somewhat abstractly), there was no way she'd be able to explain the reason for her tears. Moreover, she didn't particularly want to go into details.

'Man? He make you cry?' Jorge persisted. By this time, the other gentlemen had clambered to their feet and had gathered around her table.

'No, no man.' She'd done all her crying over Daniel back in the UK, and she certainly wasn't going to waste any more tears on the two-timing rat. Daniel she could live without – her writing was another matter.

'Woman?' Jorge asked, and one of the others tutted. 'What? It is the modern way. Man, woman, it's no matter.'

Another of the men said something, and the rest of them broke into wheezing chuckles.

'Benjo say his wife always makes him cry,' Jorge translated and pretended to wipe away tears.

Ivy gave a little smile. Bless them, they were doing their best to cheer her up. 'Work,' she said. 'Work makes me cry.'

'No work. You are on holiday, yes? No work,' he repeated emphatically. 'Come, come.' He straightened up with difficulty, wincing as he did so, and beckoned her towards their table. 'Pilar, *ron de miel, por favor.*'

Ivy took a little persuading because she didn't want to intrude and she felt rather embarrassed that the group of elderly gentlemen had witnessed her little breakdown, but neither did she wish to appear rude when they were so obviously concerned about her. So she eventually joined them and sat stiffly, not knowing what to say.

Pilar arrived with a bottle of dark golden liquid on a tray, along with several shot glasses. Oh God, they didn't expect her to do shots, did they?

They did, and she was handed a glass. She waited until the rest of them also had a glass in their hands before she took a tentative sip.

Her eyes widened in surprise. Mmm, smooth and sweet, it was definitely very moreish, and she took another sip, and another. Very soon her glass was empty and there was a warm sensation in her throat and tummy.

'What is it?' she asked, thinking this delicious drink mightn't solve her problems, but it certainly made them a little fuzzier around the edges.

'*Ron de miel*, honey rum. Is good, no?'

'No. I mean yes, very good.' She could get used to this, she thought, as Jorge filled her glass once more. She didn't mind the odd glass of wine with lunch, or the occasional gin in the afternoon, but drinking liqueurs wasn't her thing. Until now.

By the time she had downed her third, the fact that only Jorge spoke English – and not particularly well at that – didn't matter. They were all getting along famously.

It was no surprise then that by the time Ivy returned to the villa after having been comforted by the group of elderly gentlemen, she was not only feeling slightly tipsy, but her spirits had bounced back somewhat. She suspected much of that was due to the alcohol, but some of it was down to the fact that she knew her story was good. She could feel it in her bones. Even now, several hours later, she was still fizzing from the last chapter she'd written (although that also might be down to the honey rum), and her mind was filled with images of Nathaniel and Libby. More Nathaniel than Libby if she was honest – which was a good thing, because she wanted her readers to focus on the fallen angel too, and wish they were Libby.

For no particular reason other than she felt like it, Ivy decided to dress up for dinner. Not in a cocktail dress, obviously (she hadn't brought anything like that with her anyway), but in a long-sleeved top and a pair of white capri pants. The reason she told herself was because she was going to suggest they ate on the terrace and the temperature tended to dip a little in the evenings, especially at this elevation, and she didn't want to get chilled. She even wore some perfume and lipstick, along with her obligatory swipe of mascara.

Pleased with her reflection, she went outside taking a bottle of cold white wine with her and poured a glass. Drinking more alcohol probably wasn't the best idea, she should wait and have some with dinner, but what the hell? She was doing great – she deserved a little celebration. That it might be premature was something she didn't want to think about right now. There'd be time enough to consider the alternative when Nora got back to her.

A short while, and half a glass of wine later, Sebastián arrived. She heard the bike pull onto the drive and she poured him some wine as she waited for him to come looking for her. It didn't take him long and when she saw him she noticed that he'd changed out of his usual T-shirt and shorts, and was wearing faded grey jeans and a white shirt. The jeans showed off his thighs, and the shirt's sleeves were rolled up to reveal his strong forearms and the dark hairs which were scattered along them.

Ivy stared at him, remembering the feel of his muscles under his shirt as she clung on to his waist yesterday evening, and she blushed before hastily looking away.

'Are you hungry?' he asked, walking towards her, and she covered her sudden urge to tell him exactly what she was hungry for by handing him his wine and waiting until he'd tasted it before she replied.

'Starving,' she said. It was true, she'd only had a small lunch, and she needed something to soak up the honey rum and now the wine.

'What are we having?' she asked, following him into the kitchen.

'*Ropa vieja*: it is a traditional Canarian dish made from beef or chicken. My mother, she makes the best. Mine will not be as good as hers, but you will like it, I hope.'

Ivy watched as he unpacked a small bag, bringing out a can of chickpeas, a link of chorizo and a small red tin. He saw her staring at it.

'Paprika, with red chilli pepper. Not too spicy, but the *ropa vieja* is not the same without it,' he told her, while he washed his hands.

She settled herself down at the dining table which separated the kitchen area from the living space and continued to watch as he filled a large saucepan with water. While it was coming to the boil, he removed a couple of chicken breasts from the fridge and sliced them into strips.

'I usually cook them whole,' he told her, 'but it will take too long, so tonight I cut them.'

He was handy with the knife, she saw, expertly slicing the chicken before popping the meat into the water. As soon as it started to boil, he reduced the heat and placed a lid on the top. Then he set about chopping an onion and dicing a red pepper, before he peeled a couple of tomatoes and added them to the rest of the prepared vegetables.

'It will take half an hour for the meat to cook,' he said after rinsing his hands again and drying them on a towel. 'Shall we sit on the terrace and watch the sunset?'

He picked up his virtually untouched glass of wine and nodded towards the open doors. Ivy, who had drunk most of hers while she watched him work, nodded. The bottle was out there and she quite fancied replenishing her glass. This cooking business was thirsty work.

'Will it be all right on its own?' she asked, eyeing the gently simmering pot. Whenever she cooked she always felt compelled to remain in the kitchen just in case.

'*Sí*, it will be fine. I will check in twenty minutes.' He gestured for her to go ahead of him.

Thinking that if he wasn't bothered about the pan boiling dry, and he seemed to know what he was doing, then she shouldn't be either. She also consoled herself with the fact that he'd previously informed her that he often cooked for the villa's guests, so he must be at least a competent, and at best, an excellent cook. She was hoping for the latter, but the former would do – she was just ridiculously happy to have some company this evening. Not having had a lack of it in the past, it had been a bit of a novelty to be totally on her own, but now she was becoming rather fed up of it. She had been by herself for the most part during the time between discovering that Daniel had a new project in the form of Rebekkah Rain and travelling to Tenerife, but she'd been too distraught to feel lonely. Not in the same way she was beginning to feel lonely at the villa. At the time, she'd felt betrayed, abandoned, deceived… but not lonely.

'You look serious,' Sebastián said, breaking into her thoughts.

'Huh? Oh, sorry. I was miles away for a minute.' She'd been unconsciously gazing at the town spread out below in the distance, its lights coming on one by one and making the coast twinkle and sparkle in the deepening gloom. The water beyond was dark and vast, merging imperceptibly into the sky. 'It's beautiful,' she murmured. 'And the town looks so pretty from up here.'

'Garachico? It is very charming; full of old buildings. You must go there sometime. It has a marina, and a beach in a little bay, and many *piscinas naturales* – sea pools in the rocks which are safe for swimming with walkways in between.'

'I will visit it soon,' she vowed. 'It sounds fantastic. More wine?' She was amazed to discover her glass was almost empty again and he'd hardly touched his.

'No, thank you; if I have any more than this,' he held up the glass he was nursing, 'the meal will not be nice to eat.'

'I'm sure it will be,' she replied. 'Can't you handle a couple of drinks when you're cooking?'

Her tone had been light and teasing (was she flirting with him? – she thought she might be), but an expression flitted across his face so quickly, she assumed she'd imagined it. For a second there, she could have sworn she saw shame. Or might it have been regret? Maybe he had an issue with alcohol, and suddenly she felt awful for shoving the wine at him and not even asking if he wanted it. She'd just assumed he would… Thinking back, he hadn't drunk anything last night either, but afterwards she had put that down to him driving.

'I don't drink and cook,' he replied solemnly. 'The last time I did that, I had to wait two months for my eyebrows to grow back.' He waggled them at her.

'You're kidding! What happened?'

'Maybe I'll tell you another time. Right now, I have to see if the chicken is done.'

She stayed where she was, wondering what had got into her. Being friendly was one thing, but she knew she was flirting. Not excessively, and hopefully not that obviously, but she couldn't help herself. Every time she looked at him, or even thought about him, she kept getting him mixed up with Nathaniel in her head. It didn't help that her marathon-writing session last night had ended on a somewhat steamy scene where Nathaniel and Libby had got up close and personal. It was probably the most erotic love scene she'd ever written, and as she was populating the blank computer screen with words, she'd had to consciously push Sebastián from her mind and focus on Nathaniel. Then she'd spent the remainder of the night trying not to think of herself as Libby…

'Ten more minutes,' he said, taking his seat. 'You don't like cooking?'

'I used to when I was younger, but I've kind of got out of the habit. The most I can manage these days is to grill a steak.'

He took a tiny sip of his wine, and she watched him run his tongue over his lips afterwards. What would it feel like to have those lips on hers?

'You have no one to cook for?' he asked.

'No. No one,' she replied shortly.

'I am sorry; I didn't mean to offend.' He got to his feet.

'You didn't. It's just a bit of a sore subject at the moment,' she said.

'I am sorry,' he said again. Sympathy lurked in his dark eyes as they met hers, and she hastily looked away.

In the days and weeks since Daniel's betrayal, sympathy had been her undoing.

She didn't feel undone tonight, though, which surprised her. In fact, she felt slightly angry. Not at herself (been there, done that), but at Daniel. And it was one of the best feelings she'd had in a long time.

After a moment, to let this new feeling sink in, she followed Sebastián into the villa and found him finger-deep in the chicken as he shredded the breast meat. It was almost a primeval scene – a caveman tearing off ribbons of meat with his bare hands – and an equally primitive lurch shot through her.

God, he was attractive, and Ivy couldn't prevent her libido from sitting up and taking notice. Any woman with a pulse would react the same way. Maybe she should get Nathaniel to cook – and she itched to run to her laptop and start pounding away at the keys. What was that silly saying – write drunk, edit sober? She was halfway to being inebriated already, but maybe she'd leave attacking her work-in-progress for another time, since she could barely focus right now. Instead she concentrated on watching Sebastián fry the chicken in a pan together with the chick-peas, his forearm flexing as he tossed the food to ensure it browned evenly.

'I wasn't offended,' Ivy repeated, wanting to fill the sizzling silence. She didn't want things to be awkward between them. 'I've not long come out of a relationship, and it still feels a bit raw. Or at least, it did.'

'I see.'

'Daniel was also my publisher, so it was a bit of a double-whammy.'

'Excuse me?'

She realised he didn't know what she meant. 'I lost two things, my—' She had always struggled to know how to refer to Daniel. Boyfriend seemed too teenager-ish. And she didn't like the word 'partner', as it implied they were living together. She continued, 'The man I loved and the man who published my books. Hit from two sides at once.'

'I am sorry. Please accept my condolences.'

'Oh, Daniel's not dead!' she exclaimed. 'I didn't *lose him*, lose him. He left me for another woman. Another author. I'm over it now,' she said, and discovered she more or less meant it. She wasn't over Daniel completely, but she was getting there. Perhaps if he hadn't been so awful about the half-finished novel she'd shown him, she might be feeling a little differently. But for the man who she'd thought had loved her to be so derisory about her work… It almost felt like he had taken great pleasure in shooting her down.

Perhaps he had. Her success had never sat well with him, and it used to seriously rile him if a reader recognised her when they were out together, which did happen on occasion although it wasn't that often. He used to get all tight-lipped and narrow-eyed for a good while afterwards. Good luck with the rising literary star he was hitching a ride with, she thought sourly. If Rebekkah Rain was as brilliant as everyone said, then he'd have more than the occasional selfie with a reader to put up with. Still, she'd probably earn him a fair bit, and Daniel had always had one eye on the bottom line.

'I see. What about the rest of your family?' Sebastián asked. He'd moved on from tossing chicken and chickpeas, to frying the vegetables. He chopped up a clove of garlic and added it to the pan, and the smell was making her mouth water. 'Do you have any brothers or sisters?'

'Nope, neither.'

'Would you like to borrow mine? I have some to spare.' He added wine, broth and the paprika to the dish, along with some herbs, and brought the whole lot back to a simmer.

'Your family is gorgeous,' she said. 'Especially Emilia.'

His face softened. 'She is a diva,' he said fondly. 'I have to stay away from her, because she wraps me around her little finger.' He held a pinkie up, then put the lid back on the pan and turned down the heat. 'Now for the potatoes. I am going to fry them in the traditional way, but if you want to be healthy I can add them to the *ropa vieja*.'

'Fried is fine. I've eaten so much healthy food since I've been here, a bit of fried stuff won't harm me.' She deliberately ignored the image of the pizza and other food she'd consumed in considerable quantities last night.

Finally the meal was ready, and Sebastián dished it up while Ivy trotted back and forth to the terrace to lay the table.

'*Salud*,' he said, once they were seated, a fresh drink in front of them.

Ivy noticed that he chose to clink glasses with her using water and not the wine she was steadily drinking all by herself.

'Oh my word, this is delicious!' she exclaimed as the first mouthful of *ropa vieja* hit her taste buds.

Sebastián had yet to take a bite – he was too busy watching her reaction she noticed, and he seemed pleased. But it was only after she'd shoved a few more forkfuls into her mouth that he began eating, and as he ate he talked.

'You say you write books? Romance, was it?' he asked.

'That's right.'

'Have you come to Tenerife for ideas?'

'For inspiration? Not really. My agent persuaded me to come here because I'd sort of lost my way a bit. My last manuscript wasn't up to much. I didn't even finish it. She thought it would do me good to get away from everything for a while, so I could concentrate on my writing without any distractions. Which was why she picked somewhere without any phone signal or internet access.'

Ivy expected the usual questions, like what she was working on now, or where she got her ideas from, but what Sebastián said next came as a refreshing change.

'It hurts here.' He touched his chest. 'And here.' He pointed to his head. 'When you know you can do better. And you owe it to yourself to do the best you can.'

Bless him, he was so sweet trying to empathise with her. And it was also a good mantra to live by. She'd been too busy sitting on her laurels to push herself – and look at what had happened: mediocre writing and despicable plotting. Now that her back was against the proverbial wall, so to speak, she was producing the kind of stuff she'd written when she'd been as young and as hungry as Rebekkah Rain.

He waved a fork in the air. 'Is being here helping?'

'Yes, it is.' Her reply was emphatic.

'One day, when your book is published, I shall have to read it.'

Oh no, that wouldn't do at all. 'It's probably not your cup of tea,' she said hurriedly. 'This one is about angels and demons, and things that go bump in the night.' Usually a headboard or two…

'I read a lot,' he said. 'I like many types of books.' He glanced past her shoulder towards the inside of the villa, and she thought of those shelves rammed with books which lined the hall.

'Would you like to borrow any of the books here?' she offered. 'I'm sure the owners won't mind. Bookish people are usually happy to encourage a fellow reader.'

'I think I have probably read most of them already,' he admitted, somewhat sheepishly, she thought. 'At least, the Spanish and the English ones.'

'The Enid Blyton ones, too?'

He nodded and pulled a silly face. Why was she so surprised? His spoken English was very good. Excellent, in fact. Why should he not be able to read the language equally as well?

'Your English is brilliant,' she said. 'Where did you learn to speak it so fluently?' She wished she could speak another language, and she really must take him up on his offer to teach her, she thought for the second time that day.

Sebastián shrugged. 'At school, first, then from movies and English and American TV. I remember seeing *Friends* for the first time and I think I have watched every episode.'

'I'm surprised you don't have an American twang to your accent,' she laughed.

He lowered his eyes, and the shadow of his long lashes on his cheeks caught her attention. Having lashes so naturally thick and dark was deeply unfair. If she had lashes like that, she would have saved a fortune on mascara over the years. When he looked up, he found her staring intently at him, and she blushed.

In perfect American English, and with only a hint of a sexy Spanish accent he said, 'I noticed you the minute you walked in the room. Everyone did. How could I not – you're perfect.'

'That's from... no, don't tell me... *A Lavender Summer!* I haven't seen the film, but I suppose I should. It's been out for a good few years now and I remember everyone raving about it at the time. I must be the only female on the planet who hasn't!'

'Hmm.' He was staring over her shoulder, his gaze clouded and distant.

'I read the book though, that's how I recognised the line you just quoted. It's one of the best tear-jerkers ever published. When he dies in the end... I couldn't stop crying, it was so sad. Such phenomenal writing. I wish I could write something half as good as that.'

'I bet you can.' His naïve faith in her was touching, if somewhat misplaced. Her genre didn't lend itself to the same emotional range, not when the overriding requirement was a happy ending. Allowing the main male character to die in a romance wasn't the done thing; her readers would lynch her.

The house phone rang, making both of them jump.

With a frown and wondering who on earth it could possibly be, Ivy got to her feet and went into the hall. 'Hello?'

'Ivy? Ivy, is that you?' Her agent's voice was agitated.

'Nora?' An icy finger of dread traced its way down Ivy's spine. Oh God, this wasn't going to be good news…

'You've blown me away. It's bloody fantastic,' Nora gushed, and it took Ivy several beats of her thudding heart to understand what her agent was talking about.

'Do you mean the manuscript?' Her heart was now in her mouth and her palms were damp.

'Of course I mean the manuscript! Hell, girl, I need more of this and soon. Get writing! How long do you think it will take you to finish it – I need a guestimate because I'm going to pitch this bad boy to as many publishers as I can in the morning.'

'You are?'

'I am,' Nora replied firmly. 'I knew sending you to sit on the naughty step was a good idea.'

'Tenerife is hardly the naughty step,' Ivy said, bemused and dumbfounded. 'It's glorious here.'

'Yeah, well, it was either that or a yurt in Mongolia, but I thought you might prefer indoor plumbing.'

'Ha, ha. Not funny.'

'Seriously, Ivy, this is the best I've ever had from you. Your readers are going to love it! Actually, it's Nathaniel they're going to love, and every single one of them will be pretending they're Libby. The tension between the two characters is incredible already and as for Dante, he's so deliciously evil, he sets my teeth on edge. But he's also so charismatic…' She let out a long sigh. 'This one is going to be huge – I can feel it in my bones. You said five books in total? Can you make it seven? Have you got enough material for that?'

'Seven?' Ivy sank to the floor, her back against the wall. She was having a little difficulty letting it sink in. Nora *loved* it? She squealed, then clamped a hand across her mouth. Her instinct had been right, she hadn't lost her flair after all. Ivy closed her eyes and thanked whatever fairy godmother was looking out for her.

She was dimly aware of Sebastián standing in the doorway, concern etched on his handsome features, but Nora was yelling down the phone, 'Ivy? Ivy? Are you still there? Can you hear me?' and claiming her attention.

'I'm here. Let me have a think about it and get back to you. I hadn't planned on more than five.'

'Hun, five isn't going to be enough – not with characters this strong. Readers are going to lap it up, so see what you can come up with. And if you need to stay in the villa for longer, I'll see what I can do.'

'Longer?'

'Yes, sweetie, longer. If you carry on writing at this rate, the first draft of book one will be done and dusted in two months, three tops, but you'll never get all of them done in six months.'

No, she certainly wouldn't.

She hung up, feeling a mixture of relief, excitement and trepidation. She did have a few more ideas she could explore, but—

'Is everything OK?'

Ivy stared up at Sebastián. The worry in his eyes stole her breath – it was a long time since anyone had shown such concern over her. Even Nora, as good a friend as she'd become over the years, had a business to run and that business depended on the success of authors like herself. Sebastián had no ulterior motive to be worried about her, and for that reason alone she found he'd captured a little bit of her heart.

'Yes. It's more than OK. It's wonderful.' She made no move to get up. It was quite comfy here on the floor, the cool tiles under her bum and the solid wall at her back anchoring her. If it wasn't for them, she might just float away.

'It doesn't look it.' He moved near enough to reach down and hold out his hand.

After a miniscule hesitation, she took it, the warm strength of him pulling her up until she was standing so close to him she could see the lighter brown flecks in his eyes and smell his unique scent.

'I…' Words failed her. The brilliant news combined with too much alcohol and being too near to such a devastatingly attractive man had turned her brain to mush.

Without considering what she was doing, she leant towards him, and she wasn't sure whether him putting his arms around her was purely a reflex action or not. Either way, she didn't care. It was marvellous to be held again, to feel a masculine chest against her cheek, and to have the warmth of another person's breath in her hair. She felt safe and protected, and even if it was only an illusion, she didn't want it to end.

It had to eventually. Far too soon for Ivy's liking, Sebastián released her and took a distancing step back. He still wore a look of concern but it was coloured with wariness.

Oh God, she'd just made a total prat of herself with the guy who serviced the villa.

Conscious that she should give him an explanation for her needy behaviour, she said, 'That was my agent, Nora. She had some good news for me – she loves my new book.' Ivy grinned, aware she probably looked a right idiot as the smile stretched across her face.

'It is finished already?'

'Not yet. Some of it. I sent her what I'd done and the synopsis. She loved it!' There was that huge grin again, splitting her face in two and now her cheeks were aching with the force of it.

Sebastián was smiling too, and the worry had seeped out of his expression. 'I am happy for you. But why did you look so...?'

She could see he was struggling to find the right word, so she helped him out. 'Shell-shocked, scared, over-whelmed?'

He shrugged. 'That is how you looked,' he stated. 'All of it.'

Feeling silly standing in the hall, Ivy slipped past him and walked through to the terrace, where she sank onto her chair and drank the last of the wine in her glass before pouring herself another. To her relief, he joined her; she'd half thought he might take the opportunity to leave.

'I was scared because I thought it might not be any good,' she explained. 'The last stuff I wrote sucked big time. I mean, really sucked.' Tears prickled at the back of her eyes and she blinked furiously.

'But not this?' He jerked his head in the general direction of her desk. 'This is good?'

'Yes, it is.'

'And you are scared, why?'

'I'm not sure I can keep it up…'

Sebastián gazed at her intensely, his dark eyes boring into hers. 'You can,' he said. 'You know it. Everyone loses their way sometimes. Some find another path, some return to the one they were on, just as you have done. Have faith in yourself. I do.'

Bless him, he was very sweet, especially since he'd never read any of her stuff. But he was right – she did need to have faith in herself. She could do this, she knew she could. Nora knew it, too. And Nora was the best judge of a raw manuscript that Ivy knew.

She lifted her chin, new resolve coursing through her.

Time to get to work. Not tonight – tonight was for savouring – but tomorrow she'd sit at that desk and plot until she could plot no more.

There was a smidge of awkwardness on Ivy's part as she showed Sebastián out a short while later after he'd insisted on clearing away the dishes, having refused all offers of help. She kept remembering her neediness earlier and it made her wince. She'd never been needy in her life until now. But being with Daniel had chipped away at her self-confidence and turned her into someone she wasn't sure she recognised.

But ironically, there was one thing she should thank her ex for – if Daniel hadn't done what he'd done and behaved the way he'd behaved, Ivy wouldn't be in this wonderful villa, and neither would she have met Sebastián – the man who'd set her writing on fire.

Chapter 9

She'd been there ten whole days, yet to Ivy it felt as though she'd been living in the villa for months. Years, even. She found it hard to believe that less than a fortnight ago she had been attending an award ceremony and trying not to stare at Daniel, who had been sitting several tables away surrounded by his editors and other staff and a handful of authors. Of course one of them was Rebekkah Rain. And of course she had been sitting next to him. Why wouldn't she have been? She was his lover and his star attraction, after all.

Ivy had been seated with Nora and several other authors represented by the same agency, and she'd tried to avoid looking at them too, in case she saw sympathy, or worse, glee, in their eyes. The publishing world was a small one and word had soon got around of her split from Daniel Morris.

But none of that mattered any more. It seemed a life-time ago and two thousand miles away. All that concerned Ivy now was her daily routine and her work. For the past four days she'd hardly come up for air – if she wasn't writing, she was thinking about writing, and she was in that wonderful zone where the characters had taken on a life of their own and were whispering in her ear. She was conscious of them all the time, the way a medium must be aware of hovering spirits. They accompanied her everywhere, and even when she was sitting at the little cafe and pouring over her mobile, they chattered amongst themselves in her head.

Today, she was at the halfway point in the manuscript and, despite her plotting, had come to an impasse. So her planned night out at El Huerto Secreto was a welcome relief, as she needed to let what she'd written marinade in its own juices for a while; she knew from past experience that her subconscious would carry on worrying at the problem while she was going about her everyday business.

But before she went out later this evening, she intended to do a bit of exploring.

The villa's information pack provided by the owners mentioned visiting a lookout point called Mirador de Atalaya, which boasted fantastic views over Garachico and along the rugged coastline. It also informed her it was a forty-five-minute walk downhill from the villa, and an hour walk back up! Ivy thought she could reward herself with a swim in the pool afterwards to cool off and then flop on a sun lounger; a perfect way to build up an appetite for her meal later.

After ogling Sebastián when he popped in to check the pool, Ivy shared a coffee with him and, as usual, there was a friendly tussle over whether any cleaning needed doing. She'd already changed the sheets and stuffed them in the washing machine for a quick cycle, and they were now blowing merrily in the snapping breeze which swept up the mountainside from the coast, hundreds of feet below.

Ivy saw Sebastián roll his eyes as he realised she'd discovered a secret stash of fresh bed linen on a shelf in one of the wardrobes and had already remade the bed.

There was little for him to do, and he was clearly disconcerted by it. She wanted to tell him to make the most of the additional time off, but it wasn't her place to comment on his working arrangements, so she let him hover for a bit, and she told him her plans for the day.

'You will love it,' he said. 'The view is even better than this.' He swept an arm towards the distant sea. 'How is the book? Is it going well?'

She nodded. 'Very well, thanks. I've hit a bit of a block – which happens – so I'm taking the day off. It'll work itself out.' And she was confident that it would. She just needed to get from one point in the story to another, but right at this moment she had no idea how to do it. Maybe she should kill someone off? That usually worked...

After he'd left, she ate a spot of brunch while sitting on the terrace, a book propped open in front of her – an historical novel this time, set in medieval England, and with just the right amount of Gothic suspense to keep her in the mood for writing her own dark stuff. She liked a bit of sword and sorcery, and there were plenty of swords in this story.

At the end of one particularly eventful chapter, Ivy decided to pick it up later, and she got ready for her walk, packing her phone in her bag, along with a bottle of water and some sunscreen because it was particularly hot today. She wanted to take some different photos to upload to Instagram tomorrow – her followers were loving her posts so far; she'd taken loads of photos of the villa, her desk, the pool, the terrace, the bookshelves, plus the village, the cafe, a stone wall on the way, a lizard. But people didn't want to see the same things twice, and she didn't want to clutter her feed like that either.

Feeling excited to be going somewhere new, Ivy set off with a map in her hands and a spring in her step. Everything was going so well – she was loving living in the villa, her writing was going swimmingly, and she was finally putting the last few awful months behind her. She did have a vague worry that when things were going this well, the gods usually sent a bolt of something horrid to balance it out, but she couldn't see what it might be. The only thing that could possibly go wrong, and God forbid it didn't, was that her words would dry up, and she crossed her fingers and touched her hand to a wooden post as she walked by, to ward off bad luck. She might not normally be superstitious, but she didn't want to take any chances.

The sun was high and there wasn't a cloud in the sky as Ivy followed the road down the hill, but instead of taking the turning off towards the village and skirting around the side of the mountain, she carried on downwards. The slope was steep and soon she could feel a burn in her thighs at the unaccustomed exercise. Still it was worth a few sore muscles tomorrow to be out in the fresh air, with a warm breeze ruffling her hair and the scent of the ocean in her nose, along with whiffs of the most gorgeous flowery smell every so often. Tenerife didn't have a massive amount of rainfall, she knew, but there was enough precipitation throughout the winter months to allow plants other than cacti to bloom, and along the side of the road pale blossoms grew on silvery-green bushes, and daisy-type flowers nodded and danced. There was the occasional rustle in the undergrowth, which she guessed were the little green-brown lizards which were abundant, and the drone of bees accompanied her slapping footsteps as she trotted along.

When the road forked, she took a left and the tarmac disappeared and the going became rougher and narrower, as she left the main road behind.

She paused for a minute to admire a typical Canarian house with its whitewashed walls and exposed stones in the render. Actually, she couldn't tell whether the stone was exposed or whether it had been inlaid to form a random pattern, but either way it was very striking and it was perfectly offset by the green wooden doors and windows with their painted shutters.

As she resumed her walk, the gradient grew steeper and she began to consider just how tough the hike back to the villa was going to be, guessing she would be aching more than she'd originally thought tomorrow. Still, she could take her time and go at her own pace, and if it took her two hours to get back home instead of the expected one, then so be it. She had nothing to rush back for, she didn't have to leave for the restaurant until eight p.m., and she only had herself to please from now until then.

It was quite liberating, she decided, not having to consider anyone else's plans or feelings, and although she wouldn't want to live like this for ever, for the moment she was enjoying herself. She hadn't got as far as slouching around in her pyjamas all day and not bothering to brush her hair, but she found it refreshing to mooch about in shorts and a T-shirt, and to not wear any make-up. OK, just a smidge of mascara, but that was purely for her own benefit, and had nothing to do with Sebastián appearing at the villa every morning. No, siree, it didn't. Her hair was mostly gathered up into a bun to keep the strands away from the back of her neck and her feet were usually bare.

The fact that her hair suited her like that and that her feet were perfectly pedicured was neither here nor there.

As she said – liberating.

She wouldn't get away with it in London, of course, but on this subtropical island, it worked just fine.

Abruptly the scattered houses ended, as did the road, which became a cobbled footpath only wide enough for two people abreast and led to the lookout itself. It was the sound of running water which attracted her attention first – a noise which was totally unexpected on this island of very few rivers and streams, and she was drawn towards it.

It came from four metal spouts protruding directly from the hill, the cool water pouring out of them to fall into a series of stone troughs that were connected by a narrow stone canal which disappeared into the side of the mountain after a few dozen yards, taking the water with it.

Her imagination ran wild as she imagined women from the village above coming here to wash their clothes in olden days, or to collect water. There was probably a more modern explanation, but Ivy liked the one she had dreamt up, so that was the one she intended to stick with.

After dabbling her fingers under the flow and discovering how cold the water was, she turned her attention to the decked platform which jutted out over one of the steepest and highest drops she'd ever seen.

Sebastián was right – the view was astounding.

She was that much closer to the town of Garachico, and she could clearly see the rows of houses and the large church with its tall white tower in the centre. It really did look gorgeous, and she made a solemn promise to go there soon. She guessed that amongst those tightly packed streets, she'd find cafés and restaurants to die for, as well as rustic squares and narrow cobbled streets filled with unusual and quirky shops. The village was picturesque and quaint, but she suddenly craved a little more life and buzz. Despite loving her routine and adoring the fact that she was living in the most delectable villa, she was in danger of becoming a recluse. Sleepy was all well and good, but waking up now and again was good too.

The next time she had a proper phone signal she decided she would look up bus times, and if catching a bus wasn't practical, then she'd splash out and treat herself to a taxi. Having looked at the narrowness of the roads, and at how steep and winding they were, she had no intention of hiring a car. Just the thought of it made her feel a little faint.

She stayed there for a while, taking in the view and letting her thoughts drift. It would have been nice to have someone to share the view with (someone such as Sebastián?), because from up here, the sea looked huge and endless. It was extremely tranquil, with no one except the occasional bird for company, and the running water splashing into the stone troughs was the most delightful background music. Having someone to appreciate it with, would have made it even more magical.

Ivy didn't want to leave – she could have stayed there until the sun went down. But she'd already drunk half of her water, and she was conscious that the trek back up the side of the mountain was definitely going to take her longer than an hour. So it was best that she made a move before her water ran out completely.

Reluctantly, she pushed herself away from the railings and walked back to the path, taking a slight detour to splash some water on her face and the back of her neck on the way. She was tempted to refill her bottle, but considering she wasn't certain where the water came from or whether it was safe to drink, she decided against it, and after a last spatter of sparkling droplets onto her bare arms, she began the humungous hike up the hill.

The return journey took her even longer than Ivy anticipated, and by the time she reached the front door of the villa, she was gasping for breath, and she felt sticky, tired, and incredibly thirsty. She really should have taken more water with her. Or not bothered to have gone at all! No doubt she'd feel better about the escapade after a drink and a dip in the pool, but right now all she could think about was that the next time she had a notion to explore, she should have a gin instead.

Gin… ice-cold gin with tonic, a dash of lime and a handful of ice. Ooh, yum. She'd have a glass of water first though, because an alcoholic drink wouldn't be all that hydrating. Then she quickly changed into her bikini, took her gin out to the terrace and slipped into the pool's cool depths, still clutching her glass.

Slowly and carefully, as she didn't want to risk spilling any of her drink, Ivy did a clumsy one-handed breast-stroke out to the far end where she hung over the side of the pool and stared out into infinity.

Ah, this was the life.

It had been the right decision to take today off. She felt invigorated and refreshed already, although after she'd finished the gin she might very well have a little snooze on a lounger, as she had the time. A bit of dreaming about Sebastián wouldn't hurt, either.

Chapter 10

Falling asleep in the middle of the afternoon was never a good idea. When Ivy woke up, she felt really stewed and quite out of sorts. And to add to it, she'd developed a slight headache and her shoulders felt a little sore. Her mouth was dry and she bet dehydration was contributing to her headache. Her skin felt hot too, which didn't help either. In fact, her shoulders stung more than a little, and she guessed she might have had a bit too much sun. Never mind, a couple of tablets and a large glass of water should do the trick, and she could smooth on some moisturiser to take some of the heat out of her skin and help soothe it.

When she checked the time, she realised it was considerably later than she thought, so she'd have to get a move on if she wanted to have a shower, wash her hair, style it for a change and put some make-up on. She'd booked the restaurant for eight o'clock and had ordered a taxi for seven-thirty, so it only left her an hour to get ready, and to be honest, she wasn't feeling as lively as usual. That would teach her to take a siesta.

After the water and painkillers, Ivy headed to her bathroom and stripped off her bikini, throwing it in the laundry basket. It could do with a wash and as she didn't intend to go out in the sun tomorrow, she'd pop it in the washing machine in the morning.

She turned the shower on, glancing at herself in the mirror as she did so.

Oh, goodness. Her shoulders looked rather red and angry and there were two identical white lines, one on each side where the straps of her vest top had sat. There was a fainter line where her halter neck bikini top had been. Her face was quite red too, especially her nose and her forehead. She looked a right sight.

Gingerly, Ivy touched the skin on her shoulder and was concerned at how hot it felt. How had she got such a nasty sunburn when she'd taken sunscreen with her?

Hang on, she might have popped it in her bag but she'd forgotten to put any on before she set off, and she hadn't applied any all the time she was out either.

Great.

She'd rarely been sunburnt, and certainly not since her reckless, heady twenties. But now she had a good dose of it.

With a sigh, she got into the shower and— *Ow!*

Ivy winced as the warm water rained down on her sore skin, and she quickly stepped back and turned the temperature down. She also fiddled with the power shower bit too, so the spray wasn't as fierce.

The cooler water was soothing, and she stood under it for a while until her shoulders felt less hot and the painkillers had taken effect.

Feeling much better, if somewhat chilled, Ivy very carefully patted herself dry, and smothered the red burnt patches with body lotion, which her skin gratefully soaked up. She would have to put some more on later before she went to bed.

Dressed, her hair still a tad damp, but with make-up on to try to cover her red nose and glowing (but not in a good way) cheeks, Ivy was finally ready. She had just popped a cardi around her shoulders because the temperature had dropped a bit, when she heard a car pull into the drive. That would be her taxi, so she grabbed her bag, checked she had her keys, and dashed outside.

Ivy felt a little weird getting all dressed up to have dinner by herself, but the restaurant looked like the kind of place that wouldn't let you in if you were wearing shorts and flip-flops. It made a change for her to wear something nice, she thought, as she smoothed down the skirt of her floaty dress. It was flattering and summery, although it was slightly scratchy on her shoulder area, but she suspected that the discomfort was to do with her sunburn rather than the fabric.

She was conscious of the seat belt rubbing her shoulder as the taxi negotiated the winding road, and she wound the window down to let the cooler evening air waft over her, breathing in the scents of the evening.

As the car passed a large house on the side of the road, the unmistakable smell of a barbeque drifted through the open window. Her stomach rumbled loudly in response and Ivy couldn't wait to see what was on the menu. She was starving. In fact, she was so hungry she felt a little nauseous, so as soon as she was shown to her table, which was a small one in the corner, suitable for two persons at a push, she dived on the menu.

Once she had ordered, Ivy asked for the restaurant's wifi code and played on her phone until her starter arrived. She wouldn't normally look at her mobile while in a restaurant, because she didn't want to be rude, but she was acutely conscious of being alone when everyone else was in couples or more, so she kept her head down in case she spotted anyone giving her a pitying look.

Thankfully, the service was prompt and she didn't have to wait long for either her starter or her mains to arrive, and she devoured both with enthusiasm. The wine wasn't going down as well as she'd anticipated, though, so she drank mostly water instead, still thirsty from her day in the sun and from her hike. Note to self, she thought – next time take a bigger bottle of water. If there ever was going to be a next time!

When she was given the dessert menu, Ivy was stuffed. Actually, despite all the food, or maybe because of it (she had kind of wolfed it down), she felt a bit sick and shivery. Her headache was getting worse too, and the skin on the back of her neck and her shoulders was stinging and throbbing. She could feel the heat radiating from it and all she could think of was a cold damp towel and taking a couple more tablets.

Ivy made her way to the toilet, hoping to goodness that she wasn't going to actually be sick. It would be a shame because the meal had been delicious, but the thought of food—

Suddenly her stomach knotted and she threw herself into the first cubicle and hung her head over the bowl, not even having time to close the door behind her.

To her dismay and consternation, her dinner came straight back up, with heave after stomach-clenching heave. Finally, when there was nothing left inside her, she collapsed against the wall of the cubicle, shivering, her head pounding, and feeling utterly wretched.

After a while, she heard someone enter the ladies' toilets, and she knew she should make an effort to get up because she must look an absolute sight sitting on the floor, but she felt too weak and unwell to bother.

Whoever it was must have taken one look at her and had gone straight back out, because a minute later she was aware that the waiter who'd served her was bending over her and asking her questions. Unfortunately, his English was only marginally better than her Spanish, and she had no idea what he was asking her, so he retreated, leaving her to her misery.

And there she stayed, ignoring the curious stares and downright disgusted looks from the restaurant's other female clientele as they spied her through the semi-open cubicle door, until a familiar male voice sounded outside the loos and someone clapped their hands. A stream of loud Spanish sent a woman, who was trying to reapply her lipstick while staring at Ivy with a disapproving expression and therefore getting more colour on her teeth than she did on her lips, scuttling for the door.

Then Ivy was scooped up into a pair of strong arms, and Sebastián carried her gently out of the ladies' toilets into an office at the rear of the restaurant. He sat her down in a chair and knelt in front of her.

Ivy stared back at him dismally. She really did feel awful.

'Miguel says you only had one glass of wine. How much did you drink before you left the villa?'

'I'm not drunk.' She had to force the words out – all she wanted to do was to be left alone to die in peace.

'How much?' he persisted.

'One gin with tonic this afternoon. And water. Three glasses.'

'Are you sure?' He put a hand on her shoulder and she cried out.

'*Ow!* Don't touch me. That hurts.'

Sebastián rocked back on his heels, but swiftly rallied as realisation dawned on his face. Oh so gently, he peeled her cardigan back from her shoulder and hissed.

'This is not good. You have a nasty sunburn,' he said.

'I know. I think I have sunstroke too. Please—' She began to cry. 'I just want to go home.'

'Wait there. I will speak to Miguel.'

'I haven't paid him,' she said, sobbing fitfully.

'I will take care of it; I will take care of everything.'

He left her for a few minutes and when he returned he was carrying a bottle of water and a set of car keys. Miguel, the restaurant owner, was with him, wringing his hands.

Sebastián spoke to him in low tones, then clapped him on the shoulder. '*Gracias, mi amigo,*' she heard him say, before Sebastián held the bottle to her lips. 'Drink, small sips. I will take you back to the villa, but not before you have drunk half of the bottle. You are dehydrated and before I move you, I want to make sure you are well enough to travel.'

Obediently Ivy sipped, then sipped again; the water was cool slipping down her throat, and she drank until the small bottle was half empty. Then Sebastián helped her to her feet and mostly carried her through the restaurant's rear entrance and out into the car park. There, he aimed the set of keys at a small white Seat Ibiza and guided her slowly into the passenger seat.

'I am sorry,' he said, and just as she wondered why he was apologising to her when it should be the other way around, she let out a cry of pain as he eased the seatbelt over her shoulder and clicked it into place.

'It's OK,' she said through gritted teeth, cursing her stupidity. She should have applied sunscreen before she'd left the villa, she should have made sure her shoulders were covered, she should have worn a hat, she shouldn't have fallen asleep in the sun – she should have had more sense. But the breeze had thrown her, and she hadn't realised the strength of the sun, and she knew she was just making excuses. Tears trickled down her cheeks, making her want to cry harder at the waste of precious water from her body.

Sebastián drove the short distance from El Tanque to the villa as slowly as possible so as not to jar her unneces-sarily. When they arrived he helped her inside, Ivy leaning heavily on him as she tottered into the hall on shaky legs.

He settled her gently down on one of the dining room chairs and fetched her another glass of water.

'I don't want it,' she protested, trying to push his hand away, but Sebastián was insistent.

'You will drink this and then you will have a cool bath.'

'I don't want a bath. If anything, I'd prefer a shower, but I don't want that, either.' She knew she sounded petulant, but she couldn't help it.

'Sun stroke can be dangerous. We need for your body temperature to come down, and it will help with the sunburn too. I shall run the bath and you *will* get in it.'

Surprised at his insistence, having expected him to drop her off then go home, she did as she was told. It was only after she'd undressed and looked in the mirror that she could see how much damage she'd done to herself.

Her skin was incredibly red and tight-looking, worse than earlier, and it looked almost puffy, in sharp contrast to the paler skin where the straps of her top had been. Her nose was Rudolphesque and her forehead beamed like a beacon. She still felt unwell, although not as poorly as earlier, and all she wanted to do was to curl up in a ball and go to sleep.

First, though, a horrid cold bath. Sitting in it, she had to admit that although her bum and her tummy might be cold, the water didn't half feel good on her super-heated bits, and she was reminded of when she used to run her hand under the cold tap after she'd burnt herself retrieving something from the oven. That was in the days when she cooked regularly, back when she'd even been known to bake a cake or two.

Sebastián knocked on the door. 'Are you OK?'

Lord, she'd almost fallen asleep. She must have been in the tub for a while, she estimated, and she heaved herself out on slightly unsteady legs. Feeling an odd mixture of hot and chilled, Ivy delicately dried herself, wishing she had some after-sun lotion. At least the nausea had passed, she thought with relief, although she felt ropey and she should probably drink some more water, even though she didn't want to.

When she made her way into the living room, wrapped in nothing more than a lightweight dressing gown and not caring what she looked like, she was unsettled to see that Sebastián was not alone. One of his sisters was seated on the sofa next to him. Cristina was the one with grown-up children, Ivy recalled, none of whom had been at the pizzeria the other night because one was at university and the other was working in Santa Cruz.

Sebastián's sister was holding a bottle of green liquid in her hands, and as soon as she saw Ivy, she got to the feet and walked across to her.

'Come,' she said, 'I have something for the hurt. It is aloe vera for the skin. And this, too.' She held up a packet of tablets. 'It is also for the hurt.'

Aloe vera was one thing, Ivy thought, but there was no way she was popping an unknown pill into her mouth. 'Thank you, but I have some paracetamol around here somewhere; I'll take a couple more of those.'

'*Bueno*, but let me...' Cristina made smoothing motions with her hands and Ivy understood that Sebastián's sister was offering to put the gel on for her.

Knowing that she'd find it difficult to reach between her shoulder blades, Ivy reluctantly agreed, and led the way into her bedroom, where she perched uneasily on the edge of her bed and gingerly eased the dressing gown down over her shoulders, taking care to keep her boobs covered.

Feeling embarrassed and still rather ill, she allowed Cristina to gently dab the gel onto her shoulders and back, trying not to wince even though the woman had an incredibly light touch. In a few moments, though, she became aware that the gel was cooling her skin and taking some of the pain out of the burn, and she let out a small sigh. God, she'd really made a mess of things today, hadn't she? She might have known everything was going far too well.

When the ordeal was over, Ivy gave Cristina a little smile. 'Thank you so much. I really appreciate it.'

'*De nada*, you are welcome. I leave this for you.' She placed the bottle of aloe vera on the bedside table. 'Goodbye, I hope you are better soon.'

Ivy stayed in her room and listened as Sebastián spoke to his sister in the living room. Then she heard the front door open and close and the sound of a car starting up. A soft knock on the bedroom door followed.

'Come in,' she said, although her back and shoulders were bare; she couldn't face anything touching her sore skin and she had no idea how she was going to be able to sleep.

His expression tightened when he saw her red skin, and she got the impression he wanted to chastise her for her carelessness. Instead, though, all he said was, 'I have to take the car back to Miguel. Will you be all right?'

She nodded. She'd have to be. There was no one to nurse her or look after her. She was on her own with this, but thankfully she didn't feel as dreadful as she'd done earlier.

He set a full glass of water down next to the gel. 'Drink it before you go to sleep,' he said. 'Slowly, small amount at a time. Take the tablets if you are in pain, but be careful not to take too many. I will be back later.'

What? 'Oh, no, you needn't do that. I'll be fine, honestly. I'm feeling better already.' She felt her cheeks grow hotter than they already were and hoped he wouldn't notice the additional redness in her face as she blushed. 'Thank you for taking such good care of me,' she said formally. 'Although... how come you were at the restaurant?'

'Miguel phoned me. He knows you are staying in one of my— with Dream Villas and he told me you were unwell. He asked me to deal with you.'

'"Deal with me"? Those were his words?' Despite herself, Ivy felt quite indignant.

Sebastián chuckled. 'He thought you were drunk. He hoped you were, and that it was not food poisoning that was making you sick.'

Ah, she hadn't given a thought as to how her vomiting and subsequent collapse might have appeared to his other diners.

'I think he did tell everyone that the English lady had drunk too much wine,' Sebastián added.

'Is that why you questioned me about how much I'd had to drink?'

He looked away. 'It was my first thought, yes,' he admitted.

If Ivy could have shrugged without it hurting, she would have done so. He was only being logical and checking out the most obvious things first. She didn't blame him for thinking it.

'I am sorry, I should have warned you about the sun and also about taking plenty of water with you,' he said, his expression contrite.

'I'm a grown woman,' she replied. 'I should have had some common sense. I'm the one who should be apologising.'

They regarded each other solemnly for a second or two, before Sebastián nodded.

'I have to return Miguel's car and pick up my bike, but I will come back to see you before I go home,' he promised. 'In the meantime, if you are unwell or if you need me, you have my number.'

'I'll be fine,' she insisted, not totally sure that she would be, but not wanting to inconvenience him any more than she had already.

Sebastián gave her a searching look, then he nodded again, and a moment later, she heard him let himself out.

After slowly drinking the rest of the water, Ivy inched down the bed, screwed her face up as her burned skin met with the smooth sheets, and tried not to move.

She'd feel better in the morning. She was certain of it.

Chapter 11

Even breathing hurt. Throughout the night, Ivy was aware of every inhalation because any tiny movement served to chafe her already sensitive skin and disturb her. But there was nothing else she could do – she had to get some sleep, and she did manage a couple of hours, but every so often she'd wake up, disorientated in the darkness, take a drink of the water by her bedside, and drift back off into a fitful sleep.

When she finally woke for good, she'd lost count of the number of times she'd woken up, and as well as feeling very sore, she was also feeling incredibly grumpy. Thankfully, her headache had gone, and the first twinges of hunger made her aware that her tummy was painfully empty.

Carefully, with a great deal of wincing, she sat up and touched her shoulder. Gosh, that hurt; she could feel the heat radiating off her skin, so she applied some more of the aloe vera as best she could. As she waited for it to dry, she picked up the glass of water and took a drink. When she replaced it, she had a thoughtful look on her face. She could have sworn she'd drunk that glass dry at least once during the night, but the water looked as though it hadn't been touched until just now.

Surely she hadn't dreamt it?

Her bladder was telling her she most definitely hadn't, so once the gel was sufficiently dry, she dug out a loose T-shirt and slipped it over her head. A pair of leggings was OK for her bottom half, because thankfully she hadn't burnt her legs, despite not having put sunscreen on those bits, either. Slipping her feet into a pair of flip-flops, she painfully gathered up her hair and twisted it into a bun at the nape of her neck as she walked into the bathroom, every movement reminding her of her sore shoulders.

It was only when she wandered into the kitchen area, feeling slightly more human after splashing her face with cold water and brushing her teeth, that she realised she wasn't alone in the villa.

Sebastián was sprawled out on the sofa, head back and eyes tightly shut. From the gentle way his chest rose and fell, she guessed he was asleep.

Not knowing what to make of this, Ivy did nothing for several minutes. She simply stood there and studied him, loving the way his long lashes rested on his cheeks, the way a shadow of stubble coated the lower half of his face, the way his hair curled about his ears, the sweep of his jawline, the column of his neck. Without meaning to, her gaze drifted south, scanning his broad chest and flat stomach, before—

He cleared his throat and Ivy's gaze shot from where it was headed and landed on his face. Amusement danced in his eyes and her cheeks grew warm as she realised he knew exactly what she'd been staring at.

'Have you been here all night?' she asked, somewhat defensively.

He sat up and stretched, his T-shirt riding up to reveal an expanse of bare tanned stomach. Ivy hastily paid attention to the coffee table instead.

'No, Cristina was though. I came at six this morning. She had to go to work.'

'I thought she was going home last night?'

'She went to fetch some things, then she stayed with you to make sure you were all right.'

'Of course I was all right.' Ivy felt rather indignant that someone had been in the villa and she hadn't been aware of it. She was also embarrassed that Sebastián and his sister thought that she needed such care in the first place.

'You are now, but I was worried. We both were,' he added. 'I wanted to stay – there are enough bedrooms – but Cristina said it would not be right, and she made me go home.'

Thank God someone had some sense, Ivy thought. Cristina being here was bad enough – she didn't think she'd have been able to cope with the knowledge that Sebastián had babysat her.

It must have been Cristina who had refilled her glass during the night, she realised, and she was overcome with gratitude for the small act of kindness.

'Please thank her for me. I don't deserve such thoughtfulness.'

He shrugged, a gesture she was beginning to associate with him. 'Why not? We all make mistakes, we are not perfect all the time. You did not realise the strength of the sun, but it is not a crime.'

That may be, but her lack of common sense and forethought infuriated her. Ivy had made a right idiot of herself and not just in front of Sebastián, but in front of his sister, too.

'Coffee?' he asked, getting to his feet.

'I'll make it – it's the least I can do. And let me pay Cristina for her time.'

Sebastián's brow furrowed and his jaw hardened. 'She did not do it for the money. She has no need to—' His mouth snapped shut.

'Oh God, I'm sorry, I didn't mean to offend you, but I'm sure she had better things to do on a Tuesday night than take care of a silly English woman whom she doesn't even know.'

'*I* know you, that is enough for her. And she did what anyone would have done.'

Ivy seriously doubted that. When she'd been ill with tonsillitis just before Christmas, Daniel had studiously kept away, saying that he couldn't afford to catch whatever it was that she'd got, and he didn't appear on her radar again until she had returned to her healthy germ-free self. He'd not even phoned to ask her how she was. Yet here was a complete stranger spending the night at her villa to keep an eye on her.

Ivy looked away so Sebastián didn't see the tears welling in her eyes. 'Not everyone is as considerate and as thoughtful as you or your family. Let me take you out to dinner,' she added, as she fiddled with the coffee machine. 'You, Cristina and her husband.'

Sebastián gently eased her aside and took over the task of making the coffee. 'There is no need.'

'I don't care, I want to. Somewhere nice, but not El Huerto Secreto.'

'You didn't like the food?' He sounded surprised.

'Oh, no, that's not what I mean – I just don't think I can set foot in—' She gasped. 'Oh dear, I didn't pay for my meal.'

'It's taken care of,' Sebastián said.

'But I must pay. I insist. It wasn't Miguel's fault and it's not fair. He's got a business to run. I'll go to El Tanque later and—'

Sebastián held up a hand. 'You are going nowhere today. You need to rest and to let your sunburn heal. As I said, the meal is taken care of.'

Understanding dawned. 'You settled the bill yourself, didn't you?'

Sebastián didn't answer and he didn't meet her eye, either. Instead, he handed her a cup of rich aromatic coffee.

'Sebastián,' she said, warningly. 'You paid it, didn't you?'

'I might have.'

'You did! I must reimburse you. You can't be out of pocket, and El Huerto Secreto's prices aren't cheap—'

'Please, I do not want paying. It was my pleasure.'

Ivy took a steadying breath. She really wanted to insist but she could tell from his expression that he wasn't going to let her. She could hardly wrestle him to the floor and stuff a handful of notes into his pocket... Now that was an image worth keeping until later...

'Thank you,' she said. 'I hope your employer knows what a damned good guy you are. Not many staff would have done what you did. You deserve a pay rise. I've a good mind to tell him – or her – just how fantastic you are.'

Sebastián's smile made her knees wobble. 'Oh, I'm pretty sure he already knows. And, as I said, it was my pleasure. Now, it is time for me to go to work, so I am happy you are OK and I can leave you. I will see you later, no?'

'No, I mean, yes. Yes, you will. And thank you once again,' she called as he strode down the hall.

Oh dear, not only had she made a total idiot of herself, but the huge crush she had on him was turning into something deeper and far more threatening to her emotional wellbeing.

Unsettled and restless, she kept recalling the way his T-shirt rode up, and—

She shook her head. There was only one thing to do with all this nervous mental energy and emotion, and that was to write.

She had a steamy scene in mind, and she knew exactly who the starring role would go to.

Chapter 12

Ivy was sore for a good few days afterwards, but gradually the redness faded and the peeling began, revealing delicate paler skin underneath. When she eventually felt able to sit in the sun again, she did so with considerable caution and a new respect. She'd never had such severe sunburn before, and she didn't want to have it again.

She saw Sebastián in the mornings, as usual, but because she was doing most of the cleaning around in the villa herself, there wasn't a great deal to keep him there. Once he'd checked the chemical balance in the pool and cleaned it, and had swept up any fallen leaves and watered the pots, he was off.

Apart from him, she saw no one for four days, and what with either being focused on her writing, which was coming along at a rate of knots, or reading, the brief flash of loneliness she'd experienced earlier seemed to have vanished. As Ivy rediscovered her love of solitude, she was quite comfortable in her own company. It helped that she didn't feel like getting dressed, apart from the loose, cool T-shirt which she rinsed out every evening and dried in the breeze overnight. The thought of wearing a bra made her shudder and she certainly wasn't going to venture out without one, so she made do with the food already in the fridge and freezer, cooking herself wholesome simple meals. She found she was enjoying that too, and what had once been a chore gradually became an activity she looked forward to, as a demarcation between her working day and the evening.

But today, she was on a mission. And it began with Sebastián.

'Can you do me a favour?' she asked as soon as he arrived.

He was wearing his usual cut–offs and T-shirt combo, his feet in trainers, and he looked good enough to eat.

'What is it?' He accepted a cup of coffee from her with a smile of thanks.

'Can you speak to Cristina and ask her what day would be convenient to go out for a meal?' She saw his expression. 'You were hoping I'd forgotten, weren't you?' Then… 'Oh, sorry, I don't mean to be pushy, it's just that I wanted to say thank you for the other night. If it's inappropriate, I understand.' She didn't see how it could be, since she'd eaten with Sebastián and his family previously, but…

'You don't need to do this,' he said.

'OK.' She bit her lip, feeling foolish for suggesting it in the first place and then bringing it up again when it clearly made Sebastián uncomfortable. 'Sorry,' she mumbled.

There was silence for several seconds as he drank his coffee and Ivy stared out to sea. Finally he said, 'If this is what you want, I will ask her.'

'You don't have to. I shouldn't have mentioned it.'

'I would like to go to dinner with you, and I'm sure Cristina and Sergio would, too. Can I tell you tomorrow?'

'I was hoping you could let me know later today – I know I said I wouldn't go there again, but I'd like to book a table at El Huerto Secreto. I feel I owe it to them, and I know how busy they are. It could be days before they have one free.'

'Miguel will find us a table if I ask him,' Sebastián said. 'Would you like me to go ahead and book it and let you know when?'

She wasn't sure about that – it almost felt like she was asking a friend to arrange their own birthday party. But when she thought about it, it was the logical thing to do; rather than Cristina saying when she and her husband were free, only for Ivy to phone the restaurant to find they were fully booked for that date, and then have to check with Cristina again.

'OK,' she agreed reluctantly, 'but no funny business.'

Sebastián's English was good enough to understand the saying and he clapped a hand to his heart, his face radiating innocence. 'Me? I would not do such a thing.'

'Hmm.'

'You have trust issues,' he declared solemnly.

Huh, he probably wasn't too far off the mark there, not after dastardly Daniel, but she smiled anyway and cocked her head to the side.

'No funny business,' he agreed as he made to leave. 'I promise.'

And she had no choice but to take him at his word, she decided, as she washed up her breakfast things once he'd gone. Then she picked up her phone, her laptop and her bag and headed out of the door. Only to return immediately to reapply sunscreen and to pop a hat on her head. It might only be eleven in the morning, but she wasn't going to take any chances.

It felt good to stretch her legs again, as she trotted along the path leading to the village. The track wound its way across the side of the mountain, roughly following the road but far enough away so that the distant hum of traffic was drowned out by the more immediate hum of bees as they droned and buzzed from flower to flower.

She breathed deeply, the fresh air filling her lungs, and she felt at peace with the world. The rough (very rough) first draft of *An Angel from Hell* was done, and she felt cleansed and lighter, as though a burden had been lifted from her shoulders. The weight of the story inside her had been a welcome one, a cherished one, but now that it was out on paper, she felt as though she was floating on air. Was this a faint echo of what it must feel like to carry a baby inside you and then give birth to it? To see something wonderful you have created come alive? It obviously was nowhere near the same, but it was as close as she was going to get. And she'd poured her heart and soul into this particular book baby, the words had flowed from her fingers like magic, sizzling on the page, before coming to life.

Ivy had written the final sentence last night and had risen before it was light this morning in order to run her eye over the whole thing to make sure it made sense and there weren't any gaping plot holes or hideous inconsistencies. She didn't find any, but no doubt Nora would, so the sooner she sent her this rough draft, the better. Then once Nora had critiqued it, it was down to Ivy to polish the story until it shone.

She always enjoyed that bit as much as she enjoyed the initial process of creation. But before that, she'd have a break of a couple of days to let her mind settle. Maybe she'd treat herself to a trip to Garachico. She would certainly do some more reading, and some napping, too. Ivy always felt extra tired after she'd written 'The End', as though the act of finishing writing had depleted her spiritual and creative energy.

The path wound its way between rocky meadows on either side, and a low wall constructed of dark volcanic lumps of stone prevented unwary walkers from drifting onto the steep mountain slopes. Every now and again, a small tree cast some welcome shade and it was under one of these that Ivy stopped for a while to enjoy the view. To be fair, it wasn't all that different from the breath-taking views she could see from the villa, but the slight differences in the panorama below caught her attention. She didn't think she'd ever get used to the beauty and magnificence of it. It was so tranquil up here, as though she was removed from all the hustle and bustle of real life taking place more than a thousand feet below.

With a sigh of contentment, Ivy carried on with her walk until she came to the first of the houses signifying that she was on the outskirts of the little village. Waving to a woman who was pegging washing out, she practically skipped the last few yards until her feet hit the tarmac of the road proper.

Making her way through a couple of steep narrow streets, Ivy eventually came out on to the road where the pavement café was situated, with the old men, who seemed to be permanent fixtures, sitting outside it. She was greeted with smiles and nods, and Jorge pointed to her, touched his own shoulder and pulled a face. Oh dear, it seemed that news of the English woman's stupidity had travelled as far as the village, and she grimaced.

'*Bueno*,' she called. '*Mucho bueno.*' She hoped it meant 'much better' although she couldn't be sure, but the old gents seemed happy enough with her response and they smiled and raised their ever-present glasses to her.

God help them if they had already started on the honey rum – they must have constitutions of steel. She'd stick to iced coffee and maybe some tapas.

While she waited for her order, she opened her laptop, logged into the café's wifi and checked her emails. After answering a few of the more urgent ones and paying a bill or two online, Ivy finally plucked up the courage to find the document she needed and attach it to an email, which she then pinged off to Nora.

It was done. Her draft manuscript was on its way.

Ivy blew out her cheeks and leant back in her chair.

There was nothing she could do until Nora got back to her. There was no point in fretting about it (yeah, right); the best thing she could do now was to give herself a few days off and try not to think about the book until she heard from her agent.

If she hadn't heard by the end of next week, she'd make a start on the second story in the series. The ideas were there already, but she would prefer to completely finish *An Angel from Hell* first, before she embarked on the next novel. She wasn't the sort of author who could concentrate on two manuscripts at once.

It wasn't easy working on her phone, but as she ate she managed to tweet, post on Facebook, upload a couple of photos to Instagram, post a brief update on her website, as well as check out some writer forums.

Then when all that was done, she ordered herself a glass of ice-cold Spanish beer and settled down to watch the world go by. All those things which seemed to be so important and which were definitely time-consuming in London, had been reduced to just over half an hour. It made her realise how little she actually needed the internet, and exactly how much of a time-suck it was. Time that could have been spent writing, or just *being*. The way she was *just being* now, content to live in the moment and enjoy the simple pleasures. Today her simple pleasures were a cold beer, a shady umbrella and watching people stroll along the street.

So when her phone rang suddenly, Ivy almost jumped out of her skin. She scrambled to prevent her drink from spilling, as her knee banged the underside of the table, making it wobble.

'Ivy?' Sebastián said.

'Sebastián? Hi. Is everything OK?' Briefly she wondered how he knew her mobile number, then realised he'd probably obtained it from Dream Villa's booking form, and she hoped it wouldn't land him in any trouble.

'*Sí*, everything is good. El Huerto Secreto is booked for tonight at eight. Or is that too soon?'

Wow, he certainly knew how to pull a few strings. 'Eight is good.' She'd better book a taxi—

'I will come for you at seven-thirty,' he said. 'We are to meet Cristina and Sergio there.'

'Oh, OK, thank you.' She hesitated. 'Will you be on your motorbike?'

'Not if you don't want me to be.'

'Don't get me wrong, your bike is super, but...'

'*Vale*, OK. I will drive the van, so you do not have to put your arms around me.'

'That's not what I meant, I—'

His chuckle brought her to a halt. 'You want to wear a dress and not mess your hair?'

'Exactly!' Why did this man have the ability to make her blush like a schoolgirl? And he'd only been teasing her, so there was nothing to get so het up about. But she vividly remembered the way he'd felt and how he'd smelt, especially since she'd drawn on those memories to bring Nathaniel to life, and hearing his chuckle had made her knees go weak. Did he know how sexy he was?

'I will see you later,' he was saying, and she blinked as she came out of her brief daydream.

'Seven-thirty,' she agreed. 'Bye, Sebastián.'

When she placed her phone back in her bag and looked up, it was to find five pairs of eyes observing her, and most of their owners wore knowing smiles on their faces.

'What?' she said, but all she received in return were more smiles, a little laughter, and one word said with deep meaning – 'Sebastián.'

Chapter 13

That evening, Ivy took considerable care with her appearance, even going as far as to shave her already relatively hair-free legs. Thankfully the peeling of her sunburn was coming to an end, although the colour of the skin on her chest and shoulders was rather patchy, so she chose a dress which covered them up. But she couldn't do anything about her nose and forehead, she discovered, as she dabbed on a coat of foundation only to hastily remove it again. She did, however, apply eyeliner, shadow and mascara, before finishing off with a coat of coral lipstick. Her hair fell loose about her shoulders and she was pleased to see that the condition of it had improved since she'd been on the island because she had not used her straighteners once. The sun had highlighted several strands at the front and Ivy thought it suited her.

When she heard the sound of an engine, she grabbed her bag and keys and dashed outside to see Sebastián pulling up in the rental company's van. As she turned to lock the villa's door, she heard the van door open and his footsteps approaching, so it was no surprise to find him directly behind her. What did surprise her was to see him wearing a suit, and she was glad she'd made an effort. It was a deep, deep navy and the shirt he wore with it was crisp and white, and open at the collar.

Ivy resisted the urge to wolf whistle, but she was nevertheless delighted to see the appreciation in his eyes as he scanned her from her glossy hair to her painted toes.

'Shall we?' He gallantly held out his arm and she slipped a hand into the crook of it and allowed him to lead her to the passenger side and open the door for her, where she climbed in as gracefully as she could while wearing a dress and heels.

Making sure she was seated comfortably and taking care not to catch her dress in the door as he closed it, Sebastián sauntered around to the front of the van and got in beside her. For a company vehicle it was remarkably clean and tidy, she noticed. Was it always like this or had he given it a scrub for the occasion?

He scrubbed up pretty well, too, she thought. Handsome whatever he wore, he looked particularly gorgeous tonight. A suit suited him, and the one he was wearing might have been made especially for him, as it fitted so well. The fabric was of decent quality, too, and even picky Daniel, who was so particular about his appearance and especially his clothes, might have worn something similar. Her ex wouldn't have looked as good in it though, she smirked.

Ivy tried not to stare at Sebastián out of the corner of her eye as he started the engine and pulled out of the drive and onto the steep road, but it didn't work because he caught her looking and he smiled wickedly back at her.

'I don't always wear T-shirts, you know,' he teased. 'I do have other clothes.'

'And I was just thinking how handsome you looked in them, too,' she shot back, without engaging her brain first.

'Thank you, ma'am,' he drawled in an American accent. 'And I think you look beautiful.'

'I had to do something to dispel the image of me wearing vomit all down my front from poor Miguel's mind. Yours too.'

Sebastián laughed. 'I don't care what you wear – you are beautiful anyway.'

Ivy pursed her lips. 'Not with sick all over me.'

'It was only a little.' He held up his finger and thumb an inch apart. 'I did not care.'

But she did. She'd hated him seeing her in such a state, and when she'd been feeling so ill, too. However, she couldn't deny that he'd taken excellent care of her, and she was incredibly grateful to him for it.

The drive was a short one, and they were pulling into the small car park at the side of the restaurant before she could think of anything suitable to say. For someone who dealt in words for a profession, she was often remarkably tongue-tied when it came to talking, which could occasionally lead to people thinking she was being aloof, when in fact she was just nervous or shy.

Hoping Sebastián didn't think she was being stand-offish, she didn't wait for him to walk around to her side of the vehicle. Instead, she swung her legs out and was about to hop out when he reached the passenger door, leant forwards, put his hands around her waist and lifted her down.

She came up against his chest, and before she could stop herself she'd buried her nose in the open V at his throat and inhaled deeply.

God, he smelt good enough to eat.

For a second, his grip tightened as he held her close, then he released her and stepped back, leaving her wondering whether she'd imagined it.

Yeah, she probably had; he'd been making sure she was steady, that must be it. The paving stones were uneven and hadn't been put there with high heels in mind. He was most likely worried that she'd fall and break something, because with her track record so far it was a very real possibility.

Miguel greeted her at the doorway with exuberance, asking after her health and insisting they have a bottle of wine on the house. Ivy tried to refuse, but Sebastián advised her that Miguel would not take no for an answer, so she accepted with grace as he showed them to their table.

Cristina and her husband, Sergio, were already seated with drinks in front of them, and before Ivy took her own seat she went up to Cristina and enveloped her in a hug.

'Thank you so much, and I'm so sorry you had to babysit me the other night,' she cried, and Sebastián had to quickly translate what 'babysitting' meant.

'No problem,' Cristina said. 'I was happy to do it. Sebastián—' She broke off and shot her brother a swift look. 'He did not think it good he stay with you alone at night, so he ask me.'

'Of course, I understand. I wouldn't have wanted him to get into any trouble with his employer.'

Sergio chose that moment to choke on his drink and by the time he'd finished spluttering and Ivy and Sebastián were seated, the moment for her to make a proper apology was gone. Never mind, she'd thank them all again later.

Cristina and Sergio were good company, Ivy thought, as she chatted to them, with Sebastián only having to step in occasionally in his role as translator. After discovering the pair had been to London, they discussed the famous landmarks – although Ivy was ashamed to admit that she'd not been to most of them – and how Cristina, especially, had loved the shopping.

'Now, that's one thing I will miss after a few more weeks,' Ivy admitted. 'All those artisan shops, the little delicatessens, the quirky clothes shops. I've been promising myself a trip to Garachico one day soon, because I think I'm having withdrawal symptoms already. I'm going to take a couple of days off between books, so I might check it out in a day or so.'

'Santa Cruz is the best for shopping on Tenerife,' Sergio said. 'That is what Cristina tells me and she goes there often.'

'That's the island's capital, isn't it?' Ivy asked.

'The only city. It is beautiful, full of museums and art galleries, as well as the shopping. And there are many, many restaurants.'

'The one other thing I miss about London, is the way you can have French pastries for breakfast, Japanese for lunch and a Peruvian dinner if you want it,' Ivy said. 'Here, I have to cook my own meals. Except when your brother insists on feeding me. I don't like to impose though, even if he assures me that he's used to cooking for the villa's guests.'

There was a small silence and Ivy intercepted an odd look between the three of them.

'Did I say something wrong?' she asked.

'No, not at all,' Sergio replied. 'It is just we do not think he is that good at cooking. Not like his mama. Now, that lady can cook.'

'She taught me!' Sebastián objected, nibbling on a breadstick.

'You are a bad learner,' Christina said. 'He has not learnt well. I have tasted his food.' She shuddered theatrically.

Sebastián got to his feet and threw his napkin down on the table. 'That is the end. I will never cook for you again, and you are not welcome in my house.' He stalked off, leaving Ivy open mouthed; until he looked over his shoulder and winked at her.

'He's joking,' she said, relieved.

'Of course he is. He is happy when people come to dinner. It is nice to see him this way; not like before when—' Once more Cristina broke off.

Ivy's attention drifted towards Sebastián's drink – water again, with a twist of lemon. He'd more or less told her that he didn't drink alcohol, and she continued to speculate whether he might have had a drinking problem in the past. It could possibly explain why his family was a bit cagey on occasion, and why they suddenly broke off mid-sentence.

After a few minutes Sebastián slipped quietly back into his seat and Ivy sent him a reassuring smile. He grinned back. He seemed OK now, and if he had been a heavy drinker in the past then there was no sign of it on either his face or his body. Not that she'd seen his naked body (what a pity) but from what she could see of it under his clothes, he looked fit and trim, with muscles in all the right places. An image of him stretching to reveal a toned, tanned stomach with a faint vertical line of dark hairs disappearing into his shorts imploded in her mind, and she coughed.

'Better than London, you like New York for the shopping,' Sergio said to his wife, then he jumped. 'Hey, that hurt.'

Cristina glared at her husband. What was going on? Something clearly was, and Ivy guessed that Cristina must have given Sergio a kick under the table or trodden on his toe.

'I've never been to New York. I've never been to the States for that matter. What's it like?' Ivy asked, hoping to dispel the odd atmosphere. She glanced at Sebastián. His expression was neutral and he was leaning back in his seat, one hand resting casually on the table. Whatever it was didn't appear to involve him.

'Fabulous,' his sister said. 'There are many, many people, many, many shops and restaurants. I would not like to live there, but for a holiday it was very good.' Cristina was back to normal and Ivy didn't have a clue what all that had been about.

The evening eventually drew to a close after coffee and *ponche caballero*, which Ivy discovered, was a rather moreish orange and vanilla liqueur, along with the four of them vowing to meet up again before Ivy went back to the UK.

As Ivy was saying goodbye to Cristina and Sergio, the thought of returning to London made her feel rather sad and despondent. After less than a month of living on Tenerife, she realised she had lost the holiday feeling she'd had when she'd first arrived. The villa felt more like her home now; the house she owned in London was just a house, and she didn't feel at all connected to it. She put this shift in her feelings down to the fact that this time she had carried on with her writing while she was abroad. Previously, on the odd occasion she'd had a holiday, she had not done a great deal of work, although she had always taken her laptop with her in case inspiration struck. Here though, she'd done very little else apart from work, and her days were nicely structured, with a lack of distraction. She could seriously get used to this way of life.

What was stopping her, she mused as they all made their way into the car park?

Struck by an idea, Ivy halted so abruptly that Sebastián walked into the back of her.

It was one that had flitted through her mind before, and had just as quickly flitted back out again, but now it seemed to have lodged securely in her head. *What if she sold her house in the UK and bought a property over here?*

'Are you all right?' Sebastián was so close she could feel his warm breath in her hair, and she turned to look at him.

'I've had an idea,' she said.

'For your book?'

'No, I'll tell you about it on the way home.'

There was that word again – *home*. She had no idea how much a place like Villa Colina would sell for, but she could find out. It would give her a ballpark figure, so that she would know what the proceeds from her house in London would likely buy her. Ideally – and she really was fantasising now – she'd love to be able to afford to buy the villa, but that was a pipe dream and she knew it, but there were bound to be loads of other properties which were in her price range, if she were to look.

'I like Tenerife,' she announced as she buckled herself into the van's passenger seat.

'It is the best place on earth,' Sebastián said.

'You're biased.'

'Yes, I am. But I am also right.'

Ivy shook her head, smiling. 'I'd like to live here permanently, to make this my home.'

He shot her a look out of the corner of his eye. 'It is a big decision.'

'I know, but the longer I'm here, the less I want to leave.'

'Most holidaymakers feel the same.'

'But I'm not a holidaymaker, am I? I'm spending six months of my life here, so I'm not a tourist, I'm actually working.'

'There are many people who spend months at a time in the Canary Islands,' he said. 'Often they are retired, and they are usually here to avoid the English winter. This I understand. I, too, do not like the winters in your country.'

Did that mean he had visited the UK?

'But it is one thing to visit Tenerife and another to live here,' he added, before she could follow it up.

'I might start making some enquiries,' she said. 'There's no harm in that. I could get an idea of how much properties cost, like the villa, for instance.'

'Villa Colina?'

'Yes, that one. I wonder how much that would go for.'

Sebastián didn't say anything. In fact, he looked a bit out of sorts, his jaw was clenched and he kept his eyes firmly on the road. She hoped she hadn't upset him by making him think she could afford a place like the villa. Maybe she could, and maybe she couldn't – she had no clue as to house prices on Tenerife – and she'd never know unless she did some research. But she didn't want him to think she was rubbing his nose in it. Although she wasn't in the same bracket as E L James or J K Rowling, she was relatively well off, and she guessed she was considerably better off financially than Sebastián was, so she decided to down play things a bit.

'I bet it's way beyond what I could afford,' she said. 'I think I'd have to look for something much smaller, prob-ably without a pool and those gorgeous views. Maybe in El Tanque. Surely properties inland would be less expen-sive than those on the coast?'

'That is generally true.' He swung the wheel and the van turned into her driveway. 'Stay there, I will help you down.'

Ivy did as she was told; not because she couldn't manage the drop from the cab to the ground by herself, but because she wanted to feel Sebastián's hands around her waist again. She knew she shouldn't, but she couldn't help herself – it was too intoxicating. Besides, as she tried to convince herself, every time she saw him, spoke to him, came into physical contact with him, it was more material for her book.

She wiggled to the edge of the seat and watched him walk around to her side of the van, her heart thumping. This was silly; *she* was being silly. She was acting like a sixteen-year-old with a crush. If it had been Daniel who'd suggested she waited until he'd helped her down (not that he'd ever do anything like that) she'd have ignored him and hopped to the ground of her own accord. By being a gentleman, Sebastián was unwittingly fuelling her ridiculous feelings for him. No, it wasn't him but

Nathaniel. She was getting her sexy, smouldering, charismatic lead character confused in her over-stimulated mind with the admittedly handsome, kind guy who worked for the company who owned the villa. Sebastián was no Nathaniel. He was an ordinary fella—

Eek! She'd been so busy thinking about him that she'd failed to notice he'd opened the van door and was close enough to wrap his strong hands around her middle, and when he did exactly that, she let out a small squeak as he lifted her down.

'Sorry, did I hurt you?' he asked, releasing her so quickly she stumbled against him, and his arms came around her to steady her.

As she lifted her face towards him, he bent his head, and... oh God, his lips were inches from hers, so close she could almost taste them, almost feel their imagined softness compared to the rasp of faint stubble on his chin.

He stepped back, leaving her wobbling slightly, her heart thumping madly, and her breath rasping in her ears.

Dear God, she'd nearly kissed him.

She'd wanted to kiss him so badly – she still did. Her whole body was on high alert, the blood was rushing through her veins, her skin tingled and felt superheated.

'I have to... err...' He gestured at the van.

'Oh, yes! Of course. Sorry. I'll let you go. You must want to go to bed. Um...' Shit, she really didn't want to let him go, and she seriously wanted him to go to bed. Hers, obviously. And now she was making a complete idiot of herself yet again, as she stammered through more innuendos than a stand-up comedian desperate for laughs.

He waited for her to move away so he could shut the passenger door, and she tottered off towards the villa's entrance, her legs behaving like jelly. Meanwhile her brain was also doing a blancmange impression, as she tried to think of something to explain (excuse?) the fact that she'd practically offered herself to him on a plate. He must surely have been aware she had been puckering up for a snog. Not puckering exactly, but almost. She'd clearly been up for it.

No wonder he was now hopping up into the driver's seat and doing the quickest three-point-turn she'd ever seen anyone perform in a transit. He must be desperate to get away from this needy woman who'd thrown herself at him. Oh dear... he was probably thinking that she'd asked him to dinner not as a thank you for rescuing her the other night, but as some kind of a date, even when it so clearly hadn't been like that.

Groaning at her own stupidity, Ivy hastily let herself into the villa and headed straight for the gin. Drowning her sorrows was the only thing she could think of doing right now, and it would certainly be preferable to lying in bed staring at the ceiling and reliving every single embarrassing second, over and over again.

And now she had another five months of feeling like a prat every time she saw him.

Way to go, Ivy...

Chapter 14

Sebastián was late. It was most unlike him, and Ivy prayed she hadn't upset him too much last night. She was used to him arriving between nine and nine-thirty, and it was now ten o'clock. She was starting to worry that he was avoiding her. Praying that Dream Villas wouldn't send someone else instead, Ivy made a coffee and drank it on her own as she sat in the shade on the terrace, and wished that she hadn't had that last glass of gin. Or the two before that.

Three glasses of orange juice and a couple of painkillers had taken the edge off her hangover, but she was still cross with herself. Getting drunk wasn't the answer. Apologising was. She could always try to pretend nothing had happened (it hadn't though, had it, despite her wanting it to), and hope that they could carry on as before, but she guessed she'd probably need to clear the air with Sebastián. Reassure him that it wouldn't happen again. That she didn't fancy him like mad.

No, she'd not mention the fancying bit. With his looks, he was probably used to women throwing themselves at him...

Ooh, that was a thought. What about the other properties he was responsible for? Were there other sad, lonely women staying in other villas owned by the company who were offering to take him out for meals? Or worse? Was she one in a long line of hopefuls?

Probably not, she reasoned.

Just her, then, showing herself up.

Wonderful.

Where *was* he?

She checked the time again. It was now ten-thirty; he was later than he'd ever been. He might very well have seen to the other properties in his care first, leaving hers until last. How late he'd be, she had no idea, not having a clue how many other pools he was supposed to clean, or how many other gardens he was meant to sweep. She couldn't even guestimate how many properties Dream Villas had on their books, or where they were located. Maybe there was a repair or DIY emergency at one of them, and he'd been called to see to that first?

She really should get back to work; he might not turn up for ages, if at all, and she couldn't afford to waste the rest of the day listening out for his van and thinking about what she'd say to him when he eventually arrived.

But instead of writing, she found herself pottering around in the kitchen, cleaning cupboards and wiping work surfaces down. Yes, she really did feel like this was home, and it made her even more determined to check out properties for sale when she was next in the village and able to look online. As she said to herself previously, it wouldn't do any harm to look.

When she heard the sound of an engine, it took her a moment to realise that it wasn't the engine she'd been expecting. The noise was deeper, throatier and more powerful. More of a growling snarl than the chug she'd come to recognise as the Dream Villas van.

That didn't bode well, she thought, as she hurried outside. He obviously wasn't here to work, and she prayed he hadn't come to tell her that someone else was taking over the servicing of the villa. She couldn't imagine anyone other than Sebastián dibbling about in the pool as he checked the chemicals, or leaning on a brush. And she most certainly couldn't imagine sharing a morning coffee with another man. It felt disloyal to be having such thoughts.

Oh, why had she been so stupid—

He'd arrived on his bike and was dressed in full leathers, so he obviously didn't intend cleaning anything in Villa Colina today.

'Would you like to come for a ride with me?' he shouted, switching off the roaring engine and putting the kickstand down.

'Sorry, what did you say?'

In a more normal volume, he repeated, 'Would you like to come for a ride?'

That's what she'd hoped he'd said. 'What about the villa?'

'It will still be here when you get back.'

'Ha ha, very funny. I meant, what about your work?'

'I have finished for the day.'

'But you haven't seen to the pool, or…'

'Would you prefer me to do that, rather than take you to Garachico?'

'Is that where we're going?' She'd already made up her mind to say yes.

'If you like. Or we can go somewhere else.'

'Garachico is fine. I've been wanting to go there for ages.'

'I know.'

That's right, she'd mentioned it last night. *Last night* – her cheeks grew warm at the memory of what she'd almost done. At least he wasn't holding it against her.

'But what about the villa?' she repeated. 'Won't you get into trouble for not checking the pool?'

'It doesn't need to be checked every day when only you use it.'

Oh? So why did he—? The idea that he might be using the pool and the gardens as an excuse to visit every day to check that she was all right, popped into her head.

The thought made her slightly giddy until she realised he'd most likely have been told by his employer to keep an eye on the guests and that he probably wasn't interested in her in that way – which would explain why he'd hurried away last night.

But, on the other hand, he was offering to take her out today, and that definitely wouldn't be in his job description.

Annoyed at the way she was constantly second-guessing herself when it came to Sebastián, she gave herself a mental shake.

'Just let me get changed and I'll be with you in a tick.' She paused, wondering what she should wear that would give her adequate protection on the bike.

As if sensing her concern, Sebastián swung his leg over the bike and got off, then opened the top box and pulled out a leather jacket and a pair of leather trousers.

Ivy raised her brows as he held them up. The jacket was pillar box red, nipped in at the waist, and was most certainly a woman's jacket. Her first thought was to wonder who it belonged to. Her second was to hope that it fitted, because it appeared to be rather on the small side. The black trousers might be OK, though.

As much as she saw the sense in wearing them, she baulked at the idea of slipping into another woman's clothes, even if they were intended to be worn over the top of her own clothes.

'Please,' he said, seeing her hesitation. 'I will not take you, if you don't wear them. I have seen what happens when bikers come off. Not that you are going to come off,' he added hastily. 'But it is better safe than sorry, as you English say.'

Reluctantly, she caught hold of the jacket and trousers and disappeared inside to get changed. Jeans, she decided, trainers, and a flowery top, with a fleece over it just in case it was cold on the bike. She spritzed some perfume on, swiped some gloss across her lips, then picked up the trousers with a grimace.

Actually, they didn't look as though they'd been worn much – if at all – and she felt a little better about stepping into them, especially as she discovered they slipped over her hips and did up perfectly. Studying herself in the mirror, she thought she looked a bit bulky in them, but they weren't as bad as she'd expected, and Sebastián was correct on the health-and-safety front. They'd offer her far more protection than her stone-washed jeans.

Next, she turned her attention to the jacket. The leather was thick yet soft to the touch, and the inside was padded with black fabric. The back of it was slightly longer, and she realised the reason for that was to keep the lower back covered when you were hunched over the bike. The cut was exceptionally flattering, as it curved in at her waist and flared back out again. It fitted as though it had been made for her, and when she zipped it up she felt sexy, glamorous and more than a little rock-chick.

Her final act before she went back outside, was to gather her hair into a plait, hoping that she wouldn't have a biker version of hat hair when they got to Garachico.

However, she didn't miss his admiration when she stepped through the door. He was lounging nonchalantly against the bike, and his gaze swept her from head to foot. She told herself he was checking that the leathers fitted and she'd done them up correctly, but she couldn't help hoping that it was because he thought she looked good in them.

'Good, it fits,' was all he said when she walked towards him self-consciously, trying to stop her hips from swaying, in case he mistook it for flirting.

'Whose are they?' she asked, fingering the satin-smooth leather of the jacket and wishing she could keep it.

'Err, I borrowed them. From a friend. Of a friend. His girlfriend.'

The jacket also had hardly been worn. In fact, it looked brand new, and she was amazed that this friend of a friend's girlfriend had been prepared to lend it out at all. If the jacket had belonged to Ivy, she wouldn't have lent it to anyone. It was far too beautiful to risk a stranger damaging it. Maybe if it had been old and scruffy, she could understand.

Sebastián handed her a helmet, and she noticed that it wasn't the same one he'd made her wear on the night he'd driven her back from the pizzeria. This one was also black, but it had deep red roses on it. She guessed it also might belong to the friend of a friend's girlfriend. And it, too, fitted perfectly.

She allowed Sebastián to adjust the chin strap, and after he was done he playfully tapped her on the top of her helmeted head and snapped the visor down. By the time she'd pushed it back up, he was getting gracefully onto the bike and indicating that she should climb on behind him. She caught his eye and he gave her a cheeky wink. Perhaps it was meant to be reassuring, but all it did was make her heart skip a beat as she settled herself snugly against his back.

Oh boy, this felt far too good. Even through their two layers of leather, she could feel the heat of him and it sent an answering warmth through her own body. How she was going to get through the next half hour or so, she had no idea, and suspected she'd be a bit of a mess when they finally arrived at their destination.

She didn't know whether Sebastián was taking it slow in deference to having a novice rider on the back, or whether the road really was as steep and winding as it appeared, but he took his time, banking gently into the corners to give her the opportunity to adjust her position on the seat behind him.

The scenery was breathtaking but although she felt she should concentrate on it and make the most of the ever-changing views, the only thing she was able to focus on was the man who her arms were wrapped around, and whose scent was in her nose. Now and again he'd reach behind him and pat her on the knee and she'd tap him back so he knew she was OK. Despite fervently wishing he'd keep both hands on the handlebars, she would have been happy if his hand had stayed there for a little longer.

Gradually the steep gradient flattened out as they neared the coast, and the impossibly precipitous mountain slopes which had been covered with cacti and other dry-weather plants, were replaced with fields of green bananas and palm trees that dotted the landscape. Houses and other buildings became more frequent, until eventually, the bike rounded a corner and Ivy could see Garachico in front of them.

She sat up a little and peered over Sebastián's shoulder, eager for her first proper glimpse of the town, which gleamed white and terracotta in the bright sunlight. The sea was a deep blue, flecked with white crests, and the sky was a paler shade with cirrus clouds wispy and high, like mares' tails, in the stratosphere. It looked so idyllic she couldn't wait to start exploring.

Then abruptly they were there, right by the sea, as they emerged from the narrowish mountain road into a cobbled parking area next to the main coast road. Sebastián carefully drove onto the uneven stones and found a space to park the bike. Ivy got off while he made sure the machine was secure, and unbuckled her helmet as she waited. Now that they were no longer moving, she could feel the heat of the sun and, as much as she would have liked to have kept the jacket on, she took that off too along with the leather trousers, and handed them all to Sebastián to be stowed, together with his own leathers and helmet, in the top box and paniers.

She pulled her hair free of the plait and shook her head, hoping for some much-needed volume. Crikey, she bet she looked a right mess. But not Sebastián – oh no, he looked as handsome as he usually did – the ruffled-hair look suited him perfectly. She watched him pop a baseball cap on his head, then don a pair of sunglasses. The accessories complemented his faded jeans and simple crisp white T-shirt; he was mouth-wateringly gorgeous.

'Shall we?' he asked, jerking his head towards an enticing side street. When he held out a hand to her so they could dash across the road together, she took it without thinking, and they continued to hold hands as they wandered down the narrow, cobbled street. Ivy held her breath; she couldn't tell whether he'd forgotten he was holding her hand or whether he was continuing to hold it deliberately. She hoped it was the latter because, let's face it, who could forget they were clutching someone else's hand?

Conscious that they looked like a pair of lovers and thoroughly enjoying the experience, she didn't say a word, not wishing to spoil the mood as they began their saunter through the town. But she couldn't remain quiet for long – not when there were so many interesting shops and such delicious smells wafting out from open doorways. She didn't know what to head for first.

A shop with an eclectic collection of paintings, pots and gifts captured her attention, and she pulled on Sebastián's hand, dragging him across the narrow road. She halted in front of the window and gazed inside, captivated by a particularly stunning ceramic painted jug. She wasn't normally a pot person. She didn't usually like ceramics. In fact, ornaments had never really interested her, but this jug was something else. Brightly coloured, it shouted 'Tenerife', and to her it embodied everything she'd come to love about the island; she could imagine it in her kitchen and had just the spot for it.

Except… the kitchen she had in mind wasn't hers – it belonged to the villa – and the jug would be as out of place in her kitchen back in the UK as a model of a double-decker London bus would be over here.

There was little point in buying it. Or the fabulous painting of Garachico – the artist must have taken his or her paints and easel up into the mountains above the town, because the view it showed was similar to the one she saw from the villa every day. It would be a perfect memento though, and it reminded her very much of the paintings dotted throughout the villa.

'Do you like it?' Sebastián asked her as she studied it avidly.

'It's lovely.' And it was, but she still couldn't decide and it was rather expensive. 'But it's a bit too big to put in my suitcase,' she joked.

'They will ship it, if you want.'

'It's OK. I'd like to have a good look around first, anyway. There might be something else I like better.' Although she seriously didn't think she would, and as they strolled out of the shop, she kept sneaking glances at it over her shoulder. Ivy then spotted Sebastián rolling his eyes and elbowed him, but then wished she hadn't because the action reminded him he was still holding her hand, and he gently disentangled himself. Her skin felt surprisingly cold without his warm fingers folded around hers, and she rubbed her hands together to warm them, even though it must be at least twenty-five degrees Celsius in the shade.

They kept walking, and occasionally Ivy would dart into a shop, Sebastián following good-naturedly behind as she exclaimed over various items. Eventually, though, she'd had enough and, as nothing she'd found so far compared to the painting she'd seen earlier, her attention turned to food and a cold drink.

Sebastián, sensing a slump in her enthusiasm, asked, 'Are you hungry?' and she nodded. 'What would you like?'

'Surprise me.'

He raised his eyebrows but didn't say another word as he took her hand once more and led her deeper into the small town and away from the more touristy area near the sea. In a very short space of time, they were climbing a steep flight of steps carved into the very rock the town was built on, and Ivy quickly became breathless as gravity made itself felt. When she stopped for a breather and turned around, she was astonished to see they were as high as the square tower of what she assumed to be a church nearby.

'What is that?' she puffed, more to give herself a chance to recover than from a burning need to know.

'It is the church of Santa Ana,' he told her. 'Would you like to see inside it after we have eaten? It is old, built five hundred years ago, and is small, but impressive.'

'Maybe, if we've got time. What I'd really like is to go down to the sea. Here I am, on an island and I haven't so much as dipped a toe in the ocean yet.'

'You want to swim?' He sounded sceptical.

'No. Just sitting on the beach would be enough. I'd like to feel the spray on my face.'

'You want to be splashed,' he said. 'OK.' The look he gave her was one of bemusement.

She supposed it did sound a bit strange. But to her, it was stranger that she was on a sub-tropical island some- where in the Atlantic and hadn't been closer to the sea than about five miles away as the crow flies – it just didn't feel right.

'How much further?' she asked, as Sebastián hauled her up the last few steps and onto yet another narrow road.

'We are here.'

'We are?' Ivy looked around, but there didn't appear to be a restaurant in sight. There was, however, a widening of the pavement, a space that jutted out over the drop below. Here a couple of tables were arranged together, and a rather wonky sun umbrella was balanced precariously on a pole between them.

When Ivy glanced at the buildings across the road, she saw an open door and a handwritten sign saying, 'Cochina de Carla'. The sounds of pots and pans being banged about came from within, along with a woman singing loudly and out of tune.

'That is Carla,' Sebastián said, taking off his cap and removing his sunglasses. 'She cooks every day for anyone who wants to eat. There is no choice of food, you eat what she makes or you go somewhere else.'

'How does she stay in business?'

'It is not a business. She does it for the love of cooking. Some people pay if they can. Others do not. It is of no matter to her. But she is a good cook and I have been coming here since I was a child. She is a favourite of the workers in the area and the taxi drivers. We are lucky there is a table free. Shall we sit?'

Both tables were free, and Ivy chose the nearest with an amused shrug. Then they waited.

When Carla eventually appeared, it wasn't to ask them what they wanted to drink, it was to plonk a carafe of water on the table, with some ice in it that clinked madly, along with a couple of glasses.

The woman didn't say a word, and Ivy watched her stomp back inside the house where she immediately recommenced warbling to herself.

'She's not very friendly, is she?' Ivy whispered. The woman was also much older than Ivy had expected. She had to be ninety, at least. Hunched over, wearing a shapeless skirt, a baggy blouse and a headscarf all in black, the old woman didn't seem capable of cooking a meal for herself, let alone for countless others.

Sebastián poured them a glass of water each and sat back. He was clearly enjoying her bewilderment, but Ivy had never eaten anywhere like this before. It was a far cry from the restaurants and cafes of London. This was more akin to being invited to a stranger's house for a meal and then being told to eat on the pavement. Weird didn't begin to describe it.

She heard a noise behind her and twisted around in her seat to see the old woman carrying two bowls in her hands, with two spoons tucked under her armpit.

She put the bowls down, whipped out the spoons, wiped them with a cloth, and then grunted out, '*Pan?*'

Sebastián said something in return and Carla grunted again and shuffled back inside.

'What is it?' Ivy narrowed her eyes at her bowl.

'*Rancho canario*. Soup with chicken, pork, chickpeas, vegetables – whatever is available – and potatoes. It can taste different every time you make it because the ingredients are always changing.' He dipped his spool into the mixture and dug in.

It certainly looked appetising, and it smelt tasty, so Ivy picked up her own spoon and took a mouthful.

'Mmm, this is delicious,' she groaned in delight as the flavours exploded in her mouth. 'What did Carla say?'

'She asked if we wanted bread.'

'Do we?'

'There is more to come after this, so I said no.'

'Are these noodles?'

'Pasta? Yes.'

'It's all tomatoey and meaty and herby,' she declared.

Sebastián chuckled. 'I know, I am eating it, too. I am happy you like it.'

'Like it? It's my new favourite thing. I wonder how she makes it.'

'I know how to cook this. I will show you, so you can cook it also.'

Ivy wasn't sure she wanted to make it herself, but the thought of Sebastián in her kitchen giving her lessons changed her mind.

'That would be great. Thank you,' she said, thinking that the cooking lessons might go the same way as the proposed Spanish ones, although Sebastián had tried to teach her the odd phrase or two when they were drinking their morning coffee together over the past few weeks.

'It will be my pleasure.'

The way he said the word 'pleasure' made her shiver. Or maybe she was reading into it what she wanted to read into it. Yeah, that was it. Her libido was awake and being silly, and she must learn to ignore it.

But he had held her hand...

Not for long though...

She concentrated on her soup, realising that Sebastián was right – having bread with it would be too much, especially since another course would follow this first one.

When they'd finished, Carla cleared their bowls away without a murmur, then shortly returned with two plates which she thumped down on the table.

Ivy examined hers. Chicken, salad, Canarian potatoes and some red saucy stuff.

'*Pollo al salmorejo*,' Sebastián said when she pointed at the meat. 'Garlic, white wine, herbs and spices. Paprika gives it the colour and some of the flavour.'

Ivy practically swooned as she took a mouthful of the chicken and very soon she'd gobbled up everything on her plate. 'Stuffed,' she announced as she chased a cherry tomato around her plate before spearing it and popping it in her mouth. Replete, she placed her cutlery neatly together and sat back.

'You do not want dessert?' Sebastián asked, smirking.

She groaned. 'It's going to be something delicious, isn't it?'

'Probably. Although it might also be fruit, or cheese. There is no telling with Carla. You eat what she gives you.'

'Go on, then. I just won't be able to eat anything for the rest of the day. Maybe for the rest of the week.'

By the time she'd eaten a small dish of *bienmesabe*, which turned out to be a rich and creamy almond, honey and egg yolk concoction, Ivy thought she might never walk again. She even refused the coffee that Carla wanted to give them, for fear she might burst if she tried to shove anything else into her totally full stomach. Instead, she sipped some water and hoped Sebastián wouldn't have to roll her back down the hill.

'I will give Carla some money for her trouble,' he said, pushing his chair back and getting to his feet. 'I will only be a minute.'

Ivy wondered if she should offer him any money. Or might it offend him? Especially since she'd paid for everyone's meal last night, and she didn't want to flaunt her success at him. She guessed her might have brought her up here to Cocina de Carla because the restaurants down in the town were too expensive, and he'd already told her that Carla didn't expect payment, so she had to trust that Sebastián would only give the old lady what he could afford. Hoping he wouldn't notice, she slipped some euros out of her purse and folded them up in her hand. She planned to drop them on the table at the very last minute before they left.

As soon as Sebastián returned, Ivy stood up. 'This way?' she asked, expecting to go back along the same route.

'We go here, then down there, and then we will arrive at the Plaza La Libertad, which is a beautiful large square with trees and places to sit...' Sebastián drew her close and pointed it out, and Ivy followed the line of his finger to see a clump of greenery next to the church that she'd asked about earlier. 'From there, we can go to the sea and the *piscinas naturales*.' He popped the baseball cap back on his head and put his sunglasses on.

As they moved away from the table, Carla emerged from her kitchen and Sebastián gave the old woman a wave, as did Ivy, but all Carla did was squint at them. Ivy casually opened her hand, and dropped the folded notes on the table. As she did so, she caught the woman's eye.

It might have been Ivy's imagination, but she could have sworn Carla gave her a tiny nod.

Content that she'd managed to contribute towards their meal, and grateful to be in the company of such a wonderful man, Ivy didn't think she'd ever felt as happy as she did right now.

And the day wasn't over yet!

Chapter 15

The Plaza La Libertad was exceptionally charming with wide pathways, an open square, grassed areas and raised flower beds. Ivy was tempted to suggest they had a coffee at a nearby cafe, but she really did want to get up close and personal with the sea, and she couldn't even see it from there, so they carried on, dawdling down a tiny street or two until Ivy spotted the tell-tale blue of the ocean at the end of one of them.

They emerged onto a wide road with a promenade bordered by black volcanic rock and glistening water beyond.

Ivy took a deep breath of the salty air and smiled. This is what she'd been yearning for – a nice walk along a scenic sea front. And, although she knew she wasn't on holiday, today certainly felt like it. What must it be like to have this holiday feeling whenever you wanted it, she mused. She was happy enough to live up in the stunning mountains with the fabulous views as it was only a short jaunt to the seaside. Work and play, all in the space of a few miles. It was the best of both worlds in her opinion, and the more she considered the possibility of making Tenerife her home, the more it appealed to her and felt like the right thing to do.

She hardly dared breathe as Sebastián took her hand again and led her off the pavement and down a slope towards the rocks, and as she walked her eyes widened in surprise and pleasure. The crazy paved path they had stepped onto, widened out into a space for people to sunbathe, or to swim in the sea pools which were carved out of the dark volcanic rock. Walkways meandered between the pools and metal ladders like the ones seen at swimming pools allowed easy access into the water. It wasn't quite the beach she'd been anticipating, but there were benches dotted around and there was a restaurant located at the far end of the sea pools.

'Fancy a coffee?' she asked as they dodged sunbathers and wet squealing children, and headed in the direction of the restaurant. It looked to be the perfect place to sit and people watch as well as to take in the glorious view of the sea and the shoreline.

Every now and again, a particularly large wave would break against the rocks which shielded the natural seawater pools from the ocean and the resultant spray would rise into the air, sending a fine mist everywhere. Some waves gushed over the barrier rocks, freshening the water in the pools with each surge, and soaking anyone who ventured too close.

The restaurant was situated far enough away to avoid drenching its clientele, yet it was close enough for diners to enjoy the action.

'What a perfect spot,' Ivy declared, spying a free table and heading determinedly towards it, dragging a laughing Sebastián along in her wake.

She dropped down into a chair and let out a contented sigh. 'I could get used to this,' she declared. 'Work in the morning, followed by a leisurely lunch, then a walk along the sea front in the afternoon.'

'Is that what you'd like to do?'

'Maybe. I'm lucky in that I can write anywhere. I might have to go back to the UK for a book launch or a radio interview or something, but I don't have to live there to be able to do my job. Do you fancy a coffee or do you want something else?' she asked, spying a waiter and calling him over.

'Coffee is fine,' Sebastián said, and she gave their order.

'I try to do something completely different other than writing in the afternoons, such as housework or swimming – anything physical helps recharge the creative process. That's why I go for a walk to the village every day, it's not just to check my emails.'

She realised then that she hadn't checked hers at all today and had actually forgotten to bring her phone with her. It was on the table in the hall, and she couldn't remember whether it was charged or not. She regretted not having it because she could have taken a few photos, and not only for Facebook or Instagram, either. They would have reminded her what a fabulous time she was having today, and having a photo of Sebastián to hand whenever she wanted to drool over him wouldn't go amiss, either.

'Drat,' she said. 'I wish I'd brought my phone – I would have liked to take a couple of snaps.'

'Use mine,' he suggested, fishing it out of his pocket and handing it to her. 'I can send them to you later.'

'Good idea, thank you. Smile,' she said, aiming his phone at him and Sebastián dutifully smiled. 'Can you take your cap and sunnies off, please – you could be anyone under all that.'

He did as she asked and smiled again, but as soon as she'd taken a few snaps, he popped his cap back on and slipped his glasses onto his nose.

God he really, really was handsome, she thought, as she checked the image. And terribly photogenic, too. If it was at all possible, he looked better in the photo than he did in real life, and she would have thought that was impossible.

He was an incredibly good-looking guy, and quite charismatic, she thought. There was a presence about him that didn't just come from his looks or confidence, although he had both in abundance. It was something she couldn't put her finger on, but it was definitely there, and she thought others might have noticed it too, because two women seated a couple of tables over from him were having a hard time taking their eyes off him. Mind you, she told herself, that might be because he was so darned handsome; she had trouble taking her own eyes off him most of the time too, so she didn't blame other women for feeling the same way. Or men, for that matter, as she noticed a group of guys sauntering past in Speedos (why, oh why, did any man think Speedos were a good fashion choice?) and they couldn't stop staring at him either. Sebastián was attractive to both sexes, it seemed.

She took a few more snaps of the sea, and the pools, then tipped her head back and closed her eyes, feeling the heat of the sun on her face and luxuriating in the sounds of the sea and people enjoying themselves. There was no need to make conversation and she felt remarkably comfortable in Sebastián's presence without speaking.

The smell of coffee made her sit up and she opened her eyes to find a waiter decanting two cups, along with milk and sugar from a tray onto their table.

'Thank you,' she said to him, reaching for her drink, then stopping with her hand in mid-air as movement to the side of them caught her attention.

A couple were taking a selfie – which wasn't remarkable in itself – but what was unusual was that they were facing away from her and Sebastián, yet they kept glancing over their shoulders then looking back and checking the screen, as though they wanted to get something in the background.

Instinctively she leant to the side, not wanting to be in the shot. Sebastián seemed oblivious, and didn't move, so the couple took the photo anyway, and when they were done, one of them turned around and gave her a thumbs up.

She smiled, glad she hadn't photo-bombed them, although Sebastián was bound to be in it. But then so were a lot of other people who were seated at the restaurant, and she wondered if the place was ever quiet.

Ivy gave Sebastián his phone back and stood up. 'I'm just off to wash my hands,' she said, and glanced around for the ladies' loo, before spying a sign.

What a delightful day this was turning out to be, she mused, as she freshened up. It was so considerate of Sebastián to remember that she wanted to visit Garachico, and then making it happen. He was a sweet guy and, along with his good looks, it made him an irresistible combination. He was nothing like Nathaniel, even though she'd initially based her main male character on him. They were really very different, although there was a bit of the angel about Sebastián in the way he was so thoughtful, although thankfully he lacked the angel's darkness. She must remember to temper it a little in the next book, to show Nathaniel's lighter side.

And suddenly she felt it, the tingling excitement that was always there at the start of a new project, and Ivy couldn't wait to sit down at her computer and make a start on the next novel in the series.

Not today, though; today was about enjoying herself and enjoying being with Sebastián, and, as she walked back to their table, she hoped it wouldn't end too soon.

She didn't see him for a moment, coming to a halt and wondering where he'd got to. Maybe he'd decided to pop to the loo, too… Oh, there he was, sitting where she'd left him, but she'd been unable to see him because several people had been standing so close to him they'd obscured him from view.

The group began to slowly move away as she drew closer. When she resumed her seat, though, one of them aimed a phone in her direction and she could have sworn the girl had taken a photo of her.

Ah, she was being silly again. The restaurant was in such a picturesque spot, no wonder people wanted to capture it. However, it did look like both she and Sebastián were going to feature in several people's holiday snaps, and she smiled to herself.

'I should have done bunny ears,' she said to Sebastián, nodding her head at the girl. 'Or made a weird face.' She noticed he'd taken his sunglasses off again, and his eyes were narrowed against the glare. Hastily, he replaced them and called for their bill without replying.

'My turn to pay,' she said when the waiter handed it to him. 'You got lunch.'

He demurred, and Ivy rooted around for some notes and slid them under her saucer.

'Time to go, I think,' he said, taking her hand (much to her delight) and leading her swiftly back onto the pavement.

'What about the beach?' she asked him.

He shrugged. 'The one here is small. I know a better one further along the coast. Or would you rather have another look around the town? You have yet to see the church of Santa Anna.'

'The beach,' she replied firmly.

'You do know that the beaches on Tenerife are mostly rocky or black volcanic sand? They are not golden.'

'I don't care.'

'*Vale*, OK.'

They were back in the car park in no time and before she knew it, Ivy had donned her leathers and helmet and was perched snugly behind Sebastián as he aimed the bike towards the main road.

Goodbye, Garachico, she thought, giving the town a quick glance over her shoulder, when she spotted the same group of people who'd been taking photos of the restaurant walking along the pavement, phones in hands, pointing and clicking. She was reminded of how she'd been a slave to her mobile before the villa's lack of reception and wifi had cured her of her addiction. At least Sebastián had brought his with him and had allowed her to take a few photos to commemorate the day, because that's all she really wanted to do with a phone at present. It was liberating not checking her emails every few minutes or not feeling the need to view Twitter, or Facebook, or Instagram or any of the other sites she felt she should be part of.

Ten short minutes later, Sebastián was easing the bike off the road and onto a dusty verge.

'Is this it?' she asked after she'd clambered off, far less gracefully than him, and had handed him her helmet.

'I said you would be disappointed.'

'I'm not – it's just considerably quieter than I anticipated.'

'I know. That is why I brought you here.'

'Here' was a small rocky bay with a small rocky beach. Breakers rolled in and crashed against the pebbles before sucking them back out to sea, and the constant sound of the push and drag was quite hypnotic. The beach itself was almost deserted, although there was a fisherman throwing a line at the other end. He was perched precariously on the rocks and only inches from the sea.

'Do you think he'll catch anything?' she asked.

Sebastián shaded his eyes. He hadn't bothered to put his cap or glasses back on, and Ivy took it as a sign that they'd probably not stay here all that long.

'I expect he will. The fishing is good here. The current brings many fish close to the shore, and sometimes you will see them jumping to escape predators. It is those fish he will be wanting. If he has caught any, he might like to sell them to us and we can have fresh fish for dinner.' He hesitated. 'If you would like to have dinner with me? I don't want to presume.'

'Yes, please.'

His grin was wide as he replied, 'Then, I shall cook.'

'Thank goodness for that! I didn't fancy cooking anything with a head and tail still on it.' Her own smile matched his; she was thrilled that he wasn't just going to drop her off at the villa and run. He was going to spend the evening with her, and she fizzed with anticipation.

What if he made a move to kiss her?

Would she let him…?

Who was she kidding! Of course she would. Despite all her internal protestations and her own advice to be cautious, she was so attracted to him she knew she wouldn't be able to resist. Darn it – she liked him as a person, too. Very much. And if she'd met him in London at a book launch or a party, she wouldn't be agonising over it.

The beach was rather narrow and not very long, and as they strolled across it, Ivy asked, 'Is the tide going in or out?'

Sebastián glanced down at her. 'Do you know, I have no idea. Out, maybe. Or in. I cannot tell.'

'How far does it go out?' she wanted to know. She was thinking of Brighton, where the tide went out almost as far as the end of the pier.

'Not far. Twenty metres, perhaps. Maybe a little more.'

'Can I paddle?'

His lips quirked. 'If you like. The pebbles may hurt your feet,' he warned.

Ivy didn't care. She was itching to feel the cool Atlantic lapping around her ankles, so she sprinted closer to the waves, slipped off her trainers, and then rolled her jeans up to her knees.

'Ouch!' He was right – the pebbles did hurt, but she wasn't going to admit defeat, so she hobbled carefully down the beach until she was in striking distance of the waves.

When she turned to glance at him, she was brought up short by the expression on his face. Although he swiftly smothered it, she could have sworn she saw desire in his eyes, along with another emotion she failed to name.

Abruptly a wave cascaded over her feet and Ivy squealed. 'It's freezing!' she exclaimed and he laughed. 'I can't feel my feet.'

'You are being a baby.'

'I am not.' She put her hands on her hips and glared at him. 'Take your shoes off and join me,' she taunted, 'and see how you like it.'

'I have more sense,' he replied loftily, his nose in the air.

Ivy couldn't resist kicking water at him, and he danced back out of reach.

'You will pay for that,' he growled.

There was a second where Ivy could have deflected the situation, made it into something else, something light and inconsequential, but it was gone before she had a chance to think about it, and she was captured by the intensity in his eyes and the hunger on his face.

With a low groan, he took three strides forward and came up against her, wrapping his arms around her waist, his lips searching for her.

Ivy tilted her head back and her lips parted. Her arms twined around his neck, pulling his head down until his mouth crushed hers and her heart pounded so hard she thought she might faint.

Never in all her life had she thrown herself so thoroughly into a kiss. It was drowning her, sucking her into its depths, consuming her until she had no coherent thought left in her head. She was utterly lost to it and to him. Nothing else existed except his mouth, his tongue, his breath on her cheek, the cage of his strong arms holding her tight as she might have floated away otherwise. He grounded her and anchored her, yet at the same time her heart soared and dipped with the bliss of it.

He was as breathless as she when they eventually broke apart, her lips already hot and aching for another one of those luscious kisses. His eyes were unfathomably dark and she could feel the thrum of his heart reverberating against her, an answering drum of longing and need.

He stared down at her.

She stared back at him.

She was lost.

Sebastián, it seemed, had another matter on his mind. 'My feet are wet,' he said looking down at the waves splashing over his trainers.

Ivy glanced down. The bottom of her rolled-up jeans were also wet. It looked like the tide was coming in after all, and they both began to laugh.

'Shall we go back to the villa?' he asked softly.

All she could say was, 'Yes, please.'

Chapter 16

'That was delicious.' After the meal at lunchtime, Ivy didn't think she'd be able to eat another morsel for the rest of the day, but a simple dinner of baked *vieja* (or parrotfish as Sebastián informed her after he'd persuaded the fisherman to sell him a couple) and a tossed salad, accompanied by crisp white wine, went down a treat.

True to his word, Sebastián had removed all the yucky bits from the fish, such as the head and tail, before he placed the plate down in front of her, and Ivy had scoffed the lot. She'd only had the one glass of wine though, conscious that Sebastián was drinking sparkling water with lime. She didn't want to be tiddly when she kissed him next and neither did she want to breathe alcohol fumes all over him.

He hadn't kissed her again, not since that fabulous kiss on the beach – but she was hopeful. He hadn't given any indication that he was regretting it either, hence her prayer that he'd do it again. And again.

She hadn't known what to expect when they'd pulled onto the drive earlier and she'd led him inside, half-hoping he'd whisk her off to bed.

He hadn't.

What he had done was remove his wet trainers and pad around her kitchen as he prepared the fish. Then he'd made her a gin and bitter lemon and they'd sat outside for a while, chatting. And all the time she could feel the ghost of his lips on hers, the scent of his cologne filling her nose. A thrilling electricity flowed between them, sparking tremors in her tummy and making her heart flutter, and she felt like a teenager again – young and carefree.

What was she thinking? She *was* young (ish – forty-three wasn't old in the scheme of things) and she was most definitely carefree. But the way he made her feel was incomparable, and she revelled in it, not wanting the sense of anticipation to end, yet wishing it would – and soon, because this slow burning build-up was driving her slightly mad.

'It's odd to think we were down there this afternoon,' she said, pointing to Garachico. 'I can see where we parked the bike – I think, although I really could do with some binoculars right now – and there's the church, and are those the natural pools?'

He nodded. 'It is like being in an aeroplane up here, a low flying one.'

She regarded him curiously. 'Have you travelled much?'

He picked up his drink and took a long swallow. 'Some.'

'Where have you been?'

'Spain, Madrid for one. And a few other places.'

'Like where?'

'Europe...'

'Where?' she persisted. He seemed reluctant to talk about it, and she was curious to know why.

'Paris, Berlin, Milan... some other places.'

'Was it like a backpacking holiday, or a gap year, or something?'

'Something like that, yes.'

'I wish I'd taken a year out. I went from school straight into university, and then into work. I should have gone travelling instead, but the lure of hard cash won.'

'And you regret it?'

'I suppose I do. You always think you'll do it later, but later never happens.'

'Could you do it now? Visit some places?'

'I have taken holidays, but it's not the same as carrying all your possessions on your back and seeing where the wind blows you. Besides, I like my creature comforts too much now, although one day maybe I'll buy a motor home and travel the world.' She laughed. 'Listen to me – I'm too scared to hire a car on Tenerife. I'm not exactly going to buy a campervan, am I?'

'We all have dreams,' he said. 'There is nothing wrong with that, but sometimes the reality does not live up to them, or it is not as expected.'

'Is that said from bitter experience?' she asked, light-heartedly, because she sensed that it might very well be, and she didn't want to dampen the mood.

'Maybe.'

'What are your dreams?'

'I am living mine,' he replied.

'You are?' She hoped she didn't sound as shocked as she felt. She wasn't a snob, and money and material posses-sions weren't that important in the scheme of things, but he surely couldn't be earning a great deal and his job most likely didn't stretch him all that much. She'd come to realise he was an intelligent guy and she thought he could use his brains more effectively than in villa maintenance.

'I live on a wonderful island, I have a family I love, I don't have to work all day every day, so I have time to enjoy myself, like today. What more is there?' he asked.

What more indeed? Since he put it like that...

She nodded slowly. 'I must admit, I've been happier since I've been here than I have been in a long time, and I don't just mean because I'm getting over Dastardly Daniel.'

'Is that what you call him?' Sebastián laughed, and the low rumble sent a tremble through her. Even his laugh was gorgeous.

'He deserves it,' she protested. 'Although to be honest, I don't miss him, London, or my life there. Coming to Tenerife has been good for me. It's given me the time and distance to slow down and concentrate on what really matters.'

'Your writing?'

'Yes. I sent the completed manuscript off to Nora, my agent, yesterday,' she told him, feeling unaccountably shy about it.

'That is wonderful. You must be so happy.'

'I am. I can't believe I've written a whole novel in just over three weeks. That's what comes of having very few distractions.'

There was a charged silence for a moment, and Ivy had a feeling she might have said something she shouldn't have.

'Does that mean you will be returning to England soon?' he asked, his eyes focusing on the horizon.

'Nope. I fully intend to see out the full six months. As I said before, Nora wants a series out of me, and I'm hoping I can write another couple of books while I'm here.' That's if she ever left at all, she thought. This slower place of life was suiting her, and she wasn't keen to give it up.

'I am very pleased to hear that,' he said quietly, and before she could think of anything to say, he excused himself and went into the kitchen.

What was she doing? she asked herself as she listened to the gentle clink of crockery followed by the sound of a tap running. What was this *thing* between them? She couldn't even begin to describe it; it was too new, too tenuous in nature to give it a name. It wasn't a relationship – not yet – although it could become one, given time, and if that's what they both wanted.

Or was it merely lust and raw desire?

She smiled. It was more than desire on her part because she really liked Sebastián as a person, not just as someone to hop into bed with. Not that she'd ever been the bed-hopping type. Sex without deeper meaning wasn't her style. Could she risk having her heart broken again and start something with Sebastián?

There was one thing she needed to consider before they took things any further, despite her feelings for him, and that was whether she seriously intended to look for a place to buy in Tenerife. Because if she went back to the UK, then this could be nothing more than a holiday fling and she wasn't sure she was the love-'em-and-leave-'em type.

Then there was the problem of not wanting to ruin things due to her overactive imagination. Look at how she'd reacted last night when she'd thought he was upset because she'd almost invited him to kiss her. She'd been horrified, and more than a little worried that Dream Villas would schedule someone else in to service the villa this morning.

She didn't want that. She didn't want to risk not seeing him again, and it had nothing to do with Sebastián being material for Nathaniel's character.

The more she thought about it, the more she considered that suggesting Sebastián left now that the wonderful meal he'd prepared had been eaten, was a sensible idea. The only issue was that she didn't know how to phrase it so as not to offend him. She'd had a great time today and had loved being in his company, but until she had come to a decision about her future, it would be best if they remained friends. *If*, that is, both of them could pretend the kiss in the ocean hadn't happened. And considering she could still feel the pressure of his mouth on hers and the way his body had felt, the way he'd tasted, that was going to be a big ask – for her, anyway. She'd never been particularly good at hiding her feelings and she wasn't convinced she could hide them now.

Sebastián, on the other hand, seemed to be doing a sterling job of pretending nothing had happened, because he was acting exactly the same tonight as every other time they'd been together – friendly, relaxed, confident. It was as though he'd sensed her mood or had read her mind and was giving her some space to decide what she wanted to do.

Or, and Ivy thought that this scenario was far more likely, the kiss hadn't meant as much to him as it had to her. He fancied her, that much was obvious, but she didn't think their embrace had had the same effect on him. She could bet her last euro that he wasn't sitting there debating whether or not to take things further, or mulling over whether or not he should sleep with her if the opportunity presented itself. Nor was he likely to be thinking about how sleeping with her might lead to something more – or not. Most probably, to him, the kiss had just been a nice kiss. That was all. She was overthinking things, as she so often did.

'It is time I left,' he said, breaking into her muddled thoughts as he stepped back out onto the terrace. 'It's getting late, and we both have work in the morning.'

It wasn't that late, barely ten o'clock…

'Thank you for taking me to Garachico, and for lunch and everything,' she said, wincing at the last bit and hoping he didn't think she was thanking him for kissing her. 'I had a good time.'

'I did, too. And if you'd like to visit Garachico again, just let me know. I will be happy to take you. Unless you would prefer to go by yourself?'

'No, that's fine. I'd love to go with you again.'

'Good…'

'Well, then…' She trailed off. Was he going to kiss her again?

He leant over her and she tensed, but all he did was brush his lips against her cheek.

'Don't forget the leathers you lent me,' she said as he turned to leave. In her haste to change out of her wet jeans, she'd walked into the villa still wearing her leathers and had hung them on a hook near the front door.

'They can stay here,' he said. 'For the next time.' He paused and she swivelled in her chair to get a better look at him. 'If you want there to be a next time?'

Ivy caught her breath. 'Do *you*?'

A smile played about his eyes and his lips parted. 'Yes. Very much.'

'So do I.'

'*Adiós*.'

'Bye.'

She waited for the roar of the motorbike to fade after he drove off, before she slowly exhaled, all her good intentions blowing in the breeze behind him.

Oh Lord, what was she doing?

Chapter 17

'I'm not so sure it was a good idea for you not to have a mobile signal or wifi,' were Nora's opening words when Ivy answered the villa's phone the following morning.

'Hello to you, too. I was going to check my emails and messages later today. What's up?'

'Everything.'

Oh God. Ivy felt sick. Nora ringing her like this could only mean one thing – she hated *An Angel from Hell*. Ivy slid down the wall and sat on the floor, her hands clammy and her knees weak. She seemed to be making a habit of that. 'What do you mean?' she squeaked.

'As I told you, based on the five chapters you sent me and the synopsis, I approached several publishers.'

'*And?*' This was like persuading a vampire to donate some blood.

'Three of them want to see the completed manuscript.'

'Three? Out of how many?'

'Three. They are all interested. So get your arse to wherever you can get a signal because I've read the book and I've got some edits for you. How soon can you get the revised draft back to me? I'd like it yesterday.'

'Hang on a sec – when you say edits, what are we talking about? Significant rewrites, or a change of hair colour?'

'You're being facetious. Nothing major, but there's a plot hole in Chapter 28 that needs resolving, and— Look, just read the notes I sent you. When can you have them done by?'

Ivy shook her head. Nora was incorrigible. How could she possibly know how long it would take her to complete the edits until she knew what they were? 'I'll go to the cafe now and give you an estimate,' she promised. 'Before you hang up, who did you approach?'

'Sarah Elliott, Carol Morgan and Jim Chase.'

'Good, that's fine.' Ivy knew all those editors, had met each of them at various functions, and two out of the three worked for the big five publishing houses. The third, Jim Chase, was employed by an up-and-coming independent house with a sterling reputation. If anything, she was tempted to go with Jim, assuming he was willing to put an offer on the table, because the publishers he worked for had a faster turnaround. She wanted this book on the shelves as quickly as possible, and she didn't fancy waiting a year or longer for it to be released. It would all depend on Nora though, because that's what an agent was for – to get the best deal possible. And Ivy trusted her to do precisely that.

She put the receiver back on its stand and checked the time; seven minutes past nine. Nora must have called Ivy as soon as she'd arrived at the office, and excitement began to course through her. This was the confirmation she needed that the book was as good as she hoped it was. OK, none of those editors had read the whole thing yet, so there was still time for one or more (not all of them, please not all of them) to pass on it, but at least the initial interest was there.

She should leave to go to the village, so she packed her laptop into its carrycase and fetched her shoes. Should she stay until Sebastián arrived? Ivy was desperate to share her news with someone, but she wasn't sure he'd be that interested, or that he'd understand the significance of what she was telling him. Besides, she was impatient to review Nora's editorial recommendations, and if she waited for Sebastián she'd inevitably have a coffee with him, and it would be nearer to midday before she'd be sitting at her usual table in the cafe.

Leaving him a hastily scribbled note which she placed by the kettle, Ivy slipped her feet into her sandals, picked up her laptop case, and carefully made her way along the uneven and somewhat rocky track until she reached the village. For the first time since she'd made that particular journey, she didn't notice the view. Her mind was too stuffed full of thoughts of Sebastián, of making Tenerife her permanent home, of this new series, of how comprehensive the edits might be... The thoughts whirled and swooped around her brain, with not one of them landing for long enough for Ivy to grasp and think about properly.

She was mentally exhausted by the time she dropped into a chair at the cafe and nodded a greeting to the old gents. Did they turn up at opening time and not go home until the place closed? The faces did seem to fluctuate though, and there was a new one today, someone she hadn't seen before. He was looking at her curiously, and she guessed the others would soon fill him in on who she was.

A coffee and a croissant, she decided, opening her laptop and connecting to the wifi. She'd rushed out of the villa before she'd even had breakfast, and despite her inner turmoil her tummy was protesting. While Ivy waited for her order to arrive, she hastily logged into her emails and began to scroll.

There it was – an attachment with Nora's edits.

She read the notes once, then again, and let out a sigh of relief. The changes were easily doable and were relatively minor. The plot hole in Chapter 28 could be resolved with a scene change in Chapter 31, which would wrap it up nicely, but that was about it. Everything else was easily rectified by a sentence added here or by changing a word or two there.

Reading Nora's email for a third time, Ivy concentrated on the parts where her agent had said she'd loved it, and a warm glow which had nothing to do with the sun peeping around the edge of the umbrella she was sitting under, spread through her.

Nora's opinion was usually spot-on. She'd been in the publishing business for years and had buckets of experience. If her agent liked it, Ivy knew the odds were that readers would, too.

It would take the rest of today to amend the parts that Nora had pointed out, but now that she had her agent's seal of approval Ivy could go ahead and polish the writing until it sparkled. Ivy never paid a great deal of attention to grammar, spelling and punctuation when writing the first draft as all she wanted to do was to concentrate on getting the story written. There was little point in making it perfect first time around if it might have to be changed depending on what your editor advised.

Now, though, she wanted it to be as perfect as possible before Nora sent the whole thing to the publishers. She'd have to put the next book in the series on the backburner for a few days, even though she was itching to get started on it. Being here definitely was good for her creativity, as Nora's reaction to *An Angel from Hell* had proved.

So with that in mind, Ivy decided to do some research which had nothing at all to do with the nine circles of hell or the assorted demons who inhabited them. She went onto Rightmove and checked out properties for sale in her suburb of London in order to estimate what her house might be worth.

Pleasantly surprised to see the price that similar properties to hers were being sold for, Ivy then searched for estate agents in Tenerife and began reading to see what she could afford and where. A couple of hours soon sped by and she ordered another coffee and a selection of tapas – because it would soon be lunchtime and it would be a shame not to enjoy the food on offer – then she went back to her scrolling.

She'd not seen much of the island, just the north west corner and only a fraction of that, but she knew what she liked and what she didn't, and she certainly didn't want to live in a livelier area. She'd fallen in love with this quiet little village and the fantastic views, and if she could find somewhere near here, she'd be delighted. Even Garachico would be acceptable, although it was more touristy than she wanted and property prices rose quite considerably the nearer you got to the sea.

Ah, here was one... She clicked on it but was disappointed to see that the promise of the property's wonderful outside was let down by the rather shabby interior. It would need a considerable amount of work to bring it up to the standard she'd want, and she wasn't sure she was up for it. What she really wanted was something she could move into straight away, although she wasn't averse to applying a lick of paint or two if necessary.

Ivy spent a good hour or so scrolling and clicking, until she had a fair idea of what was available, what she could afford, and what she wanted. Narrowing her search down to four properties, she saved them, and then opened up a new document which she called 'Scenarios'. It had nothing to do with her writing and everything to do with planning for a possible permanent relocation to Tenerife. She listed the pros and cons of firstly renting out her property in London and renting one here for the long term, then selling her house and buying one of the ones whose details she'd saved, and finally selling in London and renting here.

Moving abroad was a huge decision and not one which could be taken lightly or without a great deal of thought. The logical option, and the easiest to implement, would be to rent out her house in London and find somewhere to rent over here. An image of Villa Colina popped into her head and Ivy gave it serious consideration, as she realised that she was comparing every property she'd seen online with the one she was currently staying in, and finding them all wanting as a result. She'd love to stay at Villa Colina indefinitely, and she knew Nora had secured a good deal for a six-month rental. Would the owners be prepared to reduce the rent in exchange for a guaranteed income for the next year or two? It was a thought and one she should consider pursuing.

However, and here was the biggest consideration of them all – did she really intend to commit to living in Tenerife, or was the compromise of renting merely a way of giving herself an out clause if she needed it?

Oh well, she sighed, she didn't need to make a decision today, although she did intend to rattle off an email to the estate agent she'd used when she'd bought her London house and have them give her a valuation, both on the sale and rental of her home. There was a key with her neighbour so access wouldn't be a problem, and she reminded herself to inform Mrs Strawbridge to give it to the estate agent. Once Ivy had an idea of how much she could sell it or rent it for, she'd have a better understanding of where she stood.

Tapas eaten and decisions put on hold (for now), Ivy was about to call for the bill, when a ping alerted her to a new email.

The sender's name made her freeze.

Daniel.

Ivy read his words, first with incredulity, then with growing anger. Who the hell did he think he was? He had no right to ask to read her manuscript. *He'd heard it was good.* Huh! He could jolly well bugger off. She didn't care if she'd just written *Pride and Prejudice* and he was the last publisher on the planet. He had no right to ask – not after what he'd done. Was probably still doing with the delectable Rebekkah Rain. He'd even had the cheek to finish the email off by telling her that he missed her and they had been a good team once, and could be again.

The rotten, lying, cheating bastard.

And he'd said it in an email; how impersonal could he get? He'd not even phoned her... Oh, hang on. In her haste to read and download Nora's edits, Ivy had forgotten to check her phone.

Daniel actually had tried to contact her, several times. She'd had a couple of missed calls (no message left) and three texts. The first one said, *Call me, we need to talk.* The second: *Please don't ignore me, Ivy. We really do need to talk.* The third: *I think I might have made a mistake. I miss you x* The kiss was so unlike her ex that Ivy burst out laughing, earning herself some bemused looks from the old gents crowd.

Trust Daniel to come sniffing around her again now that she had something to interest him. It was typical of him to think he could snap his fingers and she'd come running. The only running she intended to do would be in the opposite direction. He was going to be disappointed, because she wanted nothing to do with him or his publishing company ever again. He'd made his position clear when he'd dropped her for a younger, more literary option. He'd made it clear that he hadn't really loved her. And that had hurt.

It still did, a little. Rejection was never easy to take.

Now, though, it was her turn to do the rejecting. She was rejecting him, his company, and possibly even her old life in the UK.

But was this desire to make a new life for herself on the island partly fuelled by her budding relationship with Sebastián? It was a question she had to ask herself honestly, because if it was, then she'd be relocating to Tenerife for all the wrong reasons. Especially since she wasn't entirely certain there *was* a relationship, budding or otherwise. She'd fallen into the trap of changing her life for Daniel, so much so that it had affected her writing – would she be doing the same thing again with Sebastián? If she did make this move, it would have to be for *her*, not for anyone else.

Ivy asked for her bill, waved goodbye to the old men and made her way back home. When she let herself into the villa, and smelt the familiar scent of the disinfectant that was used on the floor, Ivy knew Sebastián had done some cleaning while she was out. She must remember to ask him about Alba, she thought as she sniffed the air, trying to catch a whiff of the man himself, then laughed at how silly she was being.

Her laughter faded when she spotted what was next to the kettle. Her note had disappeared and had been replaced by a painting.

It was the one she'd admired yesterday in Garachico. The one with the expensive price tag.

In front of it, on the gleaming countertop, was a message written in petals. They were the same shade of pink as the bougainvillea that draped itself over the walls in the garden. It said two words, and they made her heart melt.

Miss you.

Chapter 18

The edits hadn't taken as long as Ivy had thought they might, and by the following morning the amendments were done. She spent the hour before Sebastián arrived reading them through and double-checking that the chapters made sense and that events ran in the correct manner.

They did, and satisfied that the story itself was ready to go, she decided to attempt the first paragraph or two of the next book before she took a break. She knew what she was going to write and she wanted to get the words out before she forgot them.

Ivy was so engrossed in getting the first couple of sentences exactly right that she didn't hear Sebastián's van pull up. When the doorbell rang, jerking her out of the story and back into reality, she went to answer it with a frown. The door was hardly ever locked, and Sebastián usually knocked and came straight in. Apart from him and Alba (who she barely remembered) no one else had come to the house, and she was a little disconcerted to see a slim wiry man, somewhere in his fifties, wearing a pair of jeans and a checked shirt with the sleeves rolled up, standing there holding a rake.

'Señora Winter?' he asked.

'Yes, that's me.' She spied a van at the end of the drive, with the Dream Villa logo on the side. It was the same van Sebastián drove; she was certain of it.

'I am Izan. Señor de León, he ask me to…' He held up the rake and shook it.

'I see,' she said. Her disappointment was so sharp it made her stomach twist.

'He say to give you this.' Izan held a note out to her.

Ivy took it hesitantly, scared of what it might say. Was Sebastián upset with her? Maybe he was disappointed that she hadn't yet phoned him to thank him for the painting.

To be honest, she hadn't known what to say. She still didn't. It was a wonderfully thoughtful gift, but it was too expensive and, besides, she wasn't sure if it was appropriate for an employee of the rental company to give a client a gift like this. Then there was the added problem of the pair of them hardly knowing each other (but you knew him well enough to kiss him her conscience said…), and for him to buy her a painting was a bit weird. Nice weird, but weird all the same. Flowers would have been far more acceptable. She was hoping to have talked to him about it this morning, but it looked like he wasn't going to show.

Ivy waited for Izan to get what else he needed from the van, and offered him a drink, which he refused, holding up a bottle of water to show he already had one, before she plucked up the courage to open the note.

I will come for you at 7 p.m. she read. *I want to show you a lighthouse. Sebastián.*

Did he now? And what if she didn't want to see a lighthouse, or she had other plans?

Who was she kidding – as if she'd have other plans! It was rather presumptuous of him though, and she wasn't sure she liked him taking charge again.

She refolded the note and was about to put it in her pocket when she saw what he'd written on the back.

Please?

That one little word made all the difference, especially when, as Izan was about to leave he knocked on the door again and said, 'Señor de León he say, please come. He tell me to ask you.'

She had trouble keeping herself from laughing. 'Tell Sebastián, I mean Señor de León, that I'd be delighted to go and see a lighthouse with him.'

'*Perdón?*'

'Tell him "yes",' she translated.

'OK. I tell him.' He went to walk away, then paused and looked back at her. 'He will be...' He smiled widely and pointed to his mouth.

Ivy shook her head, bemused. Sebastián was like no other man she'd met before – an intriguing mix of supreme confidence and insecurity – and she knew she was falling for him despite her best intentions. He was making it far too difficult not to. How could any woman resist such a lovely personality combined with such good looks? And he didn't even seem to be aware of how damned attractive he was, either. She remembered the glances people at the sea pools had thrown in his direction, but he had appeared oblivious, and she found that endearing.

Ivy settled down to get some more writing done, and it was several hours later before she surfaced. Seeing it was close to four o'clock, she made herself an extremely late lunch then spent two more lazy hours reading by the pool, interspersed with the occasional dip.

Then she started to get ready for her... *date*, she supposed she should call it... with Sebastián. It took her a while to get dressed because what does one wear when visiting a lighthouse? And would dinner be involved at some point, because seven o'clock wasn't that far off dinner time? Ooh, wait, maybe dinner would be *in* the lighthouse? Maybe it had been converted into a restaurant? Oh dear, she wished Sebastián had given her some hint.

In the end, she settled on a pair of lightweight trousers, a flowing silky top in the most delicious shade of blue, and some pumps to go on her feet. Casual, but not overly so. Besides, she guessed the motorbike might be involved and a floaty dress wasn't the most practical thing to wear if that was the case.

It was – she soon heard the deep throaty roar of the machine and her stomach did a somersault. Sebastián was here and she was quite dizzy with excitement.

She donned the leathers he had loaned her and stepped out of the door to find him already waiting for her, holding out the helmet. As she took it, their eyes met and she wished he wasn't wearing his, because all she wanted to do was kiss him until he begged for mercy. She bit her lip and his mouth quirked into a smile that had her knees trembling, so to cover her reaction she jammed her helmet on her head and swung herself onto the saddle.

God, he felt good, she thought, as she wound her arms around him, breathing in the scent of leather, gasoline and aftershave. It was a heady mix and it made her head whirl.

It whirled even more when, after thirty or so minutes of twisty steep roads, the road levelled off a little as they reached the coast and, after going through one of the scariest tunnels (there was a danger sign at the entrance, for goodness' sake!), she was beginning to think this lighthouse wasn't a restaurant after all.

She was right.

The beacon was situated at the end of a long straight stretch of road, perched on a headland of black rock.

But what stole her breath was a series of magnificent cliffs, rising vertically out of the sea to the left of the headland, the evening sun tinting them sepia where it struck them, casting deep shadows in the crevasses between.

There wasn't another soul in sight and the sun was dipping towards the horizon, its rays painting the sky orange, purple and pink.

Sebastian brought the bike to a halt at the end of the road and cut the engine.

'Wow.' She slowly dismounted and took her helmet off, her attention on those cliffs.

'They are called Los Gigantes,' Sebastián told her. 'Six hundred metres high. Beautiful, yes?'

'Yes.' The breath hissed out of her slowly, as she slipped off her jacket and wriggled out of her trousers.

He hung the leathers and helmets on the bike's handlebars and fished around in the top box, bringing out a cooler bag, and holding it up.

Ivy cocked her head.

'Dinner,' he explained.

Oh my, she'd been right, kind of. They were going to have dinner at the lighthouse after all; not in it though, but sitting on a wooden seat just below it, staring out to sea and watching the sun go down.

Sebastián laid out an assortment of tortilla, bread, cheese, olives, Serrano ham and fruit, and handed her a bottle of sparkling apple juice before they tucked in, both of them mesmerised by the setting sun and how the colours changed as the sea grew darker and more mysterious. One by one, in the distance, lights began to twinkle as the towns along the coast beyond those impressive cliffs prepared for the coming night. A few pinpricks of light shone on the water and she guessed they came from boats.

Overhead, the stars appeared, faint at first, growing bolder as the sunlight retreated from the sky. Every so often they were bathed in a beam of light from the lighthouse before darkness descended once again.

Ivy waited until the food had more or less been eaten, before she broached the subject of the painting.

'It was very kind of you,' she said, 'but I can't possibly accept it. It's far too expensive, for one thing.'

'And for another?' Sebastián asked, and she couldn't answer him, at a loss how to put into words what she meant. Flowers were one thing, but a painting was something else.

'It did not cost me much,' he said after a while. 'I know the artist.'

She sent him a sideways look, wanting to believe him, but not sure whether she did. Besides, knowing the artist wasn't the point. The gift felt far more intimate and personal than flowers or chocolates, and there was a significance to it that weighed on her.

'He is a local man,' he continued, 'and he owed me a favour.'

'Are you sure?' She still wasn't, but it seemed churlish to keep on protesting.

He nodded. 'I am. Please take it. It is a gift. No strings, I swear. It makes me happy to think you will have a reminder of your stay here when you return to England.'

As if she needed one! She could recall every inch of the villa and every moment she'd spent with Sebastián and she suspected these images in her head wouldn't fade with time – they were too precious for that. She'd enjoy looking at the photos she'd taken of him, though... if he ever got around to sending them to her!

'I... er... don't think I am going to go back,' she told him. 'I haven't properly decided yet, but as I said to you before, I have fallen in love with the place, and I'm pretty sure I don't want to leave.'

'Is it Tenerife that you love, or the villa?'

'Both,' she replied honestly, not feeling quite ready yet to be completely truthful with him and to tell him that he might be part of the reason, too. It wouldn't be fair to burden him with that, especially since they'd only had the one kiss and she didn't know how he felt about her. 'I do understand that I'm not going to be able to afford something as exquisite as Villa Colina,' she continued. 'But I've had a look on the internet, and there are some nice properties within my budget.'

'It is a big decision.'

'Yes, it is, and not one I'm going to make lightly. I haven't made my mind up whether I'd rent out my house in London and have a long-term rental here, or whether to sell up and buy something here instead.'

'I see.'

Did he? Was he thinking that by not selling up in London, she was giving herself a way out? That she

187

wouldn't be fully committed to the move? He was quite possibly right, and that was exactly what she was doing.

'You have only been here a little more than a month,' he said. 'Is it too soon to say if you want to live here?'

'Probably,' she conceded.

More silence. Then, he said, 'I would like it if you stayed.'

She drew in a steadying breath and let it out softly. Oh my... But her decision couldn't be based on a man and a hint of a relationship, because what if it didn't work out?

Sebastián leant towards her and his eyes glittered in the darkness, his face coming closer until his lips found hers. Soft and gentle this time, the kiss fluttered between them on butterfly wings, teasing, tantalising, uncertain. The passion was there under the surface, simmering, but this kiss was all about romance, rather than desire.

This was exactly the sort of kiss she'd written about when two of her characters had fallen in love and had only just realised it. It was as if Sebastián had pulled the words from her mind and from the page, and brought them to magnificent, wonderful life.

He gently pulled away and cupped her face in his hand, his fingers stroking her cheek. 'What are you doing to me, Ivy Winter?' he murmured. 'I cannot get enough of you. I cannot stop thinking about you.'

And he kissed her again, underneath the stars, with the sound of the waves in her ears and the smell of the ocean surrounding her.

And she fell in love with him a little bit more.

Chapter 19

Ivy almost wished she'd asked Sebastián to stay when she woke up the following morning to an empty bed and a silent villa. But her heart was full and her mind was inundated with images of him and that would have to do – for now. She wanted to make sure they had a future before she took things to the next level, and to be fair to Sebastián, he hadn't made any other move on her, except to kiss her. And what those kisses had done to her was blissful enough.

She touched a finger to her lips, remembering his mouth on hers, and her arms ached to hold him again. How she was going to stop herself from diving on him the second he pulled up in his van, she had no idea. Her sleep had been restless, yet she'd never felt so alive and invigorated as she did this morning. It was as though she'd viewed the world through a veil until now, and he'd pulled it away and shown her how vibrant life could be.

Daniel? Daniel who? What she'd had with her ex hadn't been love – she could see that now.

Ivy concentrated on working out the story line for the next novel in the series until Sebastián arrived, then she saved the document and fired up the coffee machine. She popped a couple of slices of bacon under the grill and started to heat some oil. Bacon and egg on toast. Yum.

She was starving, and so, she discovered, was Sebastián, as the aroma of bacon cooking drew him into the kitchen from outside where he'd been checking the pool.

But as he enveloped her in an embrace, she guessed it wasn't breakfast he was hungry for.

'Wait, wait,' she giggled, wriggling free and turning the grill and the hob off. 'I don't want to cremate the bacon, so I'll have to cook it later when you stop harassing me.'

He pulled her back to him and trailed kisses down the side of her neck. 'Like this, you mean?'

'Mmm, yes, just like that.' She shuddered in delight as he nibbled on her earlobe, the sensation raising goose-bumps along her arms and sending her pulse soaring.

It was another twenty minutes before she switched the grill back on, and even then Sebastián kept wrapping his arms around her and planting kisses on her hair, her shoulders, her cheek, as she tried to cook at the same time. Ivy didn't mind. In fact, she relished the closeness and the intimacy of it. They were like a proper loved-up couple.

She twisted around to face him, not caring if the eggs were overdone. 'Sebastián, what are we doing?'

'Um, kissing, then having breakfast?'

'No, I mean, what are *we* doing? *Us*. Is there an "us"?'

He stopped muzzling her neck and looked at her. 'I hope so, because I don't kiss just anyone.'

'What I'm trying to say is, are we in a relationship?'

'Yes.' He was emphatic, then his expression became wary. 'Do you not want to be in a relationship with me? Is that what you are saying?'

Oh God, why were these things so complicated? 'I'm not saying that at all. I just want to know where I stand. Where *we* stand.'

'Boyfriend and girlfriend?'

'At our age?'

'Why not?' He shrugged.

Why not indeed? She liked the sound of it. My boyfriend, Sebastián, she practiced saying silently. It had a nice ring to it.

'OK, then——' she agreed.

'Um, Ivy, the eggs are burning.'

'Damn!'

He stepped back and let her carry on with making a pig's ear of their breakfast. When they were done eating (Ivy had to smother hers with tomato ketchup to make it edible, much to Sebastián's disgust), Ivy returned to her laptop and Sebastián continued to do what he needed to outside.

'Will I see you later?' he asked as he stowed his tools in the back of the van.

'If you like.' She knew she was wearing a coy smile, but she wasn't able to help it.

'Oh, I like...'

'Come over when you've finished work,' she suggested, although she only had a vague idea of the hours he worked. 'I'll cook us something.'

He gathered her to him and kissed her on the nose. 'Something? Such as?'

'No idea, but there is enough food in the fridge to make a meal out of the contents.'

'I shall look forward to it.'

'Liar!' She thumped him gently on the arm. 'I do cook sometimes, you know.'

'I am sure you do,' he laughed, retreating when she raised her eyebrows at him. 'How about I cook and you kiss me? The other way around didn't work too well this morning.'

'That's because you distracted me,' she objected. Her eyes twinkled. 'Won't you be distracted when I kiss you as you're chopping onions?'

'No.'

'We'll see...'

'Is that a threat?'

'It's a promise.'

'I am looking forward to it.'

So was she, very much. She couldn't believe how flirty and teasing she'd become. It was so unlike her, but she was starting to enjoy the new Ivy. She was much more light-hearted than the former version of herself.

That afternoon, Ivy walked to the village cafe and sat in her favourite chair at her favourite table and gave the old fellas a wave. Sebastián had sent her the photos, so before she checked her emails, she updated her Facebook page with the great snap of him that she had taken at the sea-pool restaurant along with the caption, 'wonderful day out with this lovely man' and posted it along with a few other photos as well. She wouldn't name him, because that wouldn't be fair to him, but she nevertheless had a childish urge to show all those acquaintances of hers that she was doing OK for herself, thank you very much. And Daniel, too, if he ever checked out her page, which he probably didn't.

Speaking of Daniel...

Yep, just as she thought, there was yet another email from him, this one urging her to see sense (oh, she'd seen that all right), and hinting that he'd make it worth her while if he could read her new manuscript. The cheeky bugger had even informed her that he was prepared to edit it himself, and that he was sure she could benefit from his expertise.

She forwarded it to Nora, with a series of exclamation marks, an eye-roll emoji and a LOL for good measure.

She'd say that for the guy – he was persistent. He didn't seem capable of taking a hint, either, so she sent him a one-word reply. 'No.' Then she sent him and his stupid email to 'Spam', before she adjusted her settings so that all future emails from his address would go straight into that folder. There, that'd show him.

Moving on to more important things, Ivy was surprised to see an email from the estate agent with a valuation on her house in London. That was quick – a little too quick if she was honest, because it meant that things were starting to get real. It was no longer quite so hypothetical. She now had an actual monetary figure she could work with, and she was astonished to see it was more than she'd anticipated. She could afford a slightly nicer place than the ones she'd previously researched online.

She might be able to afford Villa Colina! If it was for sale. Which she guessed it probably wasn't, otherwise there would have been a 'for sale' sign outside. But did her fixation with the villa mean that she only wanted to make her home in Tenerife if she could continue to live there? Was she prepared to live in another property?

It took her a while and some considerable soul-searching, but she arrived at the conclusion that she would live somewhere else if she had to, if it meant she didn't have to go back to England.

Of course, the ideal situation would be to buy Villa Colina and live in it with Sebastián. And, as was her wont, Ivy started to think about the other extreme of living somewhere else entirely and not having any kind of relationship with the man she had fallen so hard and fast for. How would she feel about moving to Tenerife if that was the case, she asked herself, and quickly came to the realisation that she would still do it. The pace of life here suited her, as did the climate, the people, the food – everything.

There was nothing for her in London any more, and she began to wonder if there actually ever had been. She certainly didn't miss it, although she might miss her friends in time—

What friends?

It occurred to her that none of them had bothered to keep in touch when it became common knowledge that Daniel had dumped her. Not one of them had emailed, messaged, texted, or phoned since she'd been in Tenerife, and she came to the reluctant conclusion that they'd been more like acquaintances than true friends. So, she had nothing to lose on that score, either.

There was nothing to hold her back. Nothing to make returning to the UK an appealing prospect.

Her life was here now. Her heart was here, too, and she sincerely hoped that Sebastián wouldn't break it.

Chapter 20

Whale watching wasn't quite what Ivy had been expecting when Sebastián had told her a few days later to wear her swimming costume and bring a towel for their next trip. And she hadn't been expecting to see the magnificent Los Gigantes cliffs from the opposite direction either. But Los Gigantes was also the name of the small town nestled at the other end of those rocky towers from the lighthouse, and it had a pretty little harbour and an assortment of restaurants, cafes and bars. It was also rather more touristy than Ivy had become used to.

'This is it,' Sebastián said, after leading her along the harbour front right to the very end of the jetty.

Ivy eyed the moored boat with incredulity. 'What is it?' It looked like a Disney version of a pirate ship, complete with a skull and crossbones flying from the mast.

'It's a boat.'

'I can see that.' She dug him in the ribs and giggled when he let out an 'oomph'. 'Why are we here?'

'We are going to see some dolphins and whales. I hope.'

'Really?' She'd never done anything like that before. In fact, she'd never been on anything larger than a pedalo, and that was when she was a kid.

'You cannot come to Tenerife and not go out on a boat to whale watch,' he insisted.

'I can't? You do know that I'm not actually a tourist as such, don't you?'

He put his hands on her shoulders and turned her to face him. 'I know. But this is fun, and I *like* dolphins. They also serve lunch on board, and it is a good way to see the cliffs from the sea.'

'I think you are a bit obsessed by them. They are amazing, don't get me wrong, but I've seen them from both sides now. Do I really need to see them up close and personal?'

'Yes. And there will be swimming.'

'Whales, lunch and swimming? You've sold it to me.'

She loved the banter between them; it was refreshing and totally unlike the dynamic between her and Daniel. With him it had been all about work — who'd signed who, who had a new book out, whose latest novel had bombed. If not work, then he'd loved a good gossip. It was interesting up to a point, but this felt far more authentic — even if she was about to board a boat decked out as a pirate ship, crewed by men who looked like the extras from *Pirates of the Caribbean*, along with about fifty or so other tourists.

At least this was fun!

Sebastián seated them to the front of the boat, where droplets of spray caught in her hair, and as the vessel chugged out of the harbour and into the open water, Ivy leant against him and scanned the ocean for tell-tale fins, eager for her first glimpse of a whale.

Every so often, she squirmed around to give him a kiss, and every time she did so he'd kiss her back with such tenderness it almost made her cry with happiness.

They'd been on board for about half an hour and were tootling along parallel to the coast when there was a commotion over on the other side of the boat, and Ivy got to her feet for a better view. Sebastián caught hold of the waistband of her shorts to steady her as the boat slowed and began to come about.

It turned out to be a turtle and Ivy let out a squeak of delight when she saw it. 'It's huge,' she cried as the creature floated near the surface for a while, taking little sips of air. 'It's so cute.'

'Cute?' he laughed.

'Yeah, look at his little face.'

They watched for a while until the turtle decided it had had enough attention for one day, and sank below the surface with a lazy swipe of its flippers. Then the boat started up again and continued to search for whales.

'Is that Mount Teide, Tenerife's famous volcano?' she asked, pointing to a huge conical mountain, purpled by distance and wearing what seemed to be a hat made of cloud.

'Yes, it is. One day I will take you. It is like being on the top of the world.'

It might be cheesy, but Ivy felt as though she was on the top of the world right now. Sebastián seemed to know what she might enjoy before she even knew it herself; she never would have thought of a picnic under the stars on Tenerife's most westerly point, and neither would she have considered going whale watching on a boat like this. But she was having a whale of a time (she snorted quietly at her little joke), even if there was a man standing in front of her in a striped vest, wearing a tri-cornered hat, with a plastic parrot on his shoulder. In fact, he just added to the charm of the trip.

'Look starboard!' one of the crew yelled, and Ivy glanced to her right.

'Oh, my, God,' she whispered, as three enormous dark bodies broke the surface of the ocean in a cascade of white spray.

'Pilot whales,' the same guy said, and Ivy knelt on the bench with her eyes wide and her mouth open and watched them with awe.

They'd appeared from nowhere, and she knew that whatever life threw at her in the future she'd never forget the sight of those magnificent beasts. One of them blew out a cloud of mist from its blowhole and the vapour hung in the air like fog. The sun sparkled on their wet skin as they sliced through the water. Ivy felt she could sit there all day and watch them, and she'd never become tired of it.

Quickly, she fished her phone out of her bag, and took some snaps, ignoring the notifications showing on the screen. Ever since she'd left the villa and her phone had obtained a signal, they'd been streaming in and Ivy guessed she'd had some likes and comments on those images that she'd uploaded. They'd have to wait, though – she was entirely focused on photographing the whales, trying to capture the essence of them in an image, an impossible task. Nothing could convey their majesty – they had to be seen in person – no words, no photo, no painting could do them justice.

Eventually, though, the boat, which had been slowly following alongside the whales, peeled away and headed back the way it had come, letting the whales continue their journey in peace.

'That was magnificent,' she said to Sebastián. 'Thank you so much for bringing me.'

'You're welcome, I enjoyed it too.'

But instead of turning into the harbour at Los Gigantes, the boat chugged past and angled in closer to the massive cliffs. Ivy settled back again to admire the view. From the land, it wasn't easy to see the hidden valleys secreted between towering walls of rock, but from the sea, the passengers were in a privileged position to be able to peer into the deep fissures between the cliffs and spot secluded little bays with rocky crescent beaches, accessible only by boat.

Overhead, seabirds whirled, riding the currents of air which swept in from the open ocean. They spiralled upwards on the thermals before diving sharply down to the water's surface, only to repeat the process again and again. If Ivy didn't know the birds were hunting for food, she might have thought they were playing.

A larger gap between the cliffs attracted her attention and she realised the boat was swinging inwards towards it. As the pirate ship slowed, a jetty sticking out from the beach like a finger into the sea came into view. Beyond it, she had a glimpse of a hidden valley disappearing into the mountains.

'Crikey, it looks almost prehistoric,' she said. 'I expect to see a dinosaur peering around a rock, or a pterodactyl flying up to its nest.'

'Parts of *Clash of the Titans* were filmed here,' Sebastián informed her, 'so it is not only you who thinks the same way.'

Ivy continued to study the landscape over an onboard lunch of chicken paella and bread, washed down with an ice-cold can of lemonade. It was a perfect place to have lunch, she thought, even though they were surrounded by other people. The atmosphere was jolly and everyone was having a good time.

The only sour note was the beeping of her phone that continued to inform her she had new notifications. As they were eating, with an apologetic grimace at Sebastián, Ivy quickly scrolled through them. Although she didn't automatically reach for her phone all the time any more, she still found it hard to resist its allure when she was out and about and had signal; which was why she tended to leave it at the villa these days. Today, however, Ivy had brought it with her and now she felt she had to deal with her messages.

The Twitter notifications were mostly retweets or comments on her tweets, which she could thank and acknowledge another time. Her Facebook post featuring Sebastián had more likes than she'd ever had before, and there seemed to be loads of comments, but she didn't go through them. A glance at the top one went something along the lines of 'Go, girl!' and 'Phwoar!', so she ignored the rest. She had no emails of any significance, and no missed calls. What she did have though, was a cryptic text from Daniel.

Did I tell you how much I love you? You're a doll.

Ivy was about to read it again, when a small child ran past the table she and Sebastián were sitting at and jolted her in the arm, knocking the phone out of her hand and sending it skidding underneath Sebastián's feet.

'Sorry,' the little boy shouted in English, not stopping, as Ivy bent to retrieve it, hoping the screen wasn't damaged.

Sebastián beat her to it.

Ivy didn't blame him for glancing at the screen as he picked it up. She would have done the same, if only to check that it was intact.

When she saw Sebastián's expression, she knew he'd read Daniel's text.

He handed the phone back to her without comment, and she hastily blocked Daniel's number and switched the damned thing off.

'Daniel is being a pain in the backside,' she said.

'There's no need to explain. He still loves you.'

Ivy blinked. 'He does not. Daniel only loves himself. He's hoping to get his hands on my new book, that's what he's trying to do, and he thinks that by persuading me to go back to him, I'll sign a new contract with him.' She buried the phone at the bottom of her bag and wished she'd left it at the villa. 'At least his interest tells me that the book is as good as Nora says it is. I'll say that for Daniel, he does have an eye for what will sell and what the readers will love.'

'You admire him.' It wasn't a question; it was a statement.

'Not really. Not as a person. Just as a publisher, and even then, I have my doubts.'

'Do you still love him?'

'No!' Ivy was astounded that he felt the need to ask.

'Do you want him to publish your new book?'

'No. I do not.'

He considered her answer, his gaze level. Then he nodded once and reached for her hand. Ivy inhaled slowly and let it out again in a drawn-out sigh. Damn Daniel. He'd nearly spoilt a perfectly wonderful day with his selfish games. Why couldn't he accept that he'd behaved badly and that she wasn't going to forgive him, no matter how much he tried to sweet talk her. After the meal was over, talk turned to jumping into the cool waters of the bay, but Ivy wasn't feeling quite so enamoured with the idea.

'It looks cold,' she protested, 'and I'm not too keen on the rope thing.'

The 'rope thing' was a length of rope hanging from the rigging, which dangled out over the sea, and as Ivy watched, one by one, people lined up to take hold of it, swung out and then let go with a shout and a splash.

Ivy would have preferred to ease herself into the water gently via the metal steps, but Sebastián had other ideas.

'It'll be fun,' he insisted, his attention on a young lad who'd grabbed the rope and launched himself into the air.

'No, no, you go ahead,' she said, watching him pull his T-shirt over his head.

Oh my, look at that chest. There was a smattering of dark hairs over his pectoral muscles leading down to his shorts and disappearing under the waistband, and he had a six-pack that she wanted to trace her fingers over.

She almost squealed at the sight of it. An honest-to-goodness six-pack. It wasn't overly defined, but it was definitely there.

She tried to see whether he'd noticed her ogling him, but it was difficult to tell under his sunglasses, but he did have a bit of a smirk on his face, so he may well have done.

'Come on,' he urged, holding out a hand to her. 'I will go first, there is nothing to be afraid of.'

No? How about the water temperature, which wasn't half as warm as the Med? Or what about the drop itself? It was only about three metres but still… Then there was the fact that she'd be practically naked, and her body definitely wasn't as tanned and toned as his. She had wobbly bits even though she was slim, and, although she'd lost the pearly whiteness she'd arrived with, her skin was still relatively pale under her shorts and T-shirt, as she'd been ultra-careful not to get burnt again. She admitted that she'd probably overdone it on the sunscreen since Crispy-gate.

But the main issue was that she didn't want to see the disappointment on his face when he saw her more or less unclothed for the first time, in the unforgiving, bright sunlight. It might not be so bad if it was night-time and there were lit candles, but this was two in the afternoon, and every bump, lump and blemish would be illuminated for all to see.

'Please? For me?' His hand was still stretched out to her, and with a roll of her eyes and a dramatic sigh, she took it, reckoning that he'd have to see her body at some point if their relationship moved on. She might as well get it out over with, and at least he'd know what he was letting himself in for if things ever got that far between them.

As she stood up, she slipped her feet out of her sandals and wriggled her shorts down over her hips. Sebastián was concentrating on removing his own shorts and wasn't paying her any attention, so she gathered her courage and yanked her strappy top over her head, wishing she'd thought to pack an all-in-one swimsuit and not the bikini she was currently wearing.

Finally, she was standing there in a swimming costume which she wished covered more than it did, her eyes glued on the body of the man in front of her.

His swim shorts were smaller than his other shorts had been, exposing more of his muscled legs to her eager gaze. She couldn't help but stare at those abs and the faint creases from his hip bones which dipped under his swimwear – she could so clearly imagine where they ended up and the thought made her blush.

Sebastián was ripped. Not too much, but just enough. He was perfect and she couldn't stop staring at him.

'Ready?' he asked, and she reluctantly dragged her eyes away from his body, to see that he'd removed his sunglasses and was looking at her.

Ivy met his gaze and saw a seriousness in his eyes that hadn't been there before. Sebastián deliberately, and oh so slowly, scanned her from her mouth to her toes and back again. She shivered and his attention returned to her face. When she saw his expression, she felt weak with longing. There was hunger there, and admiration, and when he said, 'You are so beautiful,' she thought she might faint.

'Come,' he said, catching hold of her hand again. 'I won't let anything happen to you. You are safe with me.'

Yes, she believed she was, and she watched as he grabbed hold of the rope, swung out above the rippling ocean, let go and plunged into the depths.

That's what she needed to do – let go and take the plunge. And she wasn't just talking about taking a dip in the cobalt waters of the Atlantic.

She paused for a moment to make sure Sebastián resurfaced, then stepped onto the wooden rail as one of the crew steadied her and handed her the rope. She took it, conscious of everyone's eyes on her – and of one person's in particular. But it was Sebastián who she looked at as she clutched the rope, leapt into the void, and let go.

Hell, that was cold!

The water closed over her head and she sank for a second before flailing for the surface, her head breaking through. She took a gulp of air, wiped the salt water from her eyes and searched for Sebastián.

He was only a couple of metres away, treading water with the ease of a confident swimmer, and he moved closer until they were almost touching.

'That was fun,' she admitted. 'I'm not sure if I want to do it again, though.' The initial shock of the temperature difference had worn off, and she was becoming more used to the cool water, but she wasn't sure she wanted to repeat the experience.

'You don't have to,' Sebastián said, grinning. 'I just wanted to see you in your swimming costume.'

'You—!' she spluttered, splashing water at him with her feet, sending a spray of white water at his head, but he was gone.

Ivy turned in a circle.

Where was he…? She knew he was about to grab her ankle and pull her under—

'Eek!' His hand grasped her foot and submerged her. She just had time to grab a quick breath, then she was face to face with him, the water as clear as crystal, the salt stinging her eyes.

She felt his hand on her waist, then her head was above water again, and he had penned her in the cage of his arms. When his lips found hers, she thought she'd drown in the bliss of his kiss.

'We had better get back to the boat,' he said after several minutes.

'Do we have to?'

He chuckled and she felt the rumble in his chest. 'Yes, we are being called in.'

She saw they had drifted some distance away from the vessel and reluctantly she swam back to it with Sebastián, only realising how chilled she was when she hoisted herself up the steps and the sea breeze played over her skin.

Sebastián placed her towel around her shoulders and gave her arms a brisk rub. Ivy was so busy focusing on the concentration on his face that at first she didn't notice the excitement at the bow of the boat. Someone, a man, had got down on one knee and was holding a small black box aloft. A crowd of onlookers were gathered around a young woman with long dark hair who was wearing a shocked expression.

Ivy was just in time to hear the man say, 'Will you marry me?' and to hear the squealed 'Yes!' as the woman launched herself at her new fiancé.

'Aw, that's so sweet,' Ivy said, nudging Sebastián, who she didn't think had noticed the event.

Ivy quickly got dressed, her attention still on the happy couple, and she was envious of the look of love on the guy's face. She could tell he adored his girlfriend and a spike of longing shot through her, no one had ever looked at her in such a way and it made her feel incredibly sad.

She turned away, not wanting her sudden melancholy to sour the day, but as she did so, she noticed Sebastián's face.

He was staring at her in the same way the guy at the prow of the boat was staring at the girl he loved. Ivy raised her chin, locking her gaze on his, and thought she must be imagining things, yet knowing she wasn't. She felt it deep down. He was falling in love with her, just as she was falling in love with him.

And, despite how wonderful today was, she felt certain tonight was going to be even better.

Chapter 21

Sebastián was everything she'd hoped and imagined he'd be — and more, if that was possible. Never had Ivy felt so in tune with another human being. And never had she felt so exhausted. She'd thought the words 'making love all night' were just that, words. She'd discovered it wasn't.

She was weary to her very bones, but it was a languid, satiated tiredness that made her feel fulfilled and extraordinarily happy. Which was why she was singing softly to herself as she prepared a (very) late breakfast of fruit and yoghurt accompanied by fresh bread and honey. Sebastián was in the shower and she imagined the water cascading over his chest, and running down his stomach to his—

'Need any help in there?' she called, popping her head around the bathroom door.

He gave her a plaintive look and slumped against the tiles. 'You are killing me with love,' he said. 'I cannot keep up with you. Could you pass me a towel?'

Slightly disappointed — he looked so incredibly sexy with his wet hair and wet body — she picked up a towel from the rail and went to hand it to him.

With a low growl, he grabbed hold of her and pulled her into the shower with him.

Ivy let out a shriek. 'I was planning on taking my clothes off first,' she said, trying half-heartedly to bat his hands away.

'Let me take them off for you,' he suggested, and for a while all thoughts of breakfast were driven from her mind very thoroughly indeed.

Eventually though, they had to emerge, and they patted each other dry with huge fluffy towels, got dressed, and padded barefoot into the kitchen for some much-needed sustenance.

'It's late,' Ivy commented in between mouthfuls as they ate what should technically be called lunch, Sebastián feeding her pieces of mango drizzled in honey with a rapt expression on his face.

'I know.'

'Won't you get into trouble?'

'No.'

'But what about the other villas?'

'They can wait.'

'My writing can't.' She had a scene in her head she couldn't wait to write.

'Are you telling me to go?' He pouted and gave her puppy-dog eyes.

Ivy threw a grape at him. 'Yes. No. I don't know. I want you to stay, but you'll distract me.'

'Yes, I most certainly will.' He sent her a cheeky grin and raised his eyebrows.

Ivy shook her head, trying to pretend she was exasperated with him, when in fact she was thrilled that he couldn't keep his hands off her.

'You are right, I do have work to do, so I must go.' He picked up his coffee cup and drained it.

'Will I see you later?' she asked, wincing internally at the neediness in her voice.

'Of course. Can I take you to dinner?'

She'd like that, but she was conscious that he'd paid for the whale-watching trip yesterday (was it only yesterday, because it seemed like a lifetime ago) and she didn't want to suggest she should pay for dinner in case it hurt his feelings. He didn't appear to be short of cash – not that she could tell – but cleaning pools and sweeping up leaves in gardens couldn't pay that much.

'How about if I make us something, then if we get *distracted*...?' she suggested.

The sudden hunger in his eyes made her go weak at the knees. 'Good idea, except I shall cook.'

'Are we going to have an argument over who's going to cook dinner?' she teased.

'Only if we make up in the bedroom,' Sebastián responded.

'Does it have to be the bedroom?'

He groaned. 'I had better leave, before you make it impossible for me to go.'

He got to his feet and Ivy ran her gaze over his body, no longer having to imagine what lay beneath his clothes. She knew exactly what was under his shorts and T-shirt and it took every ounce of willpower she had to let him walk out of the door.

Right, she thought, when she heard the motorbike's engine fade, time to get more of this next book written. And she knew precisely what scenes were coming next – all she had to do was think back to last night and let the words flow.

And flow they did. Page after page flew from her fingertips over the following hours and days.

She and Sebastián fell into a routine of him spending the night (oh, those delicious nights – and the days had their moments, too), then he would leave early to go to work and to allow Ivy to write. He'd return in the late afternoon and do whatever was needed around the villa (not that there was a great deal to be done), and then they would spend the rest of the day and all of the night together.

'I want to take you into the mountains,' he said to her one afternoon about a week later.

'I thought we *were* in the mountains?'

'This is only a hill, not a mountain. Villa Colina – *colina* means "hill" – is just six hundred metres above sea level. The highest point of the island is Mount Teide and that's over three thousand seven hundred metres.'

Ivy blinked. 'Really?' She'd guessed the mountain was a bit of a tump, but over twelve thousand feet was seriously high. 'You're not suggesting we go to the top, are you?' She liked a walk as much as the next person, but seriously?

'We can go almost to the top.'

She nodded towards the biscuits she was eating. 'I'll need more than a couple of digestives for a hike like that.'

Sebastián chuckled and brushed a stray crumb off her chin. 'We will drive up.'

'Thank goodness for that. When?'

'This evening.'

'Won't it be dark?'

'That is the point.'

He refused to give her any further details, but he did suggest that she wore a fleece under her leather jacket. 'It can be cool up there, especially at night,' he informed her. 'We will leave when it is still light so you can see the view. It is impressive.'

'Better than this?' She waived the half-eaten biscuit at Garachico and the vast ocean beyond.

He merely smiled and she was left to wonder how it could possibly get any better.

She found out just how much better the view could get later on that afternoon. They'd followed the coast road for several miles before turning the motorbike inland and beginning to climb. And climb, and climb. The road wasn't particularly steep, but the incline was relentless. It just kept going up, and every so often when they rounded a bend Ivy had a glimpse of the scenery below and she realised that they were now probably at least a thousand metres above sea level, if not more. Eventually they left the little towns and villages behind, and were riding through forests of tall trees – a species of pine, she assumed, from the number of pinecones strewn across the road.

Finally, after a few more miles, the trees thinned out and Ivy could see more of the views that Sebastián had mentioned. They were definitely spectacular, and one in particular kept drawing her attention.

'I take it that's Mount Teide?' she shouted in his ear and he nodded. It still looked incredibly far away. The conical peak was clearly visible, silhouetted by the setting sun, and the first thing that popped into Ivy's head was that it reminded her of J. R. R. Tolkien's Mount Doom. At least it didn't appear to be spewing lava.

Finally there was only a smattering of trees left and Ivy spotted a building on their right with umbrellas outside and a sign saying, 'Restaurant El Portillo'.

'Is this it?' she asked when she got off the bike.

'No, but I thought you might like something to eat first. Besides, we must wait for it to get dark.' He slung an arm around her shoulders and guided her towards the entrance.

'Are you going to tell me what all this is about?' she asked, when they were inside and had been shown to a table with a view of the mountain.

'We are going to the Observatorio del Teide,' he announced.

'The what now?'

'It is an observatory and one of the best places on earth to see the stars. We are not allowed inside, but visits are permitted to the site and small portable telescopes are provided so you can have a closer look.'

Ivy was speechless. Stargazing on the top of an island in the Atlantic Ocean with the man she was certain she was in love with, sounded impossibly romantic. She reached out to grasp his hand in hers, and he smiled lovingly at her. She smiled back and they might have stayed that way for some time if it hadn't been for a waiter interrupting them to ask if they were ready to order.

'From the observatory it is possible to see eighty-three constellations,' Sebastián told her a while later, around a mouthful of roasted cheese with mojo sauce.

Ivy tucked into melon with Serrano ham, surprised at how hungry she was. And she was already looking forward to the next course of skewered pork accompanied by a jacket potato.

As the sky gradually darkened, she felt her excitement build. There was too much light pollution around the restaurant to see many stars, but she knew they must be showing their faces overhead, and she couldn't wait to see them.

'When I was little, I wanted to be an astronaut,' she announced over dessert and coffee. 'Actually, I wanted to be Princess Leia, but that's beside the point. To think of all those millions of suns, and all those billions of planets makes me feel incredibly small and insignificant.'

'You are not insignificant to me,' Sebastián replied gallantly, and she playfully flicked him with her napkin. 'I mean it,' he added. 'You are most definitely not insignificant. In fact, I—'

'*La cuenta*, Señor de León.' Their waiter placed a folder on the table, lingered for a second, then backed away.

'What were you about to say?' she asked, reaching for the folder containing the bill at the same time as he did.

'*De nada*, it does not matter. Let me get this.'

'You got the last one.'

'I did? Are you keeping score?'

'Not really. Look, there's something I want to tell you.'

He raised an eyebrow. 'Go on.'

'I've made up my mind that I'm definitely selling my house in London and I'm going to buy a place on Tenerife.'

He didn't say anything for a few moments and Ivy had the awful thought that his take on their relationship was based on the fact that she'd be returning to England in a little over four months, which would then bring what they had to a natural end. Maybe he wasn't in this for the long haul and it was merely a fling.

The sharp sting of tears behind her eyes made her blink and she lowered her head, pretending to fiddle with her cup so he couldn't see.

'Is this because of us?' he asked, eventually.

'Of course not.' It wasn't a total lie.

'OK, then I am pleased for you.'

'Good.' She swallowed, determined to hold back the tears.

'Ivy, what is wrong?'

'Nothing.'

He leaned across the table and placed a finger under her chin, lifting her head up. 'Liar.'

'Honestly, there isn't—'

'You are not being honest,' he interrupted. 'Tell me.'

'You don't sound too pleased that I'm going to be living on Tenerife permanently,' she blurted.

'I am pleased, but I am also selfish, and I wish the only reason for this is because of me. Because of *us*.'

'You do?'

'Yes.'

'Oh. I didn't want you to feel... I don't know... pressured? Cornered?'

His smile was soft. 'I do not feel pressured or cornered, what I feel is—'

'*Señor?*' The waiter appeared at their table and Sebastián slid his credit card inside the folder.

The moment was lost and Ivy wondered what he'd been about to say.

It was fully dark when they emerged from the restaurant and made the short journey on the bike up to the observatory. She was dying to look up, but the bike helmet was too restrictive, so she waited until they parked up before she tilted her head to the heavens.

'Oh God,' she murmured. She'd never seen so many stars. And they were so *bright*. She felt she could reach up

215

and touch their icy beauty, if she just stood on tiptoe and stretched a little.

'Paulo will be out to meet us in a minute,' Sebastián said. 'He will bring a telescope and he is very knowledgeable.'

'Is this something anyone can do?' she asked, once again wondering how much this was costing him.

'Not quite. There is a tour you can book, where you are shown around parts of the observatory in the afternoon, and there are activities I believe. After that, you are taken to the cable-car base where you can look through telescopes. However, I asked a friend if he would show you the stars for me.'

She felt a little better about it, knowing that it hadn't cost Sebastián anything to bring her up here (apart from their dinner, but she'd get him back for that later), and she settled down to enjoy the incredible experience.

Sebastián's friend certainly knew his stuff, and he was really patient, aiming the telescope for her and showing her things she'd only ever seen before on TV.

'What you are seeing is Ursa Major,' Paulo pointed out as she peered through the telescope. 'Also known as the Great Bear, its brightest stars form the Big Dipper, which is one of the most recognisable shapes in the sky. The Big Dipper is also known as the Plough. And over there is Ursa Minor, with Draco, the dragon snaking through the night sky around it.'

Ivy couldn't believe that she could see Venus so clearly and that the Milky Way was also visible. The whole experience left her awed, and when Sebastián and his friend clapped shoulders and said their goodbyes, Ivy was speechless, although she did manage a quiet 'thank you,' before Paulo hoisted the telescope on his shoulder and trudged inside the nearest building.

'That was amazing,' she said softly as they made their way back to the bike. 'I've never seen anything so humbling and so majestic in all my life. Thank you so much for bringing me up here.'

'It is my pleasure. I like to make you happy.'

They came to a stop by the motorbike, and his arms slid around her, pulling her close.

'You make me *very* happy,' she told him, dragging her attention away from the heavens and back to Sebastián. 'You make me happier than I've ever been.'

'I love you, Ivy Winter,' he said.

With her eyes as full of stars as the night sky above them, Ivy replied, 'I love you, too,' and when they kissed she knew without a doubt that she had found the man she wanted to spend the rest of her life with.

Chapter 22

Ivy loved cuddling up with Sebastián on the sofa, so close that she wasn't sure where he ended and she began. This was what couples should do on a regular basis, not be out every night socialising and networking. Whenever she used to suggest that she and Daniel had a cosy night in, he'd wrinkle his nose up and present her with a million-and-one excuses why it would be better if they went out.

The only thing that would make this cuddle-fest even better would be if they were watching a good film. Ivy didn't miss having a TV in the villa as a rule, but sometimes she had a craving for a rom-com or a tear-jerker.

'Why do you think there isn't a TV?' she asked one evening a couple of weeks after their visit to Teide as she nestled into his shirt and breathed in his scent.

For a moment Sebastián looked startled, then he shrugged. 'I have no idea. Do you want a TV? You've never mentioned it.'

'It would come in handy. I would have liked to have had one for the first few weeks I was here. It got a bit lonely in the evenings.'

'Are you lonely now?' He nuzzled the top of her head.

'I haven't been lonely for weeks. Not since...' She blushed, remembering the first time they had made love. 'I wouldn't mind watching a film, though. Something like

A Lavender Summer. I was thinking of maybe a romantic comedy, but I've got to a part in my new book where I need to kill someone off, and a sad, weepy film might help me get in the mood to write a death scene and all the emotion that goes with it. Hang on, the book might be on one of the shelves in the hall. I hadn't noticed, but then I haven't been looking. I'll just go and see—'

'It's not there,' Sebastián broke in.

There was something in the tone of his voice that gave her pause.

'Are you sure?'

He shrugged.

'Is it a favourite of yours? I remember you did that fab quote from it.'

'Not really.'

'I must remember to add the film to my must-watch list.'

'You have such a list?'

'I do. I have a TBR pile, too. Books to be read,' she explained when she saw his confused expression. 'Don't you have one of those?'

'No.'

'How do you keep track of what you want to read?'

'I don't. I just pick up a book and begin to read.' He lifted up the paperback he was currently holding. *Madame Bovary*, an unusual choice for a guy like Sebastián, she thought. Nevertheless, she loved that he was so well read. Even though she loved to read, she didn't feel she could claim to be well read – she'd hardly scraped the top of the classics, tending to stick with her genre and the occasional thriller.

Ivy wasn't in the mood for reading as she'd been writing for most of the day, so she reached for her phone and began scrolling through the images she'd saved of local properties that were within her price range. Every time she visited the cafe in the village now, she would take a quick peek online at what the local estate agents had to offer and then download the images of those houses she liked the look of.

'Will you do me a favour?' she asked before Sebastián returned to his book. She had decided to wait until her London house was on the market before she made any arrangements to view properties in Tenerife, but now that she'd received an offer from the second person who had viewed it, she felt it was time to start looking in earnest at places on Tenerife.

'You know I will.'

'I'm not sure how to go about buying a house or an apartment over here, but I'm assuming I'll need a solicitor. I honestly don't know anything about the process. And...' She hesitated. 'I hope you'll come with me to view some properties.'

He sat up a little straighter and pulled his arm out from behind her back, wincing as he shook it to get the blood flowing back into it. 'You have not said anything about it for a while – I thought you had changed your mind.'

'Definitely not. I just wanted to get my house in London sorted, so I knew how much I had to play with. What do you think of this?' She showed him a picture on her phone.

'It looks nice. Where is it?'

'Puerto de la Cruz. It's a bit far from here, I think, but it has a terrific outdoor space.'

'Hmm. What site did you find this on?'

'Perfect Properties.'

'They are for foreigners. You will get a better deal if you use an agent who sells mainly to the locals.'

'Do you know of any?'

He nodded. 'Shall I make an appointment for you to speak with them?'

Ivy hesitated. 'I'd like to have a look at what they've got first, before I make an appointment.'

'OK, then tell me what it is you want, and the next time I drive past their office, I will ask them for some brochures.'

'This,' she joked, waving her arm around the living room. 'Ideally, I want this. But I know I'm not going to be able to have it, so I'll have to settle for second best.'

Sebastián looked solemn. 'Would you buy Villa Colina if it was for sale?'

'In a heartbeat,' she shot back at him. 'But from what I've seen, I don't think I can afford anything that costs as much as this.'

'You might be surprised.'

It was Ivy's turn to shuffle on the cushions until she was more upright. 'Why?' she asked suspiciously. 'Do you know how much the owners paid for it?'

He pulled a face. 'I pai— um, I am not sure.' He cleared his throat. 'How much are you prepared to spend? I will need to know this if I am to bring you details of some properties, because the *inmobiliarias* – the estate agent – will ask.'

Ivy wasn't sure she wanted to share that detail him. It was a significant amount of money, especially for someone like Sebastián, who she suspected didn't earn a great deal.

She was lucky in that she'd bought her house more than twenty years ago, when London property prices weren't as stupidly high as they were now, so she'd amassed a significant amount of equity. And with her mortgage paid off several years ago, she could afford something nice. She hoped.

But when she told him her upper limit, Sebastián didn't bat an eyelid. All he said was, 'OK, I will bring something tomorrow for you to see.'

'Sebastián...?' Ivy licked her lips nervously. 'I... er... I've got a suggestion. What would you say if I asked you to move in with me, when I buy a place of my own?'

His brows shot up to his hairline. 'I would say that we need to discuss it. It is a big step, and you need to be certain it is what you really want. We both do.'

'Fair enough.' She felt a little crushed that he wasn't leaping at the chance, but there might be all kinds of reasons why he didn't want to say yes straight away – although the only ones she could think of were of the I-don't-love-you-enough variety. He was right, they did need to discuss it.

She lay in bed that night, Sebastián sleeping deeply beside her, searching the darkness for answers and not finding any. It was reasonable, she concluded, for him not to want to move into a house she'd bought and paid for, and she didn't want him to feel like a kept man, but what other alternative was there?

It came to her suddenly that she had no idea where he lived! Sebastián had never invited her to his home, and she could only assume that he was ashamed of it. On the other hand, the villa was very spacious and comfortable, so maybe it was easier to spend the night with her there, rather than at his place. She really must press him about his living arrangements, because whenever she'd brought up his past he'd brushed her off or changed the subject. He'd done it nicely and in a way that seemed completely natural, but now that she'd come to think about it, he wasn't exactly forthcoming about his life outside of their relationship.

She knew he had an extensive family (she'd met them at the pizzeria), she knew he seemed to like his job, she knew he loved his bike. She knew he hardly drank, if at all (although he hadn't told her the reason why); she knew that his favourite food was steak and fries, that he loved his island with a passion, ditto his family. And her. He loved her: he told her constantly and showed her frequently. Yet she felt there was a part of him that was hidden from her.

He was happy to be seen out and about with her, and he'd accompanied her to the village cafe on occasion, carrying her laptop for her, which made her think he didn't have a wife hidden away somewhere, or anything equally as sinister. But he did prefer to keep himself to himself, and he liked the less crowded places, such as the beach where they'd shared their first kiss.

Yet... yet... there was something, some piece of the puzzle, that was missing. Maybe Ivy should have got to know him a bit better, before she dived in with an offer to share her life and her home with him. She supposed she could ask Sebastián outright if there was anything he was keeping from her (like the reason he didn't drink alcohol, for instance), but what if he said there was nothing? She could hardly force the issue, especially when she didn't know where to start.

The question was, did it matter? Everyone had secrets, some bigger than others. From what she'd seen of him and his family, Sebastián didn't appear to have a ruddy great big skeleton in his closet. A tiny chicken bone maybe. So, once again, she asked herself if it really mattered.

She had to conclude that it didn't. Whether he cleaned pools to make ends meet, or whether he was still living with his parents, or whatever it was that he was ashamed of or didn't want her to know about, she didn't care.

She loved him and he loved her. And that was the only thing that mattered.

Right?

Chapter 23

'No, definitely not. I don't care what he's offering, I don't want Daniel anywhere near it,' Ivy hissed down the phone, disbelief running through her. She glanced across at the group of old men who occupied their usual table in the café, hoping they hadn't picked up on her irritation.

'I don't understand, honey; why did you ask me to send it to him if you didn't want him to offer on it?' Nora's confusion travelled clearly along the line.

Ivy, for her part, was just as confused. 'I didn't ask you to send it to him. I'd never do that! You know how I feel about him.'

'I was surprised, I admit, but business is business,' Nora said.

'Not when it concerns Daniel Morris. How *is* Rebekkah Rain?' Ivy knew she sounded childish but she couldn't help it.

'I know he hurt you, but you are over him now, right? Is this what your change of heart is all about? Please don't tell me you still love him because, hon, he's not good for you. Look at how well you've been writing since—'

'Of course I am over him! I couldn't be more over him if I tried.'

'That's the ticket. So, coming back to Daniel offering you a contract for *An Angel from Hell*—'

'No, most definitely not. I don't care if he's the last publisher on earth, I'm not going to let him publish my book. And we still haven't got to the bottom of why you sent the manuscript to him in the first place.'

'Because you told me to! I've got the email here. Hang on… He sent you one asking to read the manuscript and you forwarded on it to me.'

Ivy was almost incandescent. 'Didn't you see the question marks and the emoji?'

Her agent didn't say anything.

'*Nora!* You know how he treated me, and after I expressly told you I didn't want him to read it. I don't believe it!'

'I thought the question marks meant you were asking if I could send it over to him,' Nora said, her voice subdued. 'I didn't think you were upset or annoyed judging by the eye-roll emoji and the LOL comment. I thought you just meant that Daniel was being Daniel, ha, ha sort of thing…'

'You should have checked with me!'

'Why would I do that when the instruction had come from you in the first place? Ivy, hon, I'm sorry, I really am. I misread your intention, and you're right…' Nora took such a deep breath that Ivy heard it clearly. 'I should have double-checked. But there's no real harm done. If you don't want to go with him, you don't have to, even though he's offering the best deal by far. The other three are all terribly interested, and look at it this way – Daniel must think it's good if he's so keen.'

'I suppose… I'm still annoyed that he's read it, though. And as for taking his interest as a compliment? Hmm. He most likely just wanted to make sure I'd completely lost my mojo.'

'Hardly! He'd have heard on the grapevine that your new manuscript is your best yet. Besides, he wouldn't have offered you a contract if he wasn't serious.'

True, but the thought of Daniel owning the rights to this book and the others in the series made her blood boil. He'd trashed her work (OK, she conceded, he was right to do so, but he needn't have been so mean about it), he'd dumped her, and Nora had told her that he'd been busy telling anyone who'd listen that she was a has-been. And now he wanted to publish the best book she'd ever written?

'Over my dead body,' she said. 'No, no, and thrice no.'

'OK, hon, it's your decision. I was duty bound to inform you of it, but just for the record, I think you're letting your heart rule your head. If you could just view it as a business transaction—'

'No.'

'But—'

'No.'

Nora sighed down the phone. 'I'll send you a comparison of the offers I've got from everyone, Daniel included, and a projection of earnings based on estimated sales so you can make an informed choice. Oh, and can I have a synopsis for each of the other books in the series? They want to see that before any contracts are drawn up.'

Ivy nodded to herself. She'd plotted out each of the seven books, both individually and as a whole, and she was fairly certain the story hung together to reach a satisfying (and hopefully totally unexpected and jaw-dropping) finale.

'I'll go over them again when I get back to the villa, and I'll send them to you tomorrow,' she promised.

'Great. I'll look forward to it.'

Ivy ended the call feeling cross with Nora and rather disconcerted and out of sorts. Her agent was right, there was no real harm done because Daniel couldn't take things any further without her signing a contract with him. She wondered if he'd been trying to get hold of her again, and assumed that he probably had. Feeling glad that she'd blocked his number and resisting the urge to check her Spam folder, Ivy pushed her misgivings to one side. That was undoubtedly the last she'd heard from Daniel, and with Nora telling him Ivy wasn't interested in anything he had to say or offer, then he was bound to get the message and leave her alone. Of course, it helped that she was thousands of miles away and he couldn't pop by her house and throw his weight or his charm around.

Shoving her annoyance to the back of her mind, Ivy tried to think about this evening instead. Sebastián was taking her to his parents' house for dinner – and Ivy hadn't had to drop huge hints about the fact that she wanted to know more about his life outside of their relationship, either. He'd suggested it all by himself, and she had butterflies in her stomach just thinking about it.

She knew she had met them previously at the pizzeria, but that had been when Sebastián was taking pity on one of Dream Villas' guests. Dinner tonight felt more like she was being taken to meet his parents, which was a significant step forward in their relationship. Did it mean their relationship was gearing up a notch? Or was she reading too much into it?

Ivy dressed with care, not wanting to wear anything too revealing, or too casual, or too formal… Oh heck, she didn't have a clue what she should wear.

In the end, she settled on a pleated skirt that flounced around her ankles and a silky blouse. She slung a cardigan over her shoulders and slipped her feet into a pair of ballet shoes with diamantes on the front.

Sebastián was picking her up in the Dream Villas van, so she didn't have to worry about having to stuff her skirt down the legs of the leather trousers or messing up her hair, which she wore loose about her shoulders this evening. A slick of barely-there lipstick, a light dusting of bronzer over her cheekbones and a flick of mascara, and she was out of the door.

'Ready?' Sebastián asked, as he opened the van door for her.

She nodded, and got in.

'Are you OK?'

Trust Sebastián to notice; she still felt a little out of sorts, and was cross that Daniel was still able to affect her. She nodded.

'Sure?'

Ivy bit her lip. 'Remember I told you my agent is in discussion with three publishing houses for *An Angel from Hell*?'

He nodded.

'She sent it to Daniel.'

Sebastián didn't say anything, and waited for her to continue.

'There was a bit of a misunderstanding.' Hardly a bit of one, but what was done was done. 'He's read the book and he wants me to sign a contract with him. I believe Nora thinks it's a good idea, too. His deal is the best on the table.' She paused for a moment. 'It's so good, it makes me think there's a catch.'

'Or he believes in your book. In *you*.'

Ivy glared through the windscreen. The only thing Daniel believed in was himself. She couldn't help being flattered, though. 'Nora says the same.' Not about *her*, but about the book. Daniel was a businessman first and foremost.

'Do you want to go back to him?' Sebastián's jaw was clenched.

'No. He trashed the last work I let him read.'

'Maybe he was right to do so? You said yourself that it wasn't very good.'

Just whose side was Sebastián on? He had a point though, she conceded – it had been dire and Daniel's assessment of it had been correct. He hadn't needed to have been so mean about it, though. And neither should he have dumped her for a better prospect soon afterwards.

'If it is best for you, for your career, then perhaps you should consider it. You do not want to cut your ear off to spite your head.'

Ivy giggled. Sebastián could be so cute. He could also be so right. But she'd lost all faith in her former publisher, even if she managed to move past how he had treated her in their private life. She had to look forward, not back. New book, new series, new publishing contract.

New home? New life? New love?

This was what she wanted now. And it looked like she was on her way to achieving it.

Once again, Ivy had to force Daniel and thoughts of the past out of her mind, and she vowed that this would be the last time she let him get to her.

Focusing on the evening ahead, Ivy couldn't wait to see where Sebastián's parents lived and she gazed around curiously as he drove through El Tanque, out of the other side of the town and turned off to the right, through another village. They then drove down a narrow lane with the most fantastic views of the sea on one side and pine forests on the other. They seemed to be in the middle of nowhere, and Ivy began to think his parents might live on a farm. But when the van slowed, and went through a set of wrought-iron gates, Ivy let out a low whistle as she caught sight of the house beyond them.

Painted a pale shade of terracotta with a darker tiled roof, the house was huge, and comprised of two storeys with lots of cherry-coloured wooden windows, with a wide veranda which wrapped around the front. It was far larger than Ivy had been expecting and considerably grander, too.

His mother and father were waiting on the veranda as Sebastián parked the van, and the butterflies in Ivy's stomach went into overdrive as he opened her door and then took her hand and led her towards them.

'You remember my mother, Nerea?' Sebastián said, and Ivy nodded and smiled widely at her.

Nerea, to Ivy's surprise and delight, stepped towards her and drew her into a hug, kissing her on both cheeks. Francisco, Sebastián's father, also did the same when they were reintroduced. But what was really heartening for Ivy to see, was the way Francisco hugged his son, and the way Nerea grabbed Sebastián's face and chucked him on both cheeks.

Ivy laughed as he grimaced and batted his mother away, clearly embarrassed, but the smile hovering about his lips also told her that he secretly enjoyed it, and her heart melted that little bit more.

Curious to see inside, Ivy tried not to stare as his parents led the way into a spacious hall with a sweeping wooden staircase, through an enormous living room with a wood burner at one end and out into a garden room where a table had been laid for four. As they walked through the house, Ivy had caught a glimpse of a large bright kitchen, from which the most delicious aroma was emanating, and a formal dining room beyond, which looked grand enough to cater for ten diners.

The garden room overlooked a small pool and had huge sliding glass doors so it was as good as being outside, but was sheltered from the breeze at the same time. The pool and the gardens beyond were surrounded by trees, and through their mottled trunks Ivy caught glimpses of the sea in the distance. It was tranquil and charming, as nice as, if not nicer than, Villa Colina.

His parents clearly weren't short of a bob or two, and Ivy could have kicked herself for being so presumptuous, because she'd not been expecting them to live in a place such as this.

This must have been what Sebastián had been reticent about sharing with her. She hoped he wasn't ashamed that he probably wasn't doing as well as them. The fact that he seemed perfectly happy in his job was all that mattered to her. She earned enough for both of them – but that was a discussion for another time.

Sebastián's father handed Ivy a glass of wine, while Sebastián had sparkling water, and they all sat down at the table. Nerea was up and down like a yo-yo seeing to the meal, but when Ivy offered to help, she was told that she was a guest and they didn't expect her to do anything. Nerea, with Sebastián's help as a translator, suggested that

Ivy could help in the kitchen next time, which left Ivy with a glow in her heart to think that his parents were confident enough in her and Sebastián's relationship to expect a 'next time'.

Francisco spoke better English than his wife, but it was Nerea who Ivy warmed to the most. Sebastián's mother was continually smiling and she seemed really happy that her son had brought someone home, as she kept giving Ivy a squeeze on the arm or a pat on the hand, and smiling broadly at her.

'Tell your mum she's a fantastic cook,' Ivy said, as they tucked into a delicious meal of chicken, rice and vegetables. She didn't know what the chicken had been marinated in, but it was spicy and so tender it was falling apart.

Sebastián translated and his mother nodded, smiled, and pushed the dish of vegetables across the table at her. Ivy dutifully took another portion, even though she was pretty sure she'd never finish what was already on her plate.

'My mother says thank you. She also says you make me happy. She is right – you do.' Sebastián laughed. 'She also wants to know if I am to make an honest woman of you. I told her it is a little soon to be talking of such things, but she is like the sea – relentless.'

Ivy's eyes widened. Wow, things were moving a little faster than she'd been expecting. Marriage? Now there was a thought she hadn't had until now. But once it had been put into her mind, she realised it was going to be difficult to un-think it.

She filed it away for later, but she could feel Sebastián's eyes on her and she knew she was blushing. And when she glanced at him, there was a speculative expression on his face.

She turned her attention back to her plate. One step at a time, she warned herself. Everything was far too new and fragile, and she still had to actually move to Tenerife first before she considered anything else.

Sebastián was still studying her and she blushed even more.

Nerea was also watching her while Francisco was oblivious to the effect his wife's question had had on Ivy.

'Sebastián is right,' Ivy said to her, as he translated. 'It is too soon. I need to find somewhere to live first.'

Nerea said something and Sebastián batted it away with a wave of his hand and shake of his head. 'No, Mamá.'

Ivy noticed that he didn't tell her what his mother had said.

'You want to buy a house?' Francisco asked.

'Yes, I'm selling my house in London and I'm looking to buy a place over here,' Ivy said.

'What sort of place?'

'Something like Villa Colina,' she explained. 'I've been looking online but I haven't seen anything that grabs me here yet.' She put a hand on her heart, then leaned across the table and dropped her voice a little. 'I think it's because I've fallen in love with the villa, and nothing is going to compare to it. I'm thinking of asking the owners if they'd consider selling it, but I doubt they will, and even if they were willing, then I'd be worried they'd want too much for it because they know how keen I am.'

Sebastián was telling his mum what she was saying, but he seemed to be having trouble keeping up with her, because he stumbled over the bit where Ivy said she was thinking of contacting the owners. Luckily, his father understood what she meant.

'He might sell. You should ask him,' Francisco said. He raised his eyebrows at his son.

'Does your father know who the owner is?' she demanded, turning to Sebastián. 'Can he put me in touch with him?' Excitement filled her, even though she knew it was a long shot. But at least she was a step closer if Francisco knew who the owner was. 'I don't want to make things difficult for you at work,' she added.

She was aware Sebastián's parents were staring at her curiously, but she kept her attention on Sebastián.

'Remind me, what was the offer you had on your house?' he asked slowly.

She told him, wondering where this was going and how it related to a villa that wasn't even for sale.

'You can afford to buy Villa Colina,' Sebastián said.

Ivy blinked. 'Excuse me?'

'You can afford it. I was going to tell you later; it was going to be a surprise.' He scowled at his father.

'But does the owner want to sell?' she asked, her heart beating faster and her mouth suddenly dry.

'He does.'

'Have you spoken to him?'

He shrugged. 'The enquiry was dealt with through Dreams Villas.'

That would make sense, she thought – it probably wouldn't do for the maintenance guy to go asking questions like that of the owner, so she didn't blame Sebastián for passing her query on to the rental company.

Ivy slumped back in her seat. She didn't know what to think, or how to feel. This was becoming very real incredibly quickly, and she was terrified and excited at the same time.

Ivy closed her eyes for a moment, imagining herself owning Villa Colina, and she had to grip the seat of her chair to stop herself from jumping up and down with joy.

Calm down, she told herself. There were many steps and procedures to go through before the dream became a reality, so she shouldn't get too excited just yet. But she couldn't help it if her insides were bubbling, and she bit her lip again, trying to hold in her glee.

'What do I do now?' she asked. 'Should I give Dream Villas a call or—'

'Leave it with me – I will ask them to put you in touch with the owner.'

'Thank you, thank you, thank you,' she squealed.

Sebastián laughed. 'You are happy, yes?'

'Yes! But it might take a while for the sale of my house to be finalised. Do you think the owner will wait that long?' she asked anxiously.

'I am sure he will, considering it is not actually on the market.'

His mother was chattering excitedly and his father was shaking his head, a bemused expression on his face.

'*Sí, mama, sí, es bueno.*' Sebastián said quite a lot more, but Ivy was unable to follow even a fraction of it, and when he didn't translate, she guessed he was telling his parents what had just happened.

They still looked a little confused though, and his dad was sending him frowning glances, looking from her to Sebastián and back again. His mother's lips were pursed, and Ivy had the horrible thought that Nerea wasn't in the

236

least bit happy that Ivy might buy Villa Colina. She hoped she hadn't said or done anything to upset her.

'Um, Sebastián, have I upset your parents?' she asked, worry tugging at her mind. She didn't want to fall out with his mum or dad, especially since his mother had been practically suggesting they get married earlier on.

'No, not at all. They are happy that you are coming to live here, because they know it makes me happy.'

'It does?'

'Yes, it does. Now, finish your dinner before my mother really does get upset.'

Ivy took a forkful of chicken and thanked her lucky stars; things were starting to come together – she had nearly sold her London house, there was a strong possibility she would be able to purchase the villa she'd set her heart on and, more importantly, she'd fallen in love with the most fantastic man in the world.

Life was wonderful and she felt truly blessed.

Chapter 24

The following afternoon, Ivy settled down on one of the sun loungers by the pool for an hour or so of reading. She must have dropped off because one minute she was immersed in the world of Amie-Lou Robbins and her latest amazingly convoluted psychological thriller, and the next she was opening her eyes to find the silhouette of a man standing over her.

'What's the time?' she mumbled, thinking Sebastián must be early because the sun was still fairly high in the sky and he wasn't due back until nearer dinnertime. Shielding her eyes with her hand, she squinted at him, blinking in the strong sunlight. Thankfully most of her body was still under the shade of the huge umbrella – she didn't want to risk getting sunburnt for a second time.

Ivy blinked again, trying to focus.

It wasn't Sebastián. It was—

'*Daniel?*' It couldn't be. Was she still asleep?

'Hello, Ivy. You're looking good.'

With a strangled yelp, she swung her legs off the lounger and sat up, making a grab for her sarong. 'Daniel! What the hell are you doing here? And how did you know where to find me? How did you get in?' She scrambled to her feet and wrapped the material around her, feeling his eyes on her bikini-clad body. 'I'm going to kill Nora when I see her,' she muttered.

'You left the front door unlocked. I did shout, but you obviously didn't hear me. As for knowing where to find you, don't blame Nora,' Daniel drawled. 'She didn't tell me where you were – she didn't need to. You weren't that difficult to find; not when you splash yourself all over social media.'

Ivy snatched her sunglasses from where they were resting on the top of her head and put them on, before glaring at her ex. Posting the odd photo on Instagram and Facebook was hardly 'splashing' herself, was it? Although, if she remembered rightly, there was that photo of her sitting outside the café in the village, and that one of the front of the villa with its name emblazoned on a decorative ceramic tile... Oh, damn it! How could she have been so careless?

'Leave,' she commanded, regrouping her scattered thoughts. 'You're not welcome here.'

'I don't suppose I am. It didn't take you long to dip your toes in someone else's pool, did it? Nice photo of your new boyfriend, by the way.'

Ivy gasped. The cheeky sod! He was the one who'd dumped her, not the other way around, and he had the gall to accuse her of—

'Anyway, Ivy,' he said, 'that's not why I'm here. Nora told me that you're not interested in the contract I'm offering, so I thought I'd pop along and talk to you in person.' His gaze skimmed her from face to toes and she cringed inwardly. 'To try to make you see sense.'

'I don't need you to "make me see sense", thank you. I can see perfectly fine, and personally I'm not too keen on the view.'

'Oh, I don't know, it looks pretty darned good from where I'm standing.'

Ivy glowered and shook her head.

'What? I meant *that* view.' Daniel waved a suit-clad arm in the general direction of the sea, but he kept his attention on her. 'You *have* done well for yourself, haven't you?'

'It was Nora's choice,' she said reluctantly. Why she felt the need to justify herself to him, she had no idea.

'Really?' He said it as though he didn't believe her. 'So, where did you meet him?'

'Excuse me? That's none of your business.'

'Are you sleeping with him?'

'Bugger off, Daniel. My private life is no longer your concern. Actually, nothing about me is your concern any longer, and that includes my work.'

'You're being a little melodramatic, aren't you? Anyway' – he made a little moue – 'as long as I still hold the rights to the books you've published through my company, then you *are* my concern.'

'You should have thought about that before you "dipped your toe",' Ivy made forceful quotation marks in the air, 'in Rebekkah Rain's pool. Eww.'

'Are you jealous, my sweet?'

Ivy snorted. 'Hardly. She's welcome to you.'

'I was talking about her literary success.'

'You're not exactly endearing yourself to me, you know. If you've come here to persuade me to sign your contract, then you're doing a remarkably poor job of it.'

'I am, aren't I? I shall blame it on the jet lag.'

She barked out a laugh. 'There *is* no jet lag.'

'I know, but it's nice to see that I can still make you laugh.'

'Yeah, *at* you,' she muttered, 'not *with* you. You need to go,' she added, somewhat louder.

Daniel raised his eyebrows. 'I've come all this way for a civilised conversation, and you haven't even got the good manners to offer me a cold drink. Besides, I sent the taxi away.'

'Why the hell did you do that?' She threw her hands up in the air. 'You'd better call for another one, and while you're waiting for it to arrive, I'll get you a glass of water. You can drink it on the drive.'

'I'd prefer a G and T,' he shouted after her, as she retreated into the villa.

She turned on her heel and marched back outside. 'Go,' she commanded, pointing to the French doors, and waited for him to walk ahead of her. Then she ushered him to the front door, opened it, gestured for him to walk through it, and slammed it in his face.

'Wait there. I'll get you your water,' she yelled. *G and T?* The bloody cheek of him!

Furiously, Ivy stomped back down the hall. Why did he have to turn up? Couldn't the damned man take 'no' for an answer?

She decided to change into a pair of shorts and a top before she poured Daniel his water. She didn't like the feeling of being half naked with only a length of chiffon material and a skimpy bikini covering her. And to think that she used to be perfectly happy with Daniel seeing her in far less. The thought now made her shudder, and she was delighted that he no longer had any effect on her heart. In fact, she wasn't sure what she'd seen in him in the first place.

He was quite good-looking, she conceded, pulling the vest over her head, and he could be attentive and good fun. But she should have realised long before he dumped her that Daniel Morris had only ever been interested in Daniel Morris. Even more than the kudos of having a well-known author on his arm or the money she earned for him, Daniel was only really concerned about himself.

Which made his coming all this way when he'd already been told 'no', all the more interesting.

The only conclusion she could draw from it was that her new series was even better than she and Nora had thought. Daniel was all about the bottom line and was driven by money. He must be able to see a very tidy profit indeed from *An Angel from Hell*, otherwise he wouldn't be here.

And that deduction sent her pulse soaring.

He wasn't here for *her* – she'd not for one second thought that he was. He was here to get her to sign a contract with his publishing house. Nothing more. But if he had to wine her, dine her, and woo her back into his bed to persuade her to do so, he undoubtedly would. Unfortunately for him, he wasn't making too good a job of it, and she came to the crushing realisation that he wasn't really treating her any differently now to the way he had treated her when they were still a couple – he was still overbearing, condescending and thoughtless.

It had taken a dire manuscript, an infidelity, and a man who loved her unconditionally and who treated her the way a woman should be treated, for her to realise that she'd been putting up with second – no, third – best for all this time.

Thank God, she thought, when she heard the sound of an engine pull up; Sebastián had arrived. Ivy struggled into her shorts without taking her flip flops off first and got one foot stuck. Sod Daniel's glass of water, he could go without and drop-dead of thirst for all she cared. Finally dressed, she marched out of her bedroom, down the hall and yanked open the front door – just in time to see Sebastián jam his helmet back on his head, swing his leg over the saddle and kick his bike into life.

Before she could run across the drive, he'd turned the bike around and was roaring off through the villa's gates in a cloud of dust.

Ivy rounded on her ex. 'What the hell did you say to him?' she yelled. 'What. Did. You. Say!'

'Only the truth, my sweet – that you and I are partners. More than partners, actually.' His smirk turned her stomach.

Oh Lord – she couldn't believe it. Damn Daniel. He really was an absolute pain in the backside. She needed to call Sebastián. She had to explain, to tell him what a creep Daniel was being, and that there was no way—

Daniel caught her by the arm as she headed inside. 'Don't bother. It would never have lasted. He's too much of a playboy. You're just one in a long list of women. No doubt he'll be off filming again somewhere, and you'll just be another notch on his bedpost.'

'What the hell are you talking about? Get off me!' She shook herself free and lunged for the front door, but Daniel grabbed for her again and held her back, an incredulous look spreading across his face.

'You don't know, do you?' he said, with a twist of his lips. 'You genuinely don't know who he is!' He sounded surprised and more than a little shocked. He also sounded very smug.

Ivy stopped in her tracks, confused. 'Of course I know who he is! Sebastián's no playboy, and what do you mean "he'll be off filming"? He—' She halted abruptly, not wanting to reveal that Sebastián cleaned pools for a living, because she knew what Daniel was like. He was a terrible snob and would stick his pointy nose in the air and then do his best to demean and belittle the man she loved. And there was no way she was standing for that.

'Your *Sebastián*, as you call him,' Daniel stretched out the name, 'is none other than Sebé Castile, the world-famous actor.'

Chapter 25

Ivy had heard of Sebé Castile, of course she had. Who hadn't? The actor had starred in several movies, most notably *A Lavender Summer*, the film she'd mentioned that she would have liked to have watched, the film Sebastián had quoted from once. It was one of the biggest box-office hits this century. As she'd noted before, she thought she must be the only female on the planet who hadn't actually seen the film.

Oh for goodness' sake, this was ridiculous. Sebastián couldn't possibly be Sebé Castile. Daniel was losing the plot.

Now that it had been pointed out to her, she had to admit that there was a similarity, but then again, a lot of men had dark curly hair, chocolate eyes, lantern jawlines and the stubble thing going on. They weren't all as handsome as Sebastián, of course, but just because he was incredibly good looking didn't mean he was *the* Sebé Castile. He bore a passing resemblance to the actor, that was all. They didn't even have the same name, for a start.

'You don't believe me, do you? Go on, Google it.' Daniel was practically chortling with amusement. 'I can assure you, it is him.'

'Don't be absurd.'

'Hang on a sec, I'll see if I can get him up on my phone.'

In a daze, Ivy staggered through the front door and made her unsteady way to the living area when she slumped onto the sofa.

Daniel followed her, peering at his mobile and waffling about how she *must have* known her boyfriend was him, and didn't she see the resemblance? Where had she been these last few years? Giving up on checking Sebastian out on the internet for a moment (yeah, good luck with getting a signal, she thought), Daniel stuck his head in the fridge and emerged clutching the bottle of wine she had been planning to have with dinner.

Think, think, she urged, wishing Daniel would disappear back under whatever rock he'd crawled out from. He was grating on her nerves bustling around in her kitchen. Why the hell was he here, anyway. Couldn't the stupid man take a hint?

'No wonder you don't want to talk to me, now you've got Sebé Castile's attention, but as I said, it won't last. You'd be silly to let his fame and fortune go to your head.' He slurped the wine and swirled it around his mouth in that annoying manner of his. 'Rather on the cheap side, isn't it?' he said, holding the glass up and peering at it, 'Never mind, it's cold and wet, so it'll do.'

'Go. Please, just go.' She couldn't be bothered to correct him. If Daniel wanted to believe she was dating a famous actor, let him. She didn't care.

'You don't mean that?' he wheedled. 'After all we've been through?'

'I do. I don't want you here.'

When she glanced at him, his brow was furrowed and his mouth was set in a thin line. She knew that expression and at one time it would have sent her rushing to placate

246

him. Daniel never did like being thwarted. But at long last Ivy didn't care what he thought, or if his feelings were hurt.

'You've changed,' he said. 'I don't think I like it.'

'I don't care.'

'See, that's what I mean – right there. It's not very attractive.'

'I still don't care. I want you to leave right now.'

'If that's the way you want to play it, then I shall go, and I won't be coming back either. Daniel Morris is not a man who asks twice.'

Did he just refer to himself in the third person? Ivy rolled her eyes. Clearly, representing budding stars like Rebekkah Rain had gone to his head.

'You've already asked twice,' she pointed out.

'Whatever. You've become too big for your boots. It'll all come crashing down about your ears when lover boy moves on. Men like him don't want women like you – not when they can have their pick of any girl who catches their eye. Young women, beautiful women. Not middle-aged novelists who are past their prime.'

'You really are a nasty bit of work,' Ivy said, shaking her head in disbelief. He was showing his true colours now, and she found she disliked him intensely. He was clearly jealous that she'd moved on, that she'd found someone else and wasn't moping around, lamenting his defection. Coming here like this and making silly and unfounded allegations was taking his dog-in-the-manger attitude to the extreme, though.

Anyway, what if she *was* dating the real-life Sebé Castile? It would still be none of Daniel's business, and for him to be so bitter about it showed what a horrid man he was.

Not that Sebastián *was* Sebé Castile, because it wasn't possible. As if a world–class actor would be cleaning pools in Tenerife. She didn't think so. Daniel had got it wrong, but if he wanted to believe she was in a relationship with a famous actor and get all hot under the collar about it, then let him. He was an idiot and she didn't know why she hadn't noticed it before now. Hindsight truly was a wonderful thing.

'Sebé Castile won't—' he began, but she cut him off.

'Shut up! My love life is no concern of yours, not anymore. You made that choice when you cast me aside for Rebekkah Rain.'

'*Cast aside?* That's a bit melodramatic, isn't it? I made a mistake, that's all.' In the blink of an eye, he'd gone from attacking her to being defensive; a sure sign he was on the back foot.

'What, you just happened to lose your footing and stumble into bed with her?' Ivy taunted.

Daniel sent her a hurt look. 'You're being unfair. Anyone can make a mistake. And Rebekkah was mine.'

'She's not doing as well as you thought she would, is she?' Ivy guessed, with sudden insight. That would explain why he was so het up at the thought of her dating someone like Sebé Castile and not signing his stupid publishing contract. It also explained why he was prepared to offer such generous terms – he needed her. But she most definitely didn't need *him*.

'Anyway,' she added, 'I don't care about Rebekkah, I just want you to leave. And if you don't, I'm phoning the *Policía Municipal.*'

He raised a well-groomed eyebrow. 'Listen to you, you've been here all of five minutes and you've already gone native.'

Ivy ignored him. Instead, she got up and strode into the hall. She meant what she said – if he didn't leave, she was phoning the police. She also desperately wanted to speak to Sebastián, too, but she didn't intend to do it while Daniel was lurking about and listening in on her conversation.

Daniel followed her. 'OK, OK, I'll go, but as I said, I won't be back. If you don't come on board now, it's your loss. No other publishing house will give you such good terms.'

'What part of "I don't care" don't you understand?' Ivy's shock was transforming into genuine anger. 'You trashed my previous manuscript—' She held up a hand when he tried to speak. 'I admit it wasn't my best work, but there are nicer ways of delivering criticism. You dumped me for someone else – another *younger* author, no less. By the way, how *is* that working out for you?' Once again, Ivy didn't give him time to speak. 'You publicly tell the writing community that I've lost my edge, then, when you manage to get your greedy mitts on my latest work and you see how good it is, you expect me to come running just because you've shown an interest in it. Well, let me tell you, I wouldn't want you to publish my new series if you were the last publisher on earth. I'd rather burn it first.'

Daniel hadn't moved during her tirade, except to open his mouth and close it again. Now, though, he was pursing his lips and shaking his head. 'Have you finished?'

'Yes.' She had *so* finished with him. If she ever saw him again, or even heard his name mentioned, it would be too soon.

'Good. I can see you've had your head turned and you're not going to listen to sense. It's typical of you to be unable to separate business from your private life. Don't expect me to look at any more of your pathetic scribblings in the future, because I shan't. I was only doing you a favour for old times' sake. I'm going to ring for a taxi now.' He placed the wine glass down on the hall table. 'Good luck, Ivy, you're going to need it.'

Was that a threat, or was he just spouting hot air? Ivy didn't care either way, and she watched him stalk out of the living room with weary eyes. The front door opened and closed, and she slumped back into the sofa. She felt drained, exhausted, and incredibly upset, and she couldn't wait for him to leave so she could call Sebastián and explain.

Daniel, much to her annoyance, reappeared in the doorway waving his phone at her. She really must learn to lock the front door, she thought crossly, as she saw his indignant expression.

'I still can't get a signal,' he complained. 'I'll have to use yours. And you'll have to give me the number for a taxi company. I must say,' he continued, without drawing breath, 'I would have thought you could at least put me up for the night. I don't even know when the next flight is.'

'You should have thought about that before you decided to drop in on me unannounced.'

'You were ignoring me. What choice did I have?'

'I'm sure you'll be able to get a flight this evening,' she said.

'Can you check the internet for me? It's the least you can do since I've travelled all this way.'

'I can't get online here. And there's no phone signal.' The first thing she intended to do when she bought the villa — *if* she bought the villa — was to have broadband installed.

'No internet?' Daniel cast a suspicious glance at her laptop sitting on the desk underneath the window, as if he thought she was lying.

'No.'

'My dear girl, why ever not? How do you cope?'

'Easily,' she retorted shortly. 'Look, just get a taxi — I've got a local number you can call on the landline — and go to the airport. If there are no flights tonight, I'm sure there's a hotel nearby you can book yourself into.'

She searched for the cab number and dialled it.

'Right, the taxi will be here in twenty minutes,' she said, after speaking to a woman whose English was thankfully better than Ivy's Spanish.

Never had she known such an awkward twenty minutes in all her life. She had absolutely nothing to say to her ex, and Daniel appeared to have shot all his arrows and missed, so was now sulking because Ivy had failed to fall gratefully at his feet. Professionally that is; he hadn't been clear about the personal side of things, but she suspected they went hand in hand for him.

When the taxi eventually pulled into the drive, Ivy let out a huge sigh of relief as Daniel climbed into the back of the cab, his overnight bag in hand. She waited until she heard the sound of the engine fade before she felt it was safe to phone Sebastián.

She wasn't too surprised when her call went unanswered, but she was disappointed nevertheless, her heart heavy as she wondered how long it might be before she saw him again.

Had she imagined that Sebastián had ridden off in a bit of a huff? Or had he been giving her time and space to deal with Daniel on her own? She'd wait a while before she tried again.

She rang Nora instead. 'Guess who's just turned up at the villa?' She leant against the wall, realising she felt weak and a bit shaky.

'Not Daniel?' Nora cried. 'Do you know, I had a feeling he was planning something. He went all cagey on me when I told him you had passed on the contract.'

'He tried to persuade me to change my mind about it. Unsuccessfully, I might add. He was being a right prat. I thought I'd better let you know, in case he starts trashing me again, although if he does, there's not a lot I can do about it.'

'Leave Daniel Morris to me. If he thinks he can harass one of my authors, he's got another thing coming.'

'Thanks, Nora. I've got to go – I need to… erm… sort something out.'

Ivy didn't feel like sharing any details about her relationship with Nora. Not yet. Her agent may well have spotted the same image of him on her Facebook page as Daniel had, but since Nora hadn't mentioned the new man in Ivy's life, Ivy wasn't about to either. She wanted to keep Sebastián to herself for a while longer, and she wasn't going to tell Nora about her plans for moving to Tenerife yet, either. It was all still too uncertain and precious.

Ivy tried calling him again. Thankfully, he answered this time and relief swept through her. Not for long, though.

'Ivy, you do not need to explain. I understand,' he said before she had a chance to say anything.

'You do? Thank God!'

'It is for the best. He can do so much more for you and for your career than I can.'

'Wait, what? No, no, you've got it all—'

'He still loves you, no matter what you think. I saw his text to you. And he understands your world better than I ever can.' He sounded incredibly sad.

'Sebastián, listen to me!'

'I am sorry, Ivy. I cannot do this – I cannot have this conversation right now. It hurts too much.'

'I don't want— Sebastián? Sebastián!'

But it was no use, the line was dead.

Ivy, frantic, tears trickling down her face, tried calling him back.

Repeatedly she stabbed his number into the keypad.

Repeatedly his number rang and rang.

She had no intention of leaving it there. She had to make him listen, make him understand. He'd got the wrong end of the stick entirely, and the last thing she wanted was for him to think she was going back to her ex. She had to tell him that it was *him* she wanted, not Daniel, and if she never published another book again, it did not matter.

The only thing that mattered was Sebastián and their love for each other. She didn't care if he was the guy who cleaned the pool. It was *who* he was that was important, not what he could, or couldn't, give her. Neither money, fame, nor publishing contracts meant anything. Not without Sebastián to share it with her.

Chapter 26

Ivy was going to go look for him. The drawback was that she didn't know where Sebastián lived. But she could always find out, and she knew exactly who to ask. Swiping tears from her cheeks with trembling, impatient fingers, she shoved her feet into a pair of trainers, grabbed her phone and her bag and headed towards the village, checking her mobile periodically as soon as she got a signal in case he had changed his mind and called her.

Thank God, she thought, as she saw Jorge and three of his pals sitting in their usual seats. Jorge was holding some playing cards in one hand and a half-smoked cigarette in the other, which he used to salute her with when he saw her hurrying along the pavement.

His smile became quizzical when she trotted up to their table, sweaty and probably red in the face, and came to a halt in front of him.

'Jorge, I need your help,' she blurted out breathlessly, aware that the other men were eying her curiously.

'I can try,' he said. 'What is it?'

'Do you know Sebastián's address? Or can you point me in the right direction at least?' She knew there was a chance Sebastián might not be at home (he could have been anywhere on the island when she'd spoken to him), but she had to try.

Jorge took a pull on his cigarette, inhaled, and let it out slowly, smoke curling around his head. His eyes were narrowed, but Ivy thought that might be from the effects of the cigarette smoke.

'Why?' he asked.

She should have anticipated him wanting to know, but she didn't feel comfortable telling him. There didn't appear to be any choice though, because from the way the other men had stilled and were watching her intently, she didn't think it a good idea to lie or make up some innocuous reason for wanting to know where he lived. They'd see straight through her.

One of the men dragged a chair across from an adjacent table, and making room for it, patted the seat. Ivy sat down, reluctantly because she was itching to keep moving. She wanted to sort this mess out now. Today. The last thing she wanted to do was to let it fester, and risk Sebastián arranging for someone else to service Villa Colina tomorrow.

'Pilar, *ron de miel*,' Jorge called, as Ivy hesitated. 'No crying,' he said to her. 'Drink rum.'

When Pilar placed a small glass of the sweet liquid on the table, Ivy took a sip, and felt the warmth travel down her throat and into her stomach. Jorge seemed to think that honey rum was a cure-all, but she reminded herself to be careful not to drink too much of the powerful stuff.

'Why?' he repeated.

'Sebastián and I are... we're... he's my...' Oh God, this was hard.

'What?'

'I love him,' she said.

Jorge flashed a look at his friends and said something Ivy couldn't follow. There were a couple of responses from the others and a few headshakes. 'OK, but why you want his house?'

'Because he...' She sighed. 'Look, you know I've been staying at Villa Colina.' She waited for Jorge to nod his understanding. 'I expect you know that he services the villa. Cleans the pool and tends the garden and stuff.'

Jorge frowned.

'Sebastián cleans' – Ivy mimed using a sweeping brush '—the villa.' She pretended to polish, too.

'Ah, *bueno*.' Jorge nodded and spoke to the others. There were a couple of puzzled faces, but Ivy was content that Jorge knew what she meant.

'We love each other. I love him, he loves me,' she continued.

There was more confusion, combined with doubt, and yet more frowning and headshaking.

'Sebastián and I are *l'amour*,' Ivy insisted. Or was that French she'd just used?

This last was met by shrugs and some face pulling, except for one man. He was nodding slowly and when he spoke Ivy could have sworn she heard the name Miguel and El Huerto Secreto. There was a bit more discussion before Jorge's attention came back to her.

'OK, *amor*. But why you want to know his house?' he said.

She could understand their reluctance to tell her because if someone she hardly knew wanted to know Nora's address she certainly wouldn't tell them, so she didn't blame them for being cautious and not wanting to violate Sebastián's privacy. For all they knew she could be lying – though why she'd want to do that was anyone's guess.

But she was beginning to think that going to look for him was a bad idea.

She'd give him another call, she decided, taking out her phone, but when it rang and rang with no answer, she hung up and got to her feet. She might as well return to the villa, as Jorge *et al* clearly weren't going to tell her anything.

But Jorge took hold of her hand and tugged her back into her seat. 'Drink,' he urged.

Feeling it would be too rude to just leave after they were trying to be kind, Ivy sat back down and took another small sip of the honey rum.

'Diego, he say you and Sebastián *cenaste en El Huerto Secreto*,' Jorge mimed eating. 'His brother works there, he tells him.'

'Yes, yes, we did, with Cristina, that's his sister, and Sergio.'

Jorge spoke to Diego, who appeared to confirm her story. '*Bueno*, but why his house? Call him.'

'I've been trying. See?' She held up her phone to show him just how many times she'd tried to call the man she'd fallen in love with.

Jorge shrugged. 'He not want to speak.'

'That's the problem,' she muttered.

'*Qué?*'

'He doesn't want to speak to me because he thinks I'm better off with Daniel, my ex.'

More frowns, Jorge clearly hadn't understood.

'Sebastián thinks I don't love him,' she said, as simply as she could. She wasn't entirely sure this was true, but it was the best she could do in the circumstances. 'He thinks I love another man.'

'You do?'

'No! I love Sebastián.'

'This other man, he loves you?'

'No, he...' Crikey how on earth could she explain what had gone on— Then she had an idea, and frantically typed: *I am an author. The other man was trying to publish my book. Sebastián thought he was my lover* into Google Translate on her phone. She had no idea whether the Spanish version of what she had typed resembled what she was trying to say, but that's all she had to work with.

'Ah, *entiendo. Una autora?*' Jorge pretended to scribble on his hand.

'*Sí*, look.' She clicked onto her author website and turned her phone around for the men to see. For those of them who weren't already wearing glasses, there was a bit of a scramble to find their specs, but one gent took the phone off Ivy and peered at it, before handing it to the next old man, like a digital version of pass the parcel.

'*Muchos libros*,' Jorge said, finally returning Ivy's phone to her. '*Eres famosa?*'

Ivy shook her head. 'I'm sorry, I don't understand.'

'Famous?'

'Oh, right. You think I'm famous? Only a little bit. Not like Stephen King or James Patterson.'

'*Muchos libros*,' he repeated, and Ivy supposed she had written quite a few books over the years. *An Angel from Hell* would be her twenty-seventh novel.

Ivy could see that the men were wavering, so she typed *I've been to his parents' house for dinner* into the translation box and showed it to Jorge.

He pursed his lips and scrutinised her.

She nodded. 'Big house,' she said, stretching her arms out. 'With trees all around.' She pointed to the nearest tree which was growing on the side of the pavement. 'Nerea and Francisco, lovely people.'

Diego dug around in his jeans' pocket and brought out an ancient flip-top phone. 'Francisco?' he asked her, although it sounded more like a warning, and she guessed she was going to get short shrift from him if he found out she was lying.

Ivy's attention, along with everyone else's, was focused on Diego as he dialled.

'Francisco? *Es Diego. Sí, sí—*' followed by a load of stuff Ivy hadn't a hope in hell of following.

Once or twice Diego sought her out and his eyes locked on hers, but his expression gave nothing away. Eventually, he ended the call and turned to Jorge. Once more Ivy felt left out of the conversation, especially when a kind of argument took place and she had no idea what it was about.

'Jorge, what's going on?' Ivy asked, after he had thrown up his hands and tutted loudly.

'Diego, he want to take you. But I say "no". He *no habla ingles*. Me! I take you.'

'Take me where?' Her heart was thumping, and her tummy turned over.

'To Sebastián house.'

Ivy sent a silent prayer of thanks to the heavens. Someone, she didn't care who, was going to take her to see Sebastián.

'If you just tell me where he lives, I can go by myself,' she suggested. 'I don't want to put anyone out.'

'*Perdón?*' Jorge squinted at her over the top of the glass he was emptying. How many of those had he imbibed? Was he in any fit state to take her anywhere? He didn't appear to be under the influence, but she didn't want to take any chances.

'I go on my own,' she simplified.

He wagged a finger at her. 'No. I go. Diego go.' The other two gentlemen understood and both of them started talking at once and gesticulating wildly. Jorge grunted. 'Tulio say he come, too, and if Tulio go, Paco, he come also.'

'All four of you?' Ivy held up four fingers.

'*Sí.*'

'Is it far? How many kilometres?'

Jorge held up three fingers and grinned at her.

'Are we going to walk?' Ivy asked doubtfully. Tulio used a walking stick and she wasn't sure he could manage three kilometres.

'Car. Diego have a car.'

Ah, that was why Diego wanted to take her, because he was the one who could drive. Ivy could also understand, and was thankful that Jorge was coming too, but she wasn't sure about the others. She guessed they didn't want to be left out and this was probably the most fun they'd had in a while – the mad English woman chasing after the Spanish guy.

'Come.' Jorge got to his feet and beckoned to her. The rest of them stood as well – Tulio after a bit of a struggle – and they began walking across the road towards an ancient and incredibly small white hatchback.

It was a two-door affair, and Paco opened the passenger door, pulled the back of the seat forward and clambered in. Tulio jerked his head at her.

'You want me to get in?' Ivy queried, pointing.

He nodded. With a shrug, she eased herself in and sat down on the hot plastic seat.

Tulio made shooing motions with his hand until Ivy realised that he wanted her to scoot across so he could get in the back, too. Blimey, this was going to be a squash, she thought. Her suspicions were confirmed when Tulio crammed himself in the back and jammed his walking stick between them so that Ivy was sandwiched between the two old men with her shoulders scrunched in and her knees almost to her chin. She felt quite flustered.

Jorge got in the front passenger seat and Diego eased himself behind the wheel. With much wheel turning and glancing in the mirrors Diego reversed the car out of its parking space and into the road, where he was immediately beeped at by a car coming the other way.

Ivy closed her eyes and prayed they'd make the journey without incident, because Diego didn't seem the most competent of drivers – he seemed to be blissfully unaware of any other road users, as another blast of horns and some serious shouting testified. Ivy was too scared to open her eyes, so she kept them firmly shut and tried not to be sick as the car lurched around corners and up and down hills. It didn't help that she was squashed into a space so small a cat would have trouble sitting down, nor that Tulio's stick was poking her in the ribs, or that she felt decidedly uncomfortable at being so close to two comparative strangers.

After about ten minutes Ivy sensed a change in the timbre of the noise from the wheels, and she cautiously opened her eyes to see that the vehicle was no longer on a road, but was travelling along a single-track lane with trees either side.

Abruptly, the car emerged out into a more open area and Ivy saw a sweeping white balustrade leading towards a gated drive. The gates were open and Ivy felt a surge of anticipation mixed with an equal amount of trepidation.

What if Sebastián didn't want to speak to her? What if he wasn't there? What was she going to do then?

Was this another Dream Villas rental property, and if so, would he be working and therefore unable to speak to her anyway? There wasn't any sign of the van or his bike, but Francisco must have informed Diego that Sebastián was on the premises, else why bring her here?

The car trundled up the drive, the four men talking amongst themselves and pointing things out, such as the treble garage off to the left, the large circular parking area, the sweeping marble pathway and wide stone steps. The steps themselves were canopied by metal arches, which had bright flowers climbing up them, and they led to the house.

Diego switched the engine off and both he and Jorge got out and pulled their seats forward to release the others. Ivy was the last out, and she awkwardly scooted and shuffled her way out of the back seat, almost crawling the last few inches, as she practically fell headfirst out of the car. Straightening up, she pulled the bottom of her shorts down, checked that her top hadn't ridden up, and smoothed her hair. She knew she wasn't looking her best, but right now she didn't care. All she wanted was to speak to Sebastián.

Swallowing nervously, she took a step towards the house before she realised that all four elderly gentlemen were hot on her heels. They were so close she could feel Jorge's breath on the back of her neck.

'Jorge, I need to do this on my own. Can you wait for me here?'

He cocked his head and frowned at her.

'You,' she waved a hand at them, 'stay here.' She patted the air. 'I go,' she made walking motions with two fingers, 'to see Sebastián.'

There was a general air of disappointment, but Ivy didn't care. 'Please?'

All four of them nodded, and Jorge reached into his trouser pocket and pulled out a packet of cigarettes, taking one for himself, before offering them around.

Ivy smiled her thanks and, hitching in a steadying breath, she climbed the wide shallow steps, her attention focused on the gardens surrounding the house. She expected to see Sebastián any second, but when she still hadn't spotted him by the time she reached the front door, she knew she had no other option than to knock on it. She couldn't exactly wander around the property at random; she had to make her presence known.

Hoping that whoever answered the door would be able to speak good-enough English for her to explain why she was there, she rapped on it and waited.

She gave it a couple of seconds before she knocked again, and this time she accompanied her rapping with a shouted 'Hello! Anyone home?'

Silence. It was so quiet she could hear the four amigos chatting by the car, almost as if they were standing next to her.

She called again.

OK, so there wasn't anyone home, which meant that Sebastián was probably somewhere in the grounds or seeing to the pool, because a house the size and spec of this one would surely have a pool.

Ivy had just moved away from the door and was about to chance her arm and have a scout around the property, when she heard a noise behind her and she turned around.

A young woman was standing in the open doorway.

A beautiful woman with shiny black hair, huge almond-shaped eyes and full pouty lips. She was wearing a tiny bikini on her slim, toned body and her golden skin glowed a uniform colour, unlike Ivy's patchy suntan. Ivy immediately felt scruffy and plain, and rather middle-aged.

'*Sí?*' the woman asked.

'Hi, yes, I'm sorry to bother you. Oh, do you speak English?' Ivy was blathering a bit, but she was feeling rather awkward and at a distinct disadvantage.

'Yes, I speak English.' The woman followed it up with a delicate shrug of her slim shoulders.

'I'm looking for Sebastián. The guy who services your pool?' she added when the girl (because, let's face it, the vision standing in front of her was only just out of her teens, Ivy realised as she scrutinised her) stared blankly at her. 'Is he here?'

'No. Who are you?' The suspicion in her voice was palpable.

'My name is Ivy Winter and I'm staying at another of Dream Villa's properties. I'm sorry to have bothered you. I expect I'll see him this evening. Thanks, anyway.'

'This evening? No, we go to dinner this evening.'

Ivy wasn't sure she heard the girl correctly. 'Excuse me?'

'You want Sebastián, yes? He is not here later,' she repeated, sounding a little exasperated. 'We have dinner later.'

That's what Ivy thought she had said. 'Oh, I see, um tell him I... Actually, no don't bother. Sorry to have troubled you.'

Feeling the hot sting of tears, Ivy smiled her thanks and hastily turned away, almost running by the time she had got to the end of the steps. Sebastián must have been seeing the both of them at the same time? God, she felt such a fool. He'd really strung her along and she couldn't believe she'd fallen for it. Daniel had been right – she had been just another notch in Sebastián's bed post, but not in the way her ex had meant. Did Sebastián sleep with all Dream Villa's female clients? What an utter bastard!

Choking back a sob, Ivy dashed to the car and threw herself into the back seat, curling herself into it as if she might disappear if she made herself small enough.

The four men who were gathered around the car shared concerned looks, before piling in after her.

Jorge twisted around awkwardly in the front seat to address her. 'You speak to Sebastián?'

Mutely, Ivy shook her head.

'He not there?'

'No.' Her voice was thin and tearful.

'Why cry?' He trailed a finger down his cheek.

266

'It's nothing. It doesn't matter.'

But it *was* something and it *did* matter, because Ivy had never felt so broken in her life, and she honestly didn't know how she was supposed to move on from this.

Chapter 27

'Nora?' Ivy whispered. It spoke volumes that the only person she could think of to call in her hour of need was her agent. God, her life was pathetic and such a mess.

'Ivy? Is that you? I can barely hear you, you'll have to speak up a bit. This line is incredibly faint.'

The only thing that was faint was Ivy. She felt like she was about to pass out. Who knew heartache could feel like this? To have reached the age she had without experiencing this level of pain was quite astonishing.

Ivy cleared her throat. 'Is that better?'

'Yes. What can I do for you? I haven't heard anything from Daniel since I spoke to you earlier, if that's why you're calling.'

Ivy had practically forgotten about Daniel in the drama of the previous hour or so, but now that Nora mentioned his name, she felt a weird kind of gratitude towards him. If he hadn't turned up when he did, then she would never have discovered that Sebastián was two-timing her.

'I have to come h——' She'd almost said the word 'home', but even now, feeling as dreadful as she did, she couldn't think of London as home any longer. But neither could she stay here. There were too many memories of Sebastián, both in the villa and on Tenerife itself. For her own emotional health, she couldn't stay at Villa Colina for the rest of her rental contract. 'Return to England,' she amended. 'Now. Today.'

'Why? What's going on? Is it Daniel?' Nora demanded.

'No. Yes, sort of. It's complicated.'

'Are you reconsidering Daniel's offer? Is that it?'

'God, no!'

'I don't understand – if it's not Daniel, then what is it? Are you ill?'

She was, but not in the way Nora was referring to.

'Ivy, speak to me! Do you need me to phone a doctor?'

'No, I'm fine.' The last word came out as a sob.

'If you don't tell me what's wrong...' Nora's voice carried a warning.

'I've fallen in love,' Ivy admitted quietly.

'Gosh! You never said. Who is he and why is that such a problem? Is he married? Oh, Ivy, my dear, you do get yourself into some scrapes, don't you?'

'He's not married, but he does have another woman. Maybe more than one.' He could have one in every villa he serviced, for all she knew. Though why he'd want to lavish time and attention on her when he had a gorgeous girlfriend in that other house, was beyond her.

'Oh, love, I'm so sorry. And you were getting on so well, too.'

For a moment Ivy thought Nora was referring to her and Sebastián, until she realised her agent was talking about her writing. And, yes, it was important, but she couldn't think about that now, when the only thing on her mind was Sebastián and how he'd betrayed her. No wonder he'd ridden off at the first sight of Daniel – why should he be bothered about that kind of drama and complication, when he had a woman half Ivy's age, who was so beautiful it set her teeth on edge, to run to?

'I'm going to try to get a flight tonight,' Ivy decided. 'If I can't, then I'll see if I can get one in the morning.'

'Ivy, take some time to think about this,' Nora pleaded.

'I've made up my mind.' What was there to think about? Thinking wouldn't alter the fact that Sebastián had never loved her. 'I'm sorry, I know you probably can't get a refund on the villa, but I don't care. I need to get away from here.'

Nora sighed. 'If you're sure...?' She sounded doubtful, but she had no choice other than to accept Ivy's decision.

'I'm sure.'

'OK, I'll email Señor de León and see if we can come to some sort of arrangement.' Nora was all business and efficiency now, and Ivy was grateful that—

'What did you say?' Ivy demanded, abruptly.

'I said, I'll see if I can sort something out with Dream Villas. Maybe if they are able to rent the place out again before the end of your lease, they'll be kind enough to refund the difference.'

'No, not that. The name! Who did you say you were going to email?'

'Señor de León. He's the owner of Dream Villas.'

Ivy almost dropped the phone. Her stomach turned over and she felt sick. No, no, it wasn't possible...Oh, wait... 'Is his first name Francisco?' That would explain everything – Dream Villas must be a family-run business.

'I'll have to look it up... Is it important?' Nora asked, slightly impatiently.

'Yes, very.'

She heard Nora tapping away at a keyboard, then, 'His name is *Sebastián* de León, not Francisco. Why?'

Ivy swallowed, as bile crept up her throat. She felt hot, yet clammy at the same time, and she knew she was about to be sick.

'Hello? Are you still there, Ivy?' Nora called.

'There must be some mistake. Sebastián de León is the pool and maintenance man.'

'I don't think so, hang on a sec, let me double check. Yep, that's the name on the booking form and in the company information bit. Oh dear.' The penny dropped, and Nora let out a long breath. 'It that the guy you said was gorgeous, the pool guy?'

'That's him. Sebastián.'

'Would he happen to be the same guy as the one in the photo you posted on Facebook? He's a dish. I meant to ask you about him. He looks a lot like… oh, what's-his-name, that actor, the one who starred in *A Lavender Summer*…'

Ivy closed her eyes, as sweat trickled unpleasantly down her back. 'You're thinking of Sebé Castile. Apparently, Daniel also thinks Sebastián looks like him.'

'He's right. Your Sebastián does look remarkably like Sebé Castile, so I can see where he has got the idea from. Your man is a bit older perhaps, a little more silver around the temples.'

'He's not my Sebastián.' Well, not any longer, if he ever was. He seemed to be quite a few women's Sebastián, Ivy thought bitterly. 'Look, I've got to go, I need to sort out a flight.' Which wasn't as straightforward as it sounded, considering she'd have to walk to a place where she could get a signal to make the booking, and she didn't want to return to the village in case Jorge and his friends were still there. They'd been kind enough to drop her back at the villa and had been reluctant to leave given that she was sobbing her heart out for most of the car journey home. But Ivy had insisted, and she couldn't face any more of their well-meaning sympathy today.

And neither could she take any more upset – first Daniel, then the row with Sebastián, then discovering he had another woman. Oh, and don't forget that the sneaky, lying git actually owned Dream Villas, which meant that he also owned the impressive house that Diego had taken her to earlier.

Her stomach did a slow, nauseating roll when she also realised he owned Villa Colina; he'd let her witter on about the possibility of buying it and hadn't said a word! Not a hint. He'd even led her to believe that he'd asked Dream Villas to approach the owner on her behalf! The two-timing, two-faced—

'Wait a minute…' Nora was saying. 'Er, Ivy…?'

'Yes?' The way Nora said her name didn't sound at all good and Ivy didn't think she could take much more.

'Your pool guy – his full name is Sebastián de León y Castile.'

Ivy sat down hard, the tiled floor of the hall jarring her bum. Disbelief swept through her, even as her brain was busily joining the dots. Sebastián… *Sebé Y Castile?* Dear God.

'There's more,' Nora continued. Ivy wasn't sure she wanted to hear anything else, but it was like a bad toothache that she couldn't leave alone. She had to know.

'Sebé Castile retired from public life after he'd filmed *A Lavender Summer*, and he hasn't acted in anything since,'

Nora informed her. 'There's a quote in an interview he did with one of the big magazines, that says he wanted to return to a simpler life on the island of his birth – Tenerife.'

'How long ago?' Ivy croaked, her mouth dry and her throat scratchy. Her head was pounding and she thought she might throw up at any second.

'Um... this article was written about three years ago.'

'OK.' But it wasn't OK. It most definitely wasn't. There she was, assuming the man she loved worked in a low-paid job, feeling bad about the fact she earned probably ten times the amount he did; when in fact his net worth was probably more than she would earn in a lifetime. And now that she'd worked this out, she felt an absolute idiot. A used idiot to boot. Daniel, the sod, had been right: why would Sebastián be interested in a long-term relationship with *her* when he could have his pick of women?

Ivy screwed her eyes shut in despair.

Nora let out a gasp. 'Bloomin' heck! I've just realised you've based Nathaniel on Sebé Castile!'

Oh God, she had. Ivy felt a chill sweep through her. Her whole new series was based on a man who was instantly recognisable (although not to her, she thought sourly) and world famous. How was he going to react when he found out?

It was no good hoping he wouldn't, because numerous pairs of eyes had seen the manuscript already, and it wouldn't be long before someone else made the connection, especially since Daniel knew who Ivy had been dating and she herself had posted Sebastián's photo on social media. It was a wonder her ex hadn't brought the subject up, she thought, before it occurred to her that he might well be saving that little nugget of information for later. Such as when the book had been published, and this sort of revelation could do her the most damage, for instance? So much for the clause on the copyright page which stated something about the published book being a work of fiction and that any resemblance to persons either living or dead was purely coincidental, Ivy thought in dismay. That clearly wasn't the case here, and anyone who knew about her relationship with Sebastián would see the truth straight away. Nathaniel, her dark, dangerous and sexy-as-hell bad angel, was clearly based on Sebastián de León, aka Sebé Castile!

'Nora, I might have to pull the book,' Ivy groaned. She sniffed to try to stop the tears.

'I take it Sebé or Sebastián, or whatever he calls himself, doesn't have a clue that he's playing the starring role in your new series?'

'No.' Her voice was small and there was a tremor to it.

'OK, um, let me think.' Nora was silent for a couple of seconds. 'Let's not do anything hasty. Right, you need to have a chat with your Sebastián and let him know what's what, and once you've got his take on the situation we can go from there. Besides, if you need to rework his physical description – I don't know, make his hair blonde or silver, or something – then it's not too late to do that. We can work around this, so don't worry. Everything will be fine.'

But that's where Nora and Ivy differed.

Ivy didn't believe that anything would be fine ever again.

Chapter 28

Ivy felt too sorry for herself to make the effort to leave the villa to book a flight. She was exhausted, mentally and emotionally. It was difficult to believe that only just over two hours ago she had been lying asleep by the pool without a care in the world and looking forward to a future with Sebastián at its centre.

Not now, though; now she was planning on running back to London with her tail between her legs, with her heart well and truly broken. How could her life have changed so much in such a short space of time? She felt as if today had lasted for ever – it felt like several days and not just the one, and it wasn't over yet. It was only six o'clock and she had the rest of the evening ahead, and the night to get through. She really should make the effort to find a signal so she could book herself onto the next flight to England. She didn't care which airport – any of them would do as long as she was away from Tenerife.

She contemplated curling up in a ball and staying there, but lying on the floor next to the loo where she'd managed to run to before she had thrown up wasn't that appealing. Getting unsteadily to her feet, Ivy wobbled into the kitchen to make herself a cup of tea (the thought of coffee made her stomach churn). She took the cup into the bedroom with her, fully intending to crawl under the covers and sleep for as long as humanly possible, until she caught sight of the bed where Sebastián had made glorious love to her. This was the bed where he'd told her time and time again that he loved her. This was the bed where he'd held her in his arms until she'd fallen asleep, safe in the knowledge that at last she had someone who truly cared for her.

How wrong could she have been? Ivy was filled with such deep sorrow that she thought her heart might break in two.

She couldn't possibly sleep in that bed. She wasn't even sure if she would be able to sleep in the villa.

Never mind searching for flights online – she'd do what she'd told Daniel to do, make her way to the airport and hope for the best. The irony wasn't lost on her, as she pulled her suitcases out of the wardrobe in one of the spare rooms where she'd stashed them, and began to open drawers and throw her belongings inside.

Still feeling sick and realising that it was going to take her a while to round up all her possessions which were scattered throughout the house, Ivy thought it might be a good idea to make herself some dry toast to try and settle her tummy.

She was in the kitchen, waiting for the toaster to do its job and trying not to let fresh tears fall, when she heard the unmistakable sound of a motorbike engine.

Sebastián was back!

God, what should she do? She could hardly lock him out, because he had a key (he owned the damned place, remember, she thought harshly), and she couldn't run away because there was nowhere to go.

Just then, the toaster popped, startling her, and she let out a small whimper of despair as Sebastián opened the front door. Ivy quickly turned around, and pretended to busy herself with the butter so he couldn't see the pain on her face.

What was he doing here anyway? Had he come to gloat? Or to talk? Neither was acceptable, because no reason in the world could explain away the depth of his deception.

'Ivy?' He sounded hesitant, cautious.

She ignored him.

'Talk to me? Are you leaving? The suitcases…?'

She continued to butter the piece of toast furiously, lathering on yet another layer of butter.

'Please, Ivy. We need to talk.'

Taking a deep breath, she whirled around, brandishing the butter-coated knife. 'No, we don't.'

His eyes widened as he stared at the knife, and Ivy hastily threw it in the sink. It landed with a clatter that made them both jump.

'Yes, we do,' he insisted. 'I want to know why my father had a call from Diego Salinas to ask if we were dating. I want to know why you were crying. Do not deny it, Diego told me – I saw him in the village about ten minutes ago,' he added. 'He said you were *agitada* – upset. What is going on? Is it Daniel? Is he the reason why you were crying? Did he hurt you?'

She shrugged and nodded. It was partly to do with him, because if he hadn't turned up at the villa then Ivy might not have found out about Sebastián's deception. Not just yet, anyway.

'Is he here?' Sebastián asked. 'I will kill him if he—'

'Please… stop. Just go.'

'You want me to leave?'

'Yes.' It came out as a whisper, but he heard it anyway.

'I cannot persuade you to…? No matter. I am sorry.' He bit his lip. 'I know you and he were… are…' He trailed off. 'I wish you luck, Ivy Winter. But know this, I love you with everything I have, and I always will.'

'Do you now? Is that so?' She rounded on him, suddenly furious, anger sweeping through her out of nowhere, burning her tears to a crisp and leaving bitter ashes in her mouth. 'You don't love me enough to be faithful to me, though, do you? Or to tell me you own Dream Villas? And what about loving me enough to tell me you are a famous actor?'

'*Mierda!*'

That was one word of Spanish she did know. 'Yeah, you're right, it is shit. And for your information, Daniel has gone. I kicked him out. You'd have watched me do it if you hadn't driven off thinking you know what's best for me. But do you know what? I'm glad you did, because if you hadn't, I wouldn't have known that you were dating a woman young enough to be your daughter. That's what hurts the most,' she continued, before he could open his mouth. 'That you're seeing someone else, when you said you love me.'

'I do love you—'

'Bollocks.'

He blinked at the unaccustomed profanity. He might never have heard her swear before, but if he stayed around much longer he was going to hear an awful lot worse. She dashed a tear from her cheek with the back of her hand.

'Don't you dare,' she warned when he took a step towards her. She didn't need his pity.

Ivy swallowed, her anger vanishing as quickly as it had arrived. What remained was a hurt so deep she didn't know how she was supposed to bear it.

'What woman?' he asked, his brow creasing.

She shook her head in disbelief. 'How many have you got? The one in the villa that Diego drove me to.' She looked away, her heart pounding.

'That's my home. I live there.' His frown intensified.

She screwed her eyes shut as the significance sank in. The woman at the villa had been in *his* house – she wasn't just a random guest in a Dream Villas property. She most likely lived there. With him. Oh God!

Sebastián barked out a small laugh, his face clearing. 'Ah, now I understand, the woman – the *girl* – is my niece. She is Cristina's daughter, home from university.'

'Wait, *what*?' Ivy opened her eyes. 'She's your *niece*?'

'Yes.'

'Are you sure?'

'Completely.'

'What was she doing in your house?' Ivy didn't know whether to believe him or not. He'd lied before… OK, not lied as such, but he'd omitted telling her the truth, which was more or less the same thing.

'She prefers my pool to her mother's.'

'She said you were going to dinner together. You and her.'

'We are. Also, with Cristina, Sergio, my mother, my father… the whole family. And you.'

'Me?' This was starting to become surreal.

'I came this afternoon to ask you, but Daniel was there, so I...' He inhaled deeply. 'I was scared,' he said.

'Scared? Why?'

'Daniel told me he still loved you and that you and he were back together. I drove away because I could not bear to see you with him, to know that he is better for you and your writing. I was scared because I thought he'd come to claim you, and that you had gone back to him.'

'I'm not a piece of lost property that can be claimed,' she retorted.

'I know. I am sorry.'

Ivy studied her hands, before lifting her head to meet his gaze. 'Daniel has gone,' she repeated. 'I told him to leave. I don't want anything to do with him or his publishing house.'

He closed his eyes briefly, then opened them again. Were those tears that she could see in their brown depths? 'I am glad.'

'Thank you for setting me straight about your niece.'

'You are welcome.' He hesitated. 'But...?'

'You own Dream Villas — why didn't you tell me?'

'I am a private man, or I try to be.' He shrugged. 'I do not publicise the fact that I own the business. I keep out of the public eye as much as I can. Most people have forgotten me or if they remember, there is nothing to report on me — I am far too boring now and I like it to stay that way.' Sebastián's eyes held hers fiercely, as if willing her to understand. 'But I can't take the risk that, if it was general knowledge that I own Dream Villas, I would be hounded like before and my family would suffer for it. I didn't tell you in the beginning because I did not know you at first, but when I grew to love you, there never was a good time. I was going to tell you after the meal with Cristina and Sergio, but...' He shrugged. 'I was scared, and I wanted to kiss you, but I ran away instead. If I am honest, I could have told you many times since, but it made me happy that you thought I was no one special.'

'I never thought you weren't special. You've always been special to me.'

'And now? Does it matter that I am Sebé Castile?' He said his name as though the words were poison in his mouth.

'You are Sebastián to me. I don't know anyone called Sebé,' she replied honestly.

He took another step closer to her and opened his arms. 'Can you forgive me?'

Ivy wanted to, but she wasn't entirely sure she could. He'd kept so much from her. 'Why did you come back now? You said goodbye to me?'

'Diego...' He dropped his arms, his face a mask of hurt.

'You already told me that. But if you truly thought I'd be better off with Daniel, why did you come here now?'

'When I spoke to Daniel, I was hurt. But later, after I drove off and had a chance to think, I realised I could not let you go, I *cannot* let you go without a fight. When Diego called and said you had been looking for me, it gave me hope that I might be wrong – that you might still have feelings for me. I had to see you, had to try to win your love from Daniel. If that makes me selfish, then I am sorry.'

'It does make you selfish,' she said, but a smile was growing in her mind, and hope was blooming in her heart.

'Ivy Winter, I love you. I will always love you. Can you forgive me?'

'Yes.'

He held her gaze for a long, long moment, and when he opened his arms and held them out to her once more, she did not hesitate to step into his embrace, and as his mouth found hers, she knew she never wanted to let him go.

Chapter 29

'We've missed dinner,' Ivy observed some time later. It was dark outside and she was lying across Sebastián's broad chest listening to the reassuring thud of his heart. One of his legs was over hers, pinning it down, and his arm was around her waist. She was pleasantly languid and was feeling happier than she could ever remember feeling.

'It's OK. They won't care,' he said.

Ivy felt bad about it, though; she hated letting people down, and she vowed to make it up to his family.

But first, there was one thing on her mind that she needed to share with Sebastián.

'I've got to tell you something and I don't think you're going to be pleased,' she said, screwing up her face. 'Err, I based my main character, Nathaniel, on you,' she blurted out, and winced, waiting for the fallout.

It didn't happen.

'You did?' Sebastián chuckled. 'I hope your readers like him.'

'You're not mad?'

He shook his head. 'I am flattered.'

'I thought you'd be furious. I probably wouldn't have told you at all – I'd have just changed some details – but too many people have read it now, and when Daniel has finished shooting his mouth off—'

'Daniel knows who I am?' Sebastián interrupted.

'Yes. In fact, it was him who told me who you were, because I didn't have a clue. He saw a photo I posted on Facebook. The one I took of you when we were at that restaurant in Garachico.'

'I remember. There were many photos taken of me that day.'

So there had been, but Ivy hadn't realised at the time that those people were taking snaps of Sebastián – Sebé – and not the scenery. 'Is that why you wanted to drive to that other beach?'

'Yes.'

'You must find it hard being recognised all the time,' she sympathised, kissing his chest and tasting a slight saltiness.

'You get used to it, but I don't make it easy for them.'

'The sunglasses and the baseball cap?' Ivy guessed.

'They help,' he admitted. 'Also, I avoid tourist spots when I can. Like you, most people don't recognise me when I'm not in a tux on a red carpet or the big screen.'

'That's why we had lunch in Cocina de Carla!' she exclaimed. 'I thought it was rather out of the way, although the food was great.'

'Carla needs the money. Cooking is the only thing that keeps her going. She is also a friend of my grandmother's, and I make a point of looking out for her. I cannot believe she is still making food for people every day at her age.'

'You ought to employ her to cook for your guests,' Ivy said. Then— 'You don't really cook for your villa guests, do you?'

'No. Just you.'

The warm feeling in her heart grew, and Ivy felt like singing about her happiness from the rooftops. He was so sweet and thoughtful.

'I, too, have something to tell you,' he said, regarding her seriously.

'Oh?' Ivy propped herself up on her elbow, wondering what was coming next. This day had been one which was full of surprises, and she wasn't sure she could take any more. 'Tell me what?'

'I do not drink alcohol.' He stared at a spot over her shoulder. 'I was young and foolish when I started acting – I drank too much, partied too hard, dated too many women and made too many poor decisions. So now I do not drink at all. It is easier that way.'

'I see,' she responded slowly. That explained why he hardly ever touched the stuff. Not that it mattered, because it didn't. Ivy loved him regardless and she respected Sebastián for having made the decision not to drink if he found it easier. She loved that he was honest and open with her now, and she could fully understand why he hadn't felt able to tell her about his previous life.

'It was one of the reasons I retired from acting,' he continued. 'I was losing myself and I didn't like what I had become. I came back to Tenerife, to my home and my family, and I live a much simpler life.'

Ivy smiled softly at him. 'I love a simple life, too,' she said. 'I'm so much more contented and productive without the bright lights of the city distracting me, although I do miss having the internet.'

'Ah. Um, about that… this place does have internet.'

'No!'

'It is your Nora's fault. She told me to disconnect it when she rented the villa for you.'

'The sneaky... Well, I never!' It had been the right thing to do though, Ivy acknowledged. If she'd had unrestricted access to the internet, then she would never have got as much writing done. Of course, she had become distracted in other ways – like watching Sebastián, for instance, but she was classing that as research.

There was one other thing she was curious about, though. 'Why do you clean pools and stuff when you don't have to?' she asked him. Not that she didn't appreciate the sight of him cleaning the pool, and she didn't think she would ever forget the first time she saw him, and how gorgeous she thought he was.

'I enjoy it,' he replied. 'Besides, if I hadn't cleaned Villa Colina's pool then I would never have met you.'

He had a point. And if he enjoyed the more hands-on side of his business, then that was up to him. She didn't care what he did as long as it made him happy.

'Why a holiday rental company?' she asked. With his success she bet he'd never have to work again.

'Because I have to have something to do with my time, and I need to keep working. After I bought the house I now live in, I bought one for my parents, and I found I enjoyed searching for properties to buy. It was fun.'

'Maybe you should have started an estate agency?' Ivy suggested.

'I did think of it, but buying property is a much better investment. And if I decide to do something else, I can always sell the villas.'

'Is there anything else I should know about you?' she asked.

'I like to paint.' He sounded quite sheepish, as though it was a secret he was ashamed of.

'You do? That's wonderful! You'll have to show me—' Ivy stopped and shook her head. '*You* painted the picture you gave me, didn't you?'

He pulled a face. 'Yes.'

She sat up and twisted around to look at the framed painting, where she had hung it above the bed.

There was a scrawled, almost illegible signature in the bottom right-hand side, and Ivy leant forward for a better look.

It bore his name.

'You are a man of many talents,' she said. 'Actor, artist, gardener, businessman.'

'Lover?'

'That, too.'

'Am I a better lover than artist?' he asked, coyly.

'Hmm, let me see... I think I'll have to study your other paintings first, then— Eek!'

Sebastián pounced on her and Ivy fell back against the pillow.

'I think I might have to show you again how much better a lover I am than a painter,' he said, pinning her to the bed and nibbling her ear.

'Ooh, yes please,' Ivy cried, and Sebastián proceeded to do exactly that, much to her delight.

Chapter 30

All of Sebastián's family had gathered at Villa Colina for dinner. Ivy had initially wished that she and Sebastián weren't hosting the meal, because she wasn't too keen on cooking for such accomplished home cooks. Which was why Sebastián had persuaded Carla to come cook for them that evening, and the little old lady was happily ensconced in the kitchen, singing to herself while bashing pots and pans around. Ivy hoped she would be forgiven for not doing any of the actual cooking herself. His family should know by now that Sebastián was a better chef than she was; his parents had visited the villa enough times over the past five months to discover that about her, and they didn't seem to hold it against her, although his mum kept trying to give Ivy lessons.

Alba, who had returned from nursing her sick sister, was helping clear up, and Ivy gave the woman a smile as she trundled past, her hands full of dishes. Alba had actually returned after only a few weeks, but Sebastián, Ivy had discovered, had quite enjoyed having Ivy all to himself and didn't want to share, so he'd carried on cleaning Villa Colina himself, and deployed Alba to another one of his properties.

Marta glared first at Sebastián, then at Ivy.

'Do you love him?' Sebastián translated his grand-mother's question, blushing slightly. Aww, that was so cute.

'Err, yes?' Ivy said. It was her turn for her cheeks to flush. The old woman was very direct.

'You don't sound certain. Don't you know?' Sebastián translated again, a smile on his lips. Marta continued to glare, but this time it was directed solely at Ivy.

Ivy made a face, but all Sebastián did was chuckle. His grandmother was one determined lady, and nothing was going to deter her from questioning Ivy. The fact that she'd roped Sebastián in to translate for her, made the situation even more awkward.

'Yes, I do love him; with all my heart,' Ivy said, trying not to look at Sebastián, and blushing madly.

'*Bueno*,' Marta said, then the old lady stretched out her hand and pinched Ivy's cheek. Ivy smiled, trying not to show how much it hurt. For an oldie, Marta had incred-ibly strong fingers.

She heard Sebastián's laughter beside her, and resisted the urge to poke him in the ribs. She was trying to be on her best behaviour, and having his whole family here was scary enough, without his irascible grandma asking such personal questions in front of everyone.

'Let's go outside,' Sebastián said, abruptly.

'Now? But—?' She gestured towards his family, not wanting to leave the table. They'd think she was incredibly rude, even though everyone had finished eating and were lingering over coffee.

'*Please?*' Sebastián caught hold of her hand, pulled her to her feet and led her out onto the terrace. It was fully dark by now, and the stars were coming out to play overhead, like so many fairy lights. Garachico was a blanket of twinkling lights below, and beyond the town the sea and the sky had become one. The night was incredibly beautiful, made even more so by the fact that Sebastián had forgotten to switch on the outside lights.

'How are the reviews?' he asked, clearing his throat.

Ivy tilted her head slightly and stared at him. Why did he need to bring her out here to ask her that? Oh, wait a sec, maybe he thought he should ask her in private in case the advance reviews hadn't been as good as she had hoped. Her heart swelled with love. He could just have waited until his family had left to ask though, but it was marvellous that he was taking such an interest in her work.

'Fantastic! I've only had a dozen so far from the advance readers, but they've all been glowing. Fingers crossed that the rest of the public will like *An Angel from Hell* just as much. I think it helps that when they read about Nathaniel, they can visualise you,' she added, mischievously.

The story of their romance had 'broken' as Ivy had guessed it would, and for a short while the press had focused on Sebé Castile's new girlfriend, but that was old news now, and the media had moved on, except for the occasional mention of Ivy's new book, which was due to be released in two months' time.

'I am pleased, and I am even more pleased that you have made your home here. Living on Tenerife is good for your writing, yes?'

'It's good for my love life, too,' she smiled at him. 'I couldn't imagine living anywhere else, or loving anyone else.'

'Are you happy?' Sebastián asked.

'You know I am. I've never been happier.' And she meant it.

He gazed into her eyes and she melted into his, seeing herself reflected in their depths and knowing that was where she wanted to be for the rest of her life.

Her lips parted and she waited for him to take her in his arms and steal a sneaky kiss away from the inquisitive eyes of his family. They couldn't stay out here long, because they'd soon be missed.

A squeal from Emilia made her glance towards the open patio doors and Ivy saw the whole family gathered there to watch them. When she turned back to Sebastián to ask him what was going on, it was to find him kneeling on the ground.

It took her a moment to realise what he was doing, and by the time she understood, Sebastián was holding out a small box, and the look of love on his face made her want to cry with joy. She clapped her hands to her mouth and stared at him, her eyes wide, her heart pounding.

'I love you, Ivy Winter, from now and until the stars fall out of the sky. Will you marry me?'

Ivy thought she was going to explode with happiness as Sebastián opened the box and revealed the most exquisite ring she had ever seen. The sapphire was so dark it was almost black, with two sparkling diamonds on either side, set on a platinum band. Sebastián took the engagement ring out of its velvet nest and Ivy held out her hand. She was trembling and she thought she might pass out.

Sebastián slipped the ring on her finger and pulled her to him. 'Look.' Sebastián pointed, and Ivy looked up to see the night sky alive with stars. 'The sapphire represents the night, the diamonds represent the stars,' he told her. 'See there, the constellation of Draco, the dragon, do you remember?' Ivy followed his finger as he pointed. 'See those two pinpricks of light close together, in the middle of the dragon? I have named those two stars after us, so we are bound together for eternity in the heavens.'

She let out a sob of pure happiness, tears trickling down her cheeks.

'Will you marry me?' he asked again, and Ivy realised she had yet to accept this wildly romantic and wonderful proposal from the man she loved more than life itself.

'Yes,' she said. 'I want nothing else in the world.' And it was true. Nothing else mattered except him. Ivy had written Sebastián into her stories, her life, and her heart, and he had written them both into the stars.

'Actually, there is one thing,' Ivy said cheekily, oblivious to the cheering and clapping of his family who were now pouring out of the house in congratulation. 'Didn't you promise to sell me Villa Colina?'

Sebastián didn't answer. He was too busy kissing her.